The Cavern

Lug

(Written By Henry Graham Docherty.)

Whiffyskunk.com Publishing.

Contact Admin@whiffyskunk.com

The Setting for this Fantasy is a real place. All characters, names and events are completely fictitious, any resemblances to actual persons living or dead, is entirely coincidental.

Whiffyskunk.com Books.
First Published as an E-Book 2008 by https://www.whiffyskunk.com.
Paperback Edition 2009 Whiffyskunk Publishing.

British Library Cataloguing information in Publication Data.
A record for this book is available from the British Library.

ISBN 978-0-9558333-5-9

Dedicated to my son Graham and daughter Lisa.

Acknowledgements

Annie, thanks for all the assistance, support and encouragement. Thanks also to Ed Chapman, Scribe at Othergods.org (Grove of the Other Gods, ADF) for his generous help, and thanks also to Amanda L Valentin for helping in the editing of this work.

INTRODUCTION by the AUTHOR

Most horror stories I have experienced centre around Gothic folktales, Vampires, Werewolves, Frankenstein creations, Mummies, the Supernatural or cultural Mythology - particularly Greek. With the exception of Banshees and Leprechauns in Irish folklore, there is very little that I have read which draws from Celtic Mythology: a source boasting volumes of tales with heroes and villains, gods and monsters, fantastic worlds and incredible characters. This story redresses this situation somewhat, albeit merely scratching the surface of a treasure trove of legend and fantasy.

I am not an authority on Celtic Mythology nor do I pretend to be. This tale is a work of fiction. Many experts may criticize my 'embellishment' of stories handed down through generations - collated, translated and interpreted. My reading gave me the impression that no-one can be 100% certain as to accurate translation, as I found various alternatives and sometimes contradicting 'historical' documentation, depending on where the author derived his or her source. Accordingly, I feel no compunction with regard to exercising my own self-assumed 'Poetic License'!

All the places and place names mentioned in the novel are real. The people and events are not! I have set the bulk of the narrative in and around Bathgate in Scotland, because that is where I am from and grew up. The focus of the story revolves around Cairnpapple, deep in the Bathgate Hills, simply because it has fascinated me since I was a young boy. The best guess is that it was a burial ground for Beaker

People dating back over 5000 years ago…there just has to be more history there than anyone knows, or perhaps more than anyone is telling. Why there? What is the significance of the hill? What about the holes, the stones, the ditch and ramps? Theories abound. Check it out on the Internet, by searching for "Cairnpapple", you'll find an amazing place, and a great location for my tale.

Move over Gothic, Celtic has arrived!

Myths that are believed tend to come true…

George Orwell.

LEVEL 17

Light from twenty-four headlamps turned as one towards the horrendous screeching and groaning coming from the coalface, the beams accentuated by the belching black cloud of coal dust. The whole area was pitched in blackness surrounded by a cacophony of coughs and curses as the clawing dust storm penetrated the miners' lungs and eyes. Gradually the dust began to settle enough for beams of light to permeate the darkness only to reveal a gaping black maw in the centre of the coal seam, the peripheral walls framing the unbelievable, an impossibility; the figure of an entity, dark and malevolent, dressed in black, its long cape swirling about it in the artificial air.

oooOOOooo

A few minutes previously...

"What time is it now, Sandy?" yelled Joe Turner in his broad Scottish accent.

"Its time you got yourself a watch! That's what time it is!" Yelled back the other miner.

"Aw, come on. You know I broke mine over a week ago." Pleaded Joe.

"There's half an hour to the end of shift. And it can't come soon enough! I could murder a pint!" Replied Sandy.

"Aye and me. I'm dying for a smoke too!" Joe added.

The miners continued shovelling fallen lumps of coal onto the small rail cart. They had been friends since they were boys; gone to the same school, lived in the same neighbourhood in Bathgate, home to Easton Colliery, where they had both worked since leaving school almost fifteen years ago. Despite being of similar age, it was difficult to tell, Sandy being tall and slim with a full head of dark brown hair, while Joe was short and stubby, prematurely bald and sported a few scars on his face from a mining accident a few years previously.

Joe and Sandy could tell you just how much mining had changed in their short tenure. Today, technology had new means for handling most tasks, controlled by hydraulic machines that moved by robotics. A huge cutting machine could be heard now; a whirring, circular mole spinning at goodness knows how many revolutions per minute. It was about six feet in diameter with rows of sharp, steel teeth extending around its perimeter. It was used extensively to form tunnels or excavate the coal seams.

Electricity, once they had developed safe means to introduce it to the depths they worked at, was a boon to all the miners making their helmet lamps almost obsolete. Unfortunately, the down side to all these improvements meant that many jobs were lost. There was no need for so many men with shovels and picks hacking away at the coalfaces or others scooping their endeavours into hutches. Nowadays, all they had to do was follow the cutter, fill the small trucks and they would be rolled to the end of the line and hoisted on railed elevators to the surface. And even this was only for a small percentage of coal that fell off the automated conveyor belt. The majority of the cut mineral fell onto these belts and was carried along to a dump location where it simply tumbled off the end into the waiting trucks. All the miners had to do was ensure there was a sufficient line of rail buggies available to catch the coal.

Joe and Sandy, being fifteen years experienced, were part of this specially chosen twenty four man crew to pave the way in the exploitation of a new deeper section recently opened; Level 17 - a record depth at twelve hundred feet. There were sixteen levels above them but many more tunnels since they ran off at a myriad of tangents following the productive seams. If improvements had been made in efficiency, technology, safety and other spheres, there was apparently no great leap forward in noise containment. There was a constant unnatural symphony of hydraulic hissing, truck rumbling, equipment whirring and whooshing, all playing background to the ripping, crunching, grinding, cutting machine. This was what the miners had to yell over.

Sandy checked his watch one more time. Less than fifteen minutes to go. Suddenly, the pitch of the grinder changed. All the miners stopped what they were doing and looked towards the coalface; this was unusual. The pitch increased to a high whine making the workers cover their ears, then the whole machine base began to vibrate and resonate. With an almighty deafening final shriek, it spun out of control leaving a huge gap in the coal face as if it were suddenly free wheeling, making no contact with the surface. It spun on its own axis and toppled over, the steel teeth biting at the tunnel floor and spinning the whole thing around until it came to a grinding halt trying to bury itself. One of the teeth severed the electricity feed, plunging them into darkness.

Jock Archibald returned to his cabin from the office washrooms. He was a big man approaching sixty years old. Some time ago, nearly twenty years now, there had been a partial tunnel collapse and a few men had been injured. None too seriously, but Jock was unfortunate enough to have one of his vertebrae crushed, which had rendered him unable to carry out lifting duties. He had been quickly retrained as the standby cage operator, and had taken over the role full time almost sixteen years ago. Now, his only exercise at work was getting to and from the toilet due to his irritable bowel syndrome.

He dropped back into the control room chair; it groaned under his weight. He checked his watch - five minutes to two, time to send the cage down for the Saturday day shift on Level 17. Jock checked his dials to ensure no doors were open, indicating that there was no one in or around the cage. Satisfied that all lights were green, he pushed the descend button, and sent the huge elevator on its way.

His 'travel' orange light flashed until he saw Level 17 on the control panel. He slowed the cage until it rested on the tunnel floor and the limit switches recorded a green light for safe location. That was his signal to open the door. In around five minutes time the miners would be accounted for by the shift foreman, who would then call Jock to begin the ascent.

Jock waited for eight minutes, then, "What the Fu...?" he cursed. "If this is one of Joe's practical jokes, I'll have his guts for garters!" He picked up his phone and pushed the intercom button to the cage. No one answered.

"Shit! What do I do now?" Jock panicked. He picked up the internal phone and punched in three numbers, anxiously tapping on his desk until finally the shift supervisor answered.

"Ian Strathearn."

"Ian, its Jock. Got a bit of a problem; Level 17 crew are not responding. What should I do?"

"Weird; any alarms from down there?"

"Nope, none."

Ian realized Jock was under stress.

"OK, contact the rescue team and tell them to meet me at the cage access. Is the cage down there? Bring it up if it is. I'll be there in five."

Jock made a few more calls to the on-shift firemen then retrieved the empty cage.

"If this is someone having a lark, I'll kill 'em!" He said to himself.

Ian and the emergency squad were fitted with protective gear and air tanks and were ready to descend within seven minutes. The supervisor signalled for Jock to take them down.

As soon as they reached Level 17, they did gas checks and found nothing untoward so Ian authorised entry. The group moved in slowly and carefully since there was no lighting, having only their helmet lamps and flash-lights. There were shouts and yells as they spotted the overturned cutter and the havoc it had wreaked, but all were incredulous to find no one in the vicinity, not a living soul. There was no evidence of a gaping cavern; just a smooth, almost polished looking, black wall.

"This is out of my depth." Confessed the supervisor. "Let's get the hell out of here!"

They returned to the cage and got Jock to return them to the surface. Ian went straight to the phone and called the emergency handsets on the other two levels that were being worked that Saturday. He asked the foreman of each team whether they had seen anyone from Level 17 in their section. No one had recorded any sighting.

"Damn!" Cursed Ian. "Jock, get me the boss."

"But...he's at home." Whined Jock.

"I don't care where he is! I need to talk to him, right now!"

Jock dialled the home number of the colliery manager. As soon as he heard the receiver being lifted on the other end, he handed the phone over to the supervisor. Ian took it, hearing "Hello... hello? Who is this?" from the handset.

"Harry? It's me, Ian. You'd better get down here; there's been an acci...I mean, an incident on Level 17."

"What do you mean? An accident, a fire, gas?" enquired the pit boss.

"I'm not entirely sure. There seems to have been a malfunction or something with the cutter, but that's not the main issue; the whole shift seems to have disappeared. I know this sounds crazy, but I really think you ought to see this for yourself. I don't know what to do." Ian blurted out.

The manager was confused. "You're not making sense. Disappeared! What does that mean? Never mind! I'm on my way. I'll be there in half an hour."

Harry Grant was almost fifty years old, rotund with a reddish complexion, a round face and a balding head. He had been educated in Edinburgh and had gone into the Civil Service, National Coal Board, as an executive officer at the tender age of eighteen.

Following a slow progress up the ranks, eventually taking him to the headquarters at The Whins in Alloa, he was appointed as assistant manager at Kinneil Colliery in Bo'ness where he served his managerial apprenticeship for six years before being promoted to manager at Easton four years ago. He had been doing a good job, had a rapport with the unions and had consistently returned profits for the company. He had never had a major incident in either of his positions; that is, until now. He recalled he had had a bad feeling about opening up the seam at Level 17, something about the geological surveys - he couldn't put his finger on it, it just didn't seem right.

He changed clothes, scribbled a note to his wife, and jumped into his Ford Poplar car. Harry entered the colliery almost exactly thirty minutes from when he received the call.

ooo000ooo

Within minutes of Harry's arrival at the main offices of the colliery, and having been briefed of the incident, he, Ian, and the earlier squad, were checking out Level 17.

"Don't touch a thing." Harry warned the rescue crew personnel. "Just look. Observe." Harry was stumped. How could this be?

"We need to get the police in on this, it's beyond our ken." Harry said to his supervisor. "Did you see the coal face? How smooth

13

it is? I've never seen anything like it. Get Jock to contact the police; I'll advise the area manager while you get hold of Brian and Hamish. I think we need their heads on this one too."

Bathgate Police Station on South Bridge Street was sparsely manned. It was Saturday afternoon and weekends were generally quiet. WPC Allison Weir took the call from Jock. At first, she could not make out what he was trying to tell her. An incident down the pit? Men missing? Disappearing? An accident? No, no one injured. No, wait, they don't know, they can't find anybody. Eventually she put the incredible story together and called PC Alex Phillips to hear his opinion. There were only five of them on shift that afternoon; herself, Alex and Sarge, who was out doing rounds and two other constables on duty at a local football match down at the Creamery Park.

The young policeman thought for a minute and concluded.

"We won't be able to get hold of Sarge for a while, better call the guv'nor."

"Er, no!" She protested. "You know he hates getting calls when he's off duty. You do it, you're the senior officer!"

"Me? All of a sudden two years seniority is important, huh? What a cop out! Pardon the pun." He chided and forced into a corner, he reluctantly dialled the Police Inspector's home number.

Bob Mathieson was tidying up a flowerbed. He enjoyed gardening, especially around this time of year. He was a relatively tall man, just short of six feet, and in spite his fifty-five years he was remarkably fit. Bob was born in Stirling and had joined the police force at an early age but felt he needed to broaden his horizons after a few years on the beat. He applied for a position with the Metropolitan

14

Police and after a couple of interviews and a long wait, transferred there when he was twenty-four. It was there that he met Sandra, then a clerical assistant, and made her his wife. They had three children, who were now grown-up with lives of their own. He missed Sandra and longed for her from time to time, anger building inside him because of the fact that in this day and age there was still no cure for Leukaemia. She had finally been taken from him four years since, just two years after he was promoted to his current position as head of police in Bathgate Burgh. He lived in a two-storey, stone built, detached house in Balbardie Street, the rich area of town. He had a large garden and kept it neat and tidy. Bob sighed with frustration when he heard the phone ring and sauntered back to the house.

"Yes, who is it?" he enquired impatiently.

"It's Phillips, Sir. Sorry to bother you..."

"Phillips? This had better be life or death!"

"Well, it could be Sir, you see..."

"What do you mean 'could be'? What is going on down there?"

"Well, we have had a strange garbled message from Easton Colliery...it appears that some men have disappeared..."

Alex held the phone away from his ear in anticipation of the response.

"What? Disappeared? What do you mean? How many men? Where from? Speak up lad, what are you talking about?"

"About twenty-four men as far as we can make out Sir."

"What? Where is Sergeant Morrison?"

"He's out on his rounds. We don't expect him back for an hour

15

or so."

"OK, I'm coming in. Give me a minute to change, meanwhile get me a full coherent, do you hear? Coherent...report for my arrival." Click.

Alex stood up and gave a straight armed salute to the telephone-

"Ya vool Herr Commandante!" He mimicked Sergeant Schultz from *Hogan's Heroes*; Sandra could hardly contain her giggle.

The police inspector went indoors, washed his hands and started stripping off his gardening clothes as he headed upstairs to his bedroom. He opened his wardrobe doors to reveal three pressed uniforms and a row of starched white shirts. He smiled as he thought of his housemaid, Eleanor. She was a godsend; well over sixty, but still managed to conquer the hill from Belvedere every day to clean for him. She had been recommended to him during Sandra's illness and she had never let him down. Fifteen minutes later, he was driving his Ford Escort into the reserved parking space behind the police station.

Alex Phillips was as tall as his boss, but youthfully muscular and fit; at weekends, he played for the West Lothian Police football team. He was twenty-four years old, a three-year graduate from Tulliallan Police College. He and Allison both jumped to attention when the inspector stormed into the reception.

"Weir! Tea, and make it snappy. Phillips! Where's this report?" he bellowed.

Alex pulled his notes out of the typewriter, almost tearing the paper and the carbon copy in his haste. Bob read the statement, harrumphed, then asked.

16

"Is the manager or anyone sensible available at Easton?"

Alex replied that he believed the manager was now in attendance.

"Well, don't just stand there! Get him on the blower for me. I'll take it in my office. Weir! Where's that tea?"

Soon after, the head of police, having been fully briefed by the colliery manager, suitably refreshed by the tea and accompanied by PC Phillips, was on his way to Easton Colliery.

ooo000ooo

While the Police were getting their act together, Harry Grant had called the area manager, Tommy Graham, and explained the situation, so far as they knew it. By now, Brian and Hamish, the site's surveyor and engineer, had arrived, visited Level 17 and were just as confused as everyone else. Neither could explain the cause of the cutter malfunction nor the anomaly of the smooth seam face. Tommy agreed with Harry's decision to call in the police and asked for the manager to keep him posted. In the meantime, he advised that he would try to reach his nephew, an excellent mining geologist, whom he would try to have sequestered to their service by the following Monday.

Bob Mathieson was seriously frustrated. He had never come across a case anything like this in all his time in the forces. He had visited the tunnel with the mine officials and, having given the OK for further inspection, they had all eventually returned to the administration building convening in the small conference room.

17

"Any ideas at all, Gentlemen?" he had begun. His reply was a panorama of blank faces.

"Just doesn't make sense," opined Harry Grant eventually, "but we are going to have to have some answers pretty soon; I've already fielded a couple of phone calls from the miners' wives, asking about their whereabouts. Obviously, I've had to close the whole operation down and send everyone else home with no real excuse except that it's a 'safety' issue. But, you know, rumours spread."

Brian, the surveyor, chipped in, "I've never seen anything like this either, the only logical reason I can give is paradoxically totally illogical for this country...an earthquake opening up the ground, swallowing them then re-sealing itself."

"Show me those drawings again." Bob asked, ignoring Brian. "And there is no other way out? Could they have come up in the cage earlier?" it was more of a statement than a question.

"No way!" Said Jock emphatically. "There's logs of cage trips, both manually and electronic. I checked both and there are no unaccounted movements."

"Hmmm." Thought Bob. "And what are these things here?" he asked, indicating square shapes on the survey plans.

Brian explained, pointing to each in turn.

"These, here and here, are air shafts; and these, here, and here, are vertical conveyors, one for carrying the loaded trucks up to the central level, the other for transporting empties back to floor level. There is no way anyone, other than maybe James Bond, could use them for anything else."

"So," continued Bob, "what is anyone doing about all this, and where do we go from here?" he added.

"From my perspective, I have twenty-four missing persons and I do not want anyone corrupting the scene until I have brought the experts in. By the same token, I anticipate you will want to bring in your own mining investigation team of specialists. I don't want to impede anything that can throw some sort of light on this, so my decision, for the moment, is to allow no unauthorized personnel into that level until we have people who can assist. I suggest setting up this conference room as an incident headquarters and I intend leaving an officer here twenty-four hours a day. Nobody does anything without my say so, OK?"

They all nodded agreement, Harry advising that Tommy Graham was already on the ball trying to raise a team of experts.

"In the meantime," added the Police Inspector, "our spin on this is that there has been an incident and the miners are being held in quarantine for their own safety pending investigations. Got it? That, and nothing more, without my authorization." More silent nods.

"No doubt we will have the press and all sorts circling like vultures within hours; be prepared." He continued. "Now, Phillips, when we get back to the police station, you can work out a rota for twenty-four hour vigilance...bring people back off leave if you have to, this is serious."

"Yes Sir." The Constable replied without a great deal of enthusiasm.

"The colliery is closed and strictly off limits to anyone other than our investigation team, so be sure to log any strange occurrence, noise, vibration, whatever." The Inspector concluded. "I suggest we

19

continue searching other areas of the mine for now and look at this again first thing tomorrow. Keep lines of communication clear and advise me of anything, I mean anything, that anyone thinks may be of value to this investigation."

With that, they all sauntered out of the room amid shaking heads and indistinct mutterings. Eventually those not on duties made their way home but neither they nor those remaining had much rest that night.

GOING HOME

TRINGGGG! TRINGGGG! TRINGGGG! TRINGGGG! The young man stretched out from under his duvet, blindly groped for and grabbed the receiver. "This had better be good!" He barked into the wrong end. Having adjusted it correctly, he sat up in bed. "Hello, yes?" "Peter? Sorry to wake you, but you are going on an urgent trip."

The voice said.

"Huh? Trip? Who is this?"

"It's Eric, Eric Wynne." The irritated voice belonged to Peter's boss.

"Ah, what can I do for you Eric, and what's this about a trip?"

"Peter, I had an important phone call last night, I tried to reach you, but there was no reply." Peter had a quick flashback of singing, drinking, dancing and a taxi home.

The voice continued.

"Seems they have a problem up north and need your expert advice. Your uncle apparently has some clout with our area manager and has asked for you specifically."

"Tommy, up north? Where?"

"Not sure exactly, Easton mean anything to you?"

"Colliery? Easton Colliery? It's in my home town."

"Well, get up and get dressed and packed; you're going home! Call me when you're more coherent and I'll brief you further." Click.

Peter Graham replaced the handset and sat staring at it. What was going on, and why him? He was going back to where it all began

21

so many years ago, Bathgate, his place of birth. He had travelled a long way since then, school, university, geological trips and surveys around the world, then a resident position with the Yorkshire Mining Corporation where he had been for the past two years since his graduation. Uncle Tommy had been almost like a father to him, adopting the role after Peter's parents had died in a car accident in December of 1968. Peter had been at Edinburgh University at the time and Tommy had come to see him to break the news. They became close after that, his uncle recommending that he pursue his chosen scientific path in the coal industry.

Peter had followed his advice and made his uncle proud. Now he was living in Doncaster in a small but comfortable one bedroom flat near the centre of town. He checked the clock, and headed for the shower. Half an hour later, dressed, clean but unshaven, he was downing a cup of strong coffee. He finally felt ready to call his boss. When he had finished the call, he was indeed intrigued. What the heck had happened up there? He couldn't wait to see for himself.

He dragged his suitcase down from the top shelf of the wardrobe and dumped it on his unmade bed. He started to pack absent mindedly. Fortunately, it was Sunday and he had picked up his washing from the laundrette the day before, so everything was clean and already folded. He made mental notes as he went along, things he might need, depending on how long he was going to be there. According to Eric, that information was unknown at this stage. He was finished by noon, just in time for him to nip out to the local supermarket for his extras, and to drive the ten minutes into town to pick up essentials from his office; the tools of his trade. Peter wanted to make an early start in the morning, so he drove his maroon Ford Capri into his usual service station and topped up the fuel, oil and checked his tyre pressures.

He spent the rest of the afternoon making phone calls to people, advising them of his new assignment and that he would be gone for an indeterminate amount of time; his friends from work, his football team and a couple of casual female acquaintances. Fortunately, he didn't have a girlfriend, so was free to come and go as he pleased. He went out to eat that evening, a simple mixed grill at his favourite steak house; had a couple of glasses of house red wine and some of their delicious coffee. All the while through his meal, he had bouts of nostalgia and resurgences of forgotten memories. It was more than four years since he had set foot in Bathgate, for the funeral of his parents, which was still painful to him. On a happier note, he thought of his old friends, his time at school, his girlfriends, his first car, and…Annie.

He tried to forget about her, but here she was again in the forefront of his mind. No matter what he did for the rest of that night, she would return again and again. He went home around nine and checked everything. Satisfied, he opened a bottle of red wine and poured himself a healthy shot - his only option since he had no wine glasses and was using a tumbler. Mellowed by the wine he went to bed early, conscious of an early start on Monday morning. As he settled for the night, Annie came back into his thoughts. He didn't fight them this time; he went with the flow, the first time they met.

It was at Bathgate Pally, the Palais de Danse, to be precise, and he had gone with his friend Big Al. He ventured upstairs to the balcony cafeteria and there he saw her. She was conspicuous, the new girl in town. She also stood out because she wore her hair long to her shoulders as opposed to the fashion then of high, bouffant beehives, held together with gallons of hairspray. Her hair was a soft, shiny chestnut colour, more a Marianne Faithful than a Dusty Springfield. She was standing with some friends of his so he was accepted in their midst. During a lull in the music when the band had finished their poor rendition of 'Satisfaction' (the Rolling Stones they were not), he asked Sheila to introduce him to the new girl. Annie turned to face him and held out her hand.

"Annie," she said, "Annie Wilde, Wilde by name, wild by nature."

She gave him a genuine smile. He looked her up and down subconsciously, taking in the tight fit of her midnight blue dress, the hint of cleavage and her perfect form tapering off to beautifully shaped legs.

"Ahem," she coughed, "see anything you like?" Peter stammered an apology saying his mind was elsewhere, which only made it worse when she asked, "Can I have a guess where?"

Quickly he changed the subject. "Your accent, it's not from around here is it?"

"Ah," she mocked, "an observant boy, I want him!"

Peter blushed again, much to the amusement of Big Al and the rest of the teenagers. After that, the night went better and he had a few dances with Annie whom, she had told him, came with her parents to Bathgate where her Father had a long-term contract in the building sector. She hailed from Helensburgh, in the west part of Scotland and accordingly had a delightful western lilt in her voice and accent.

24

It turned out that, not only was Annie going to the same school as Peter, but they shared a couple of classes too. The opportunity was there for them to see much more of each other and they took advantage of it.

Peter took driving lessons as soon as he reached seventeen years old and passed his test a month before his eighteenth birthday. On that day in May 1966, his parents presented him with a little second-hand Morris Minor car. He loved that car and took great care of it, using it whenever he could, budget allowing. He and Annie travelled all around the place, the town, the county, and even the country: Knock Hill, Linlithgow, Edinburgh and Glasgow.

A few months later, on Annie's eighteenth birthday, she persuaded him to take her to the Knock Hill after a Friday night dance where, in the back of the car, in the moonlight, she gave her virginity to him.

However, their euphoria only lasted another month when, out of the blue, Annie's Father informed her they were returning to Helensburgh. His contract had finished and he had taken up a permanent position back home. Peter had been successful in obtaining a place at Edinburgh University where he had assumed Annie would join him, now it appeared that Annie had to go to Strathclyde University on the other side of the country. The young couple were devastated, but swore their undying love with promises to meet whenever possible and to write every week.

Initially, the letters were frequent but soon slowed down to once a month. Then Peter had to go to America on a six-month geology survey at the Grand Canyon. He wrote to Annie saying not to write to his old address, but he would let her have his temporary address in the States. He sent her a postcard from there with his new details but heard nothing in return. When he returned to Edinburgh, he expected some old mail; but there was none. After that, his studies and field trips kept him occupied and travelling; rock formations in Hawaii, volcanic magma in the Philippines, various mining locations at home and abroad. Soon, Annie became a distant memory. The geologist settled into an uncomfortable sleep with disturbing dreams involving loss and searching.

ooo000ooo

On Monday morning, he awoke early a few minutes before his alarm rang. He showered and dressed, had a light breakfast of toast and coffee, then began to carry his gear down to the car. Two trips were sufficient and he looked around his apartment as a final check, then, on an impulse, opened up his bedside cabinet and took out his passport. You never know, he thought. He locked up and backed his car out of the garage and, checking his rear mirror drove off smoothly with a smug grin on his face, pleased with his organization. Two minutes later, he was back at his flat having forgotten his wallet. He drove off again, not feeling quite so smug.

He headed north on the A1 having calculated that he would miss the rush hour around York; a straight run to Newcastle where he would stop to eat, then over the hills to Scotland, heading through Jedburgh towards Edinburgh where he would veer west on the A8 and follow the turn off for Bathgate. He reckoned five hours driving and

26

another hour eating which would get him to his home-town by one or two in the afternoon.

His timing was pretty accurate such that it was almost eleven thirty when the Capri climbed the Cheviot Hills to the border with Scotland. Peter had driven various ways to his homeland, but he preferred this A68 route by far, over the boring A1 eastern coastal road or the A74 on the west side. He loved reaching the top of the pass and seeing the borders of Scotland displayed before him. He stopped the car and stepped out to breathe in the fresh air. He smiled when he remembered Annie and the trip they had here in the old Morris Minor.

There was the ten-foot tall granite stone, marking the border; England, in large metal letters embedded in the rock on its north side and Scotland, emblazoned on its south side. Annie hopped from one side of the stone to the other, chanting "Scotland, England! Scotland, England!" As she skipped. Then she laughed and said, "Can you imagine their faces at school when they ask what I did this weekend and I tell them I went to England - twenty times!"

Peter got back in his car and drove with a smile on his face through Jedburgh, Laurie, and Dalkeith to the outskirts of Edinburgh before taking the Ring Road West. Within half an hour, he had driven past Newbridge, Broxburn, Uphall, Dechmont, Boghall, and was heading down Edinburgh Road towards the centre of Bathgate. He saw the Fairway Motel on his right where he would be staying for the duration of his time here, but he decided not to check in as yet. It was almost two o'clock, giving him plenty of time to visit the Colliery and introduce himself first.

He found the way mostly from his own memory, but also from

27

the map that his boss had given him. As he drove into the access street, he was not prepared for the sight before him. The entrance gate was obscured behind a swarm of families and the media, hustling for whatever news might be given out. He had to slow down to a crawl as he approached the gates, people reluctantly moving out of his way, peering into his car to see if they recognized him as someone who might feed their hunger for information. Eventually he got to the gate itself and gave his I.D. to the young policeman on duty. He gave Peter a serious look, and then signalled for the gate to be opened, the police keeping the throng at bay.

Once inside, Peter was led to the administration building where Lizzie, the receptionist and the manager's administrative assistant, showed him into the main office. Harry shook his hand and offered him a seat. Peter could see the manager was under severe stress.

"What the heck is going on?" he asked.

"Oh," moaned Harry, "it's been like this since yesterday. The Press and families of the missing shift want to know what is going on, they are not going for our 'spin' story any longer."

"Wow. No pressure, huh?" was all Peter could say.

Harry gave a tired smile. "You must have driven all the way here? Let me get you a drink at least - tea or coffee?"

Peter opted for the coffee and Harry was just about to hit the intercom to Lizzie when it buzzed at him.

"Yes?" he asked impatiently punching the button.

"Mr. Grant, sorry, but it's Jock; he is desperate to see you, and he looks very agitated and ashen. I think you should see him right

28

away." She blurted out.

"What now? OK, let him come in. I'm sorry Peter, I don't know what all this is about, and it shouldn't take a minute."

Jock barged into the room and stammered,

"I just got a buzz on the emergency phone from Level 17. They want the cage down there right away."

"Who buzzed you? There should be nobody down there!" Harry yelled.

"It's them, boss...Saturday's day shift. They're back, Mr. Grant! All of 'em...they're back!"

"I'm sorry; I don't understand any of this." Confessed Peter.

"You and me, both!" Sighed Harry. "Jock, are you saying all the men from Saturday's shift are now back?"

"Yes, boss," nodded Jock, "this is some weird shite."

"They're still at Level 17? You didn't bring them up?"

"They're all still down there, I didn't know what to do, I just ran straight here."

"Have you told anyone else?"

"No, Mr. Grant."

"OK Jock..." Said Harry, thinking as fast as he could, his brain trying to compute the new information.

"Call the incident room and get me Inspector Mathieson. No one else, you hear? If he's not there, tell them to find him! Then make sure the elevator room is clear of anybody. Get those lads up. Tell them nothing except not to leave the lift foyer until I get there. Is that clear?"

"Yes, boss." Whimpered Jock, rushing back to the control room.

Peter stood up, amazed and Harry was in a spin.

"I need them all together; this place won't do, too small. The Canteen! Yes! The Canteen!" He said to no one in particular.

He looked at Peter and saw his confusion, but did not have the answers just yet. The intercom rang and Harry explained to Bob Mathieson what had occurred and his plan to have the men assembled in the canteen. Bob agreed but also suggested medical support might

30

be advantageous, sending Alex Phillips to locate the on-duty doctor as well as the Police Physician. Within minutes, Harry, Bob and Peter were making their way to the lift room, picking up Hamish and Brian on their way.

The cage door opened and Saturday's day shift poured out grumbling and complaining. Harry ticked off their names one by one. When it was concluded that all were present, he advised them that there was a situation concerning their welfare and that for their own protection, they were required to go to the canteen to await instructions.

As the men ambled off, still grumbling, the police inspector said to Harry, "We have to make some sort of statement to the crowd outside. Do you want me to handle it?"

"Would you?" asked the distraught manager. "It would be greatly appreciated, thank you."

"Right," said Bob, "I'll just tell them all are safe, but have to undergo precautionary medical examination before they can be released. And they ought to be back with their families in a few hours."

Harry set off down the corridor towards the canteen while Bob went in the other direction towards the people waiting outside at the gate.

The crowd were happy with the update, but still hostile with the continued delay and the lack of answers. Bob finished his statement and returned to the offices amid howls of protest. Things were no better in the canteen either. The manager and his staff were having great difficulty keeping order amid a barrage of questions and complaints. The miners all wanted to know what the hell was going on

31

and how long they were to be detained there. Some were yelling that they were starving, others that they were gasping for a cigarette. Harry told them that there were staff on duty at the canteen and if they were patient, they would rustle up some food and, due to the circumstances, he was allowing them to smoke in the normally 'No Smoking' eating area. This, at least, brought subdued cheering.

The canteen was large enough to seat forty-eight people around eight six-seater tables. Harry had sat the men down while he and the others stood at the serving end in front of the kitchen. Bob took his place among the managers on his arrival.

"What have you told them so far, Harry?" he asked discreetly.

"Absolutely nothing, Bob. How do you tell twenty-four men they have lost two days of their lives and no-one can explain it?" he whispered despondently.

Bob sighed, "OK," he said, "here we go."

He banged on the stainless steel servery with a large spoon.

"Gentlemen! I'm afraid I have disturbing news for you. It appears that by some strange circumstance you have all been part of an inexplicable phenomenon and have been absent for forty-eight hours. For those of you who have not yet realised, it is now 2:30 pm, Monday 29th May."

There was pandemonium in the cafeteria. Bob's next words were swamped by protest and disbelief, Bang! Bang! Bang! Bob waited for quiet.

"Unfortunately we know as little as you do. We have no answers, no theories. That's why you've been kept here. We need to interview all of you, one by one, and then we'll have you medically examined to try to bring some sense to this madness. After you have eaten, we will conduct interviews and medical examinations when the doctors arrive."

There were more yells of protest.

Yelling above the din, the police inspector added, "This is in your own interest, and the more you cooperate, the quicker we will finish and you can all return to your families!"

The noise lessened as the men, now dazed and close to shock, restricted the protestations to those around them. The canteen workers asked if they could serve tea, and producing the beverage was enough to temporarily quell the noise.

During the light meal that followed Alex returned with the two doctors, Andy Lennon, a young local Practitioner, and Paul Stewart, the portly Police Medical Advisor who had been on duty at Bangour Hospital on the outskirts of Bathgate. They set up emergency examination rooms, one in the First Aid room adjacent to the canteen, the other in the canteen manager's office. Meanwhile, Bob and Alex along with Peter and Brian had set up tables and chairs for interviewing in the games room behind the café.

The room was relatively quiet while the men ate, save for the usual clatter of plates, clinking of cutlery, and muted conversation between mouthfuls of sausage and egg. Most comments were incredulous affirmations punctuated by the normal expletives, others expressed fear and concern, while yet other comments ranged from theories to rumour mongering; touching on all things weird from alien abduction, underground attacks by Russia or China to the supernatural and witchcraft. At least one table saw humour in all this as Joe Turner

33

made his dining companions laugh by calculating how much overtime the company owed him for the two extra days.

When all were done eating, Harry explained that names would be called and each miner would undergo an interview followed by physical tests. Once they had been given the all clear, they could all go home. This was greeted with a mixture of cheering and jeering, some happy to be going home, some chagrined by the delay.

The interviews at first were taking ten minutes or more, but soon became shorter as it was apparent the feedback was unanimous in its lack of knowledge. The medical examinations took longer, but Dr. Lennon's assistant, Peter MacMahon, had arrived too, and within just two and a half hours all the men had been seen and passed healthy. The police inspector, to a loud cheer, announced they could all go home.

While the miners rushed out to tearful reunions with family and barrages of questions from the media, the remaining doctors, police and staff wandered back to the conference room to analyse their findings.

Harry, who had sat in on a number of the interviews, looked around the faces next to him and across the table; shrugging his shoulders he said, "Well, who wants to go first?"

Peter couldn't help noticing the tiredness that had crept over the Manager's face since he had first met him only a few hours before. Now, his eyes were sunken and darkly rimmed, his skin drawn and pale.

"In a nutshell," volunteered Bob, "we are no further forward whatsoever! You heard some of the statements; they all had the same ring to them. No one saw or heard anything untoward. None of them

34

could even remember any incident or accident with the cutter machine. All they remember, and that went for all twenty-four of them, was going down on shift at 6 am on Saturday morning and coming back up eight hours later. The fact that they were two days late still hasn't sunk in with them. Some were afraid, some are still in denial, others were whinging about missing nights out or darts matches...it defeats me, it really does! In police terms, the interviews were inconclusive to say the least."

Harry sighed then looked over at the doctors.

"You guys come up with anything?"

The younger doctor picked up his notes and leaned forward then, as an afterthought, sat back down and offered the floor to his senior, Dr. Stewart. The police doctor immediately gestured carry on intimating that, at this point he was merely an observer.

Dr. Lennon nodded then read from his notes.

"We found medical evidence of the lost days in the tests we made; slight dehydration, minor nutritional deficiencies, a few cases of minor shock (which is understandable since it's not every day you learn you have been missing for forty eight hours and know nothing of it). Apart from that, they were all remarkably fit and none the worse for the experience, in fact, better for it."

"What do you mean by that, doctor?" inquired Bob.

"Well," Andy looked over to the older doctor who nodded encouragement.

"There is one instance of concern and curiosity. Sandy McLeod. I know Sandy; he's a patient of mine, and a diabetic. He requires insulin injections twice a day else his blood sugar gets out of whack and he loses consciousness and if not treated, can fall into a coma; in extreme circumstances, it could actually prove fatal. We had a scare last year at the New Year when Sandy got drunk and forgot his injection."

"Yes?" prompted the senior policeman.

"Well, that's just it, Inspector. He didn't have insulin with him. His last injection was the morning before he went on shift. Instead of a jab every twelve hours, it's now been almost sixty hours since his last! I gave him a shot, just in case, but he had no symptoms whatsoever to indicate anything adverse. All his sugar counts and other tests proved normal. Under normal circumstances, he'd be dead by now."

There was silence round the table until, "Doo doo doo doo, doo doo doo doo..." Sang the young constable in a poor parody of 'The Twilight Zone'.

"Shut it Phillips! We're not amused!" Yelled the inspector.

"Sorry Sir." Alex whispered.

"Hmmm," broke in Brian, "perhaps the lad's got a point there?"

"How do you mean, Brian?" asked Hamish.

Brian had his head down, concentrating on destroying a plastic cup he was toying with. He looked up at the white tiled ceiling of the meeting room, then slowly round the table.

"Let's face it. There is something weird going on here. We have some of the best minds in the coal industry here at this table. We have years of experience and we have the detection skills of the police. Yet we can come up with nothing! We have no explanation, so why not the paranormal?"

36

"Come on now, Brian; don't tell me you believe in all that mumbo jumbo?" Bob Mathieson said sceptically.

Undaunted, Brian continued.

"Just what do we have, Bob? I've heard more theories today just listening to the men at dinner than anything we could come up with. Off the wall sure, Bermuda Triangle, time warps, aliens - you name it. I know it sounds batty, but we can't close our minds to anything at this stage."

Bob sighed and scratched his head. "Look, we are all getting tired. I think anything further we propose tonight will be pure conjecture or hypothetical. I suggest we all get a good night's sleep and bend our minds round this tomorrow. What say we all meet here at 8 am?"

There were nods of agreement round the table.

"Yep." Conceded Harry. "I for one am completely knackered. Tomorrow we can all go back down there and have another look-see; young Peter here can take his samples and analyse that wall. Maybe something will come of that. I don't know. Anyway, the danger seems over, so I'll get the men back to work tomorrow, but we will leave Level 17 well alone."

"OK, that does it for me." Concluded Bob, "Except, someone needs to make an official statement to the media out there…Harry? Your turn!"

Harry groaned and rolled his eyes to the ceiling as they all gathered their notes and prepared to leave. As they meandered out of the room, Lizzie, still at her reception desk, waved frantically at her boss.

37

"I'm sorry, Mr. Grant, I couldn't stop them. They insisted on seeing you before you left."

"Who did?"

"Crawford and Robertson, you were all in the meeting room, so I told them to wait in your office."

"Shit!" Harry spat the word out, then sighed, "Ah well, it was to be expected. No farce is complete without Heckle and Jeckle."

He headed for his office, walked straight in and sat down, settling himself before acknowledging the union reps before him.

"Listen guys, I'm really tired, can't this wait till morning?"

"Mr. Grant." began Tam Crawford, ignoring Harry's request,

"We've heard rumours that shifts start again tomorrow?"

"Yes, that is my intention. Is there a problem with that?"

"Unless you think twenty-four men missing isn't a problem?"

"Look, they are all accounted for and passed medical fitness.

There was an incident on Level 17 and it's out of bounds until investigations there are complete."

"Well, we want compensation for going anywhere near this 'incident'."

"Aye!" Agreed Jim Robertson. "Come on guys!" Harry protested. "You've had two days paid holiday, I've had two days lost production." Tam leaned across the boss's table and whispered loudly,

"We've heard things. Like 'aliens' and that sort of thing."

"Aye!" Supported Jim.

"I'll bet!" Roared Harry in exasperation. "Typical mine grapevine, if you haven't heard a good rumour by ten o'clock, start one, right boys?"

He sat back in his chair and held his head in his hands, massaging his temples.

"Tell you what," he suggested after a moment, "we're two days behind in our weekly quota. I'll allow overtime to try and catch up, and if you do, I'll pay one pound bonus per man next week."

"Overtime at double time?" asked Tam.

"No way! Time and a quarter!"

"Time and a half?" Tam countered tentatively. Harry was too tired for prolonged negotiations. He gave in.

"OK." He said.

"Now can you two please leave? I have to make a statement to the press now and I want to get home."

"Fair enough, Mr. Grant, but I'm warning you. One more 'incident' and I'm calling everyone out!"

"Aye!" Agreed Jim yet again.

"Does he say anything other than 'Aye'?" The Manager asked Tam.

"Aye!" Replied Jim.

"Believe me, Mr. Crawford." Harry said emphatically between clenched teeth. "Another incident like Saturday and I'll have them all out, before you even know it happened!"

ooo000ooo

Peter drove back to the Fairway Motel, his mind buzzing. He had been awake since six a.m. and had driven around three-hundred miles.

The Fairway was new to him, a recent business that had opened since he was last in Bathgate. It stood on Kings Road on the corner with Academy Street, a smallish building consisting of two storeys of brick interspersed with the pinkish hue of Fife stone mix. It had only six letting rooms on the second floor above a bar, a restaurant and the manager's flat.

"Yes, Mr. Graham, we have your reservation. Will you be staying long? It doesn't say here."

The matronly wife of the manager multi-tasked as receptionist and barmaid.

"I'm not sure at this stage, sorry. A few days perhaps?" he answered.

"Aye, well, if you could let us know soon as, it's just we have a big golf competition on the weekend, we need to know if your room'll be free." She smiled at him.

"I'll be sure to tell you," he said. "Do I need to leave a deposit or anything?"

"That won't be necessary; the booking's covered by the Coal Board. I just hope they settle it quicker than the last time. Will you be wanting a meal here tonight? It's just that you're the only guest till Friday, and I need to let the kitchen staff know."

Peter smiled since he was sure this attractive middle-aged woman was also 'the kitchen staff'.

"Yes please, but nothing too much...something simple would be fine."

She supervised him signing the register then said, "Would you be wanting a drink from the bar now?"

"No thanks," he said, "I'll just get to my room and shower and change first."

"Well, there's a fridge bar in your room if you prefer. Would 7:30 be OK for dinner?"

Peter looked at his watch: it was 6:30.

"Sure, that will be fine." He replied.

"Here's your key, it's the first on your left at the top o' the stairs."

The motel (or inn) seemed pleasant enough. It had red tartan carpet throughout, juxtaposed with plain, cream wallpaper. The guest's lounge was sparse; a few wooden coffee tables and accompanying lounge chairs in plain dark green upholstery with wooden arms. The walls were festooned with a myriad of framed photographs featuring golfers receiving trophies.

His room was typical of most hostels springing up around Scotland, having only recently moved into the motel business, American style, away from the boarding house concept. It was roomy; a large double bed with an elaborate bedspread, a coffee table, desk, television, bedside tables and lamps, two armchairs and a drinks fridge. Peter was relieved to see that the red tartan flooring gave way to neutral grey carpeting in the rooms. He spotted the en suite bathroom complete with a shower.

He dumped his bags on the floor, and was half-undressed before he reached the bathroom. He turned on the shower and adjusted it, then stripped off the rest of his clothing and stepped in, letting the water cascade over his head and body. As he showered, thoughts of the day swamped his mind. His eyes screwed up tight as he tried to assemble his mind into some form of pattern, attempting to apply some logic to the scramble it was.

Just what had he gotten into? What was going on? Nothing made sense. Disappearance, then reappearance, memory loss. It was all a jumble. He had thought he might make a nostalgic trip around his home-town tonight, but now he just felt tired and hungry. Mentally filing away the events of the day, hoping they might make more sense in the morning after a good night's sleep, he decided to have his meal, unpack, sort his clothes for next day and check the equipment he had brought. Happy with his agenda, he dried himself off and, throwing on a casual t-shirt and jeans; he went down to the dining room.

While Peter was relaxing, later that evening, in the hills behind him a few miles away, Martin Preston was in his car with Sheena Watson.

"Woooooohooooooo!" Sheena squealed. "Those Moscow Mules certainly have a kick, I shouldn't have had so many! Was it five or six?"

"You had three, Sheena." Martin answered with an undertone of annoyance.

"Whatever!" She giggled. "Maybe it was the grass then?"

"You only had a few tokes." He reminded her.

"I feel sooo good! C'mere, lover!" She laughed as she dragged him across the front seat of his five-year-old Ford Cortina.

"Hey!" He howled in pain. "Watch it! The gear stick's jabbing into my leg!"

He sat back rubbing his thigh.

"Let's get in the back, then!" She whooped. She hastily opened the passenger door, practically falling out in the process.

He watched her scramble out and stagger to the back door in the dark. He liked Sheena. She was fun and pretty, with brown hair to her shoulders; ample tits but maybe just a bit too much beef on her backside. She had a great sense of humour, was loud and extroverted but when tipsy, a great lay, or so he had been told.

Martin was twenty years old, to her nineteen. He was medium height, thick, black, curly hair and slim build. He worked at the Iron

43

Foundry, having just newly served his apprenticeship, while she worked part-time at Boots the Chemist. That's where they had met, a couple of months ago when he visited the pharmacy for headache pills.

He let himself out the driver's side. He figured he had brought her here for a reason: So what if she was a bit tipsy. So what. He was horny and she seemed up for it tonight, drink or no drink. He stepped out into the cool air (Cairnpapple was never the warmest place on earth) and looked around him. In the dark, he could just make out the shapes of the hills; the Knock to his right and Cockle Roi hill in front, towering over him like a sentinel, guarding the burial ground at its base. In the sparkle of periodic silver light as the moon scurried between clouds, he noticed the glint from the granite stones surrounding the ancient burial grounds. This was Martin's favourite spot to bring girls. No one ever came here at this time of night, and the car park for visitors to the mound was perfectly placed behind a curtain of pine trees. It was the closest you could get to absolute privacy.

He opened he back door of the car and Sheena dragged him inside. He fell on her, his face in her cleavage. She laughed, and picking his head up by his hair, began smothering him with kisses.

"Hang on!" He protested. "Take it easy. Slow down. Let's do this properly, or one of us is going to get hurt."

She released him and he sat beside her, catching his breath. He looked at her, and she gave him a teasing, inviting smile.

"OK." She said, holding his gaze. She slowly began to remove her light blue, cashmere cardigan, one button at a time. He watched enthralled, his penis beginning to stir as she uncovered her white bra and slipped her hand seductively inside one of the cups.

44

Crack!

"What the fuck was that?" he jumped, his head spinning round to the back window.

"Now what?" Sheena wailed in frustration.

"Didn't you hear that?"

"Hear what?"

"Sounded like someone was out there."

"No, I didn't. Look, you want to do this or what?"

Martin relaxed, and turned his back to her-

"Sure, Baby," he whispered as he stroked her bare leg all the way up her thigh under her denim skirt. She moaned at his touch and pulled his head onto her breasts, running her fingers through his hair. Suddenly she pushed him away from her as she sat bolt upright.

"What is it?" gasped Martin.

"I heard it that time Martin, someone is out there! I heard rustling, like footsteps, honest!"

"Shite!" Cursed Martin. "I'll sort the bastard out! Friggin' peepin' Tom!" He threw himself out of the car.

"Oi!" He yelled. "Who the fuck's out there?" but there was no reply.

He walked to the driver's side and, slipping his hand through the half-open window, he flicked on the headlamps. He gasped as he saw in their beam a misshapen entity. A thing dressed in black, but looking like neither man nor beast. It was large, very large, but appeared smaller in its crouched position as if ready to run...or attack. It held its arms (or wings) up over its face, shielding its eyes from the glare of the headlamps. Then, it turned and took off at alarming speed

45

in a loping, leaping motion. Sheena screamed.

"Holy fuck!" Yelled Martin, shocked and frightened.

"What was that?" he shouted to her.

"I've no idea, but let's not try to find out! Let's get the hell outta here, Martin!"

Martin paused briefly, and then they both jumped into the front seats of the Cortina, the tyres screeching on the tarmac as he reversed back into the car park then soared onto the main road.

ooo000ooo

Long before Peter's alarm clock went off the next day, and long before Sheena and Martin decided to report their experience to the police, Jamie Wardrope was in the milking shed fitting the automatic suction caps to his cows. He was muttering to himself.

"That's the second good milker I've lost this year!" He said, whilst staring at the newly empty berth in his shed.

He had had a herd of twenty good dairy cattle up to this morning, but when he and his black and white border collie, Jess, had gone to bring them in for milking there was a gap in the fence and only nineteen cows remaining.

"Well," he continued, speaking to no one except perhaps Jess, who inclined her head as if listening to the old Farmer, "we can take a walk after breakfast and check out the old silver mine acreage. See if she got herself lost or stuck down there. I'd swear these Hamilton's in the next small holding had something to do with this...but I hear they lost a sheep themselves last month."

46

True to his promise, he and Jess set off on a hike after Jamie had milked the cattle, let them out into the north paddock to graze, loaded the milk churns onto the pick- up platform for the dairy truck to collect, and shared his toast and marmalade with his canine companion.

The Wardrope farm had been in the family for generations, it covered over three hundred acres of land, hills, valleys and meadows. At one time, it was arable, but the Forestry Commission had made an offer to turn the majority into timber plantation where it now yielded a substantial income in fence posting and building contracts. It served Jamie well since it was low maintenance farming, and allowed the ageing character to potter away with his few head of cattle and lease out the remainder of his prime grazing lands.

Mrs Wardrope, had long since passed away, that fever 'flu of the 50's'. His two sons had gone to Agricultural College to learn animal husbandry and had gone into business together south of Edinburgh, breeding racehorses. They honoured their father with occasional visits and unsubtle suggestions that he should sell out while the going was good, and go live with them. Jamie wasn't having that. He steadfastly refused to move away. He was born there, and he would die there and that was the end of it.

As he and Jess left the huge, old, stone farmhouse, built by his grandfather before the end of the last century, Jamie looked around him. He would never tire of this view; winter, spring, summer, autumn. Each three months brought with them a variance of colour and texture, as if an artist had arrived at the end of one season to paint the next. All around him were the gentle slopes of the Bathgate Hills, the highest point being only one thousand feet above sea level.

Some hills were bare and rocky; others covered in lush grass, while others wore their dark, evergreen forests like huge capes wrapped around them, protecting them from the biting winds. His farm stretched almost from Linlithgow in the north to Beecraigs Reservoir in the south. To the east was Mackenzie's land in the valley, and still put to crops. On the other side of the road, the back hill road between Bathgate and Linlithgow, was the old Campbell farm. Campbell himself having sold out to the Scottish Heritage Society years ago when they wanted to secure Cairnpapple for posterity as a site of, 'archaeological and historic interest', and to protect the public right of way to both the Knock and Cockle Roi Hills. The Heritage Society, not having the means or the manpower to farm the lands they had bought, leased out the areas they didn't require to 'smallholdings'. One farm hence became three small self-sufficient 'holdings' of around ninety acres each.

Harris had the south section adjoining the major spread of Beecraigs and he kept it in fair order, still sewn to crops (mainly turnip and barley). Scott held the central portion, and was, in Jamie's opinion, a real pain. He thought he knew everything, always trying something new, but would always come unstuck and be hammering on Jamie's door for help with this, or to borrow that. The north section however, being mainly on the foothills and lower slopes of Cockle Roi, gave old Wardrope his biggest headache- Hamilton and his blasted sheep!

It was a beautiful morning for a walk. The sun was shining and there hadn't been rain for a few days, so the ground wasn't too wet or muddy. Jess ran on ahead as usual, investigating scents, and then

48

haring back to Jamie to check that he was still going in the same direction, to race off again. The old farmer enjoyed his walks, preferring to cut across fields rather than use the roads. That way he could stay private while checking on stock or fences at the same time. It also gave him time to walk and whistle and think of happier times, times when he had walked his land with Eileen by his side, or watch his sons scampering ahead with the dogs. He followed the route he thought a cow would follow if it were allowed to roam free.

On the down slope from his home, he saw the lake by the Silver Mine glistening in the morning sun both picturesque but dangerous. No one quite knew why it was called the Silver Mine; there was a cave there on the far side of the lake, cut into the rock - part nature, part man-made. Was it a cave or a mine? No-one living knew for sure, not even his grandfather. Tin mining was the popular bet, but it was never certain when (or if) it had begun or ended. One thing he did know was that it wasn't anything now.

He and his brothers (and latterly, his sons) had all explored the cave and found it to be less than forty yards deep, with an entrance tall and wide enough for maybe two or three persons to enter at a time. Inside was a dangerous, rocky under footing, and the more adventurous who reached the end found themselves facing a man made concrete wall.

Jamie, unbeknown to anyone except his dear departed wife, was a bit of a romantic at heart, and often liked to think the valley had got its name not from silver or mining, but from the small loch guarding the cave entrance. On those beautiful, balmy, summer nights when the moon was full, Jamie and Eileen had often walked to the end of the farmhouse perimeter fence, where they could look over the valley.

There, they saw the lake bathed in reflected moonlight as if it were a huge reservoir of pure silver. Jamie was distracted from his reminiscing as he spotted another damaged fence.

"Hmmm," he thought, "she did come this way, but what the heck is a cow doing breaking down fences like that?"

He followed the trail all the way down to the water, expecting to see his beast any minute or, at worst, to find her carcass in the deep pool. Jamie knew the 'lake' was no such thing and was constructed by man hundreds of years ago to provide a capture for water for whatever activities took place at the cave. He knew also that it was small, fed only by a tiny natural spring and dammed at the north end, but had steep banks and became very deep very quickly.

There were no signs of the wandering bovine, but Jamie was startled when he heard Jess barking furiously and darting back and forth from the cave entrance. She was behaving as if she was on the scent of something, but the old farmer had never seen her so agitated before.

He went to explore Jess's inkling and discovered, about four feet from the opening of the tunnel, a relatively fresh cowpat. He stood and leaned on his staff, took off his cap and scratched his baldhead.

"How strange," he said to the barking Collie, "how very strange."

He gave it plenty of thought on his way back to the farmhouse, mulling over possibilities from the sublime to the ridiculous, and came up with no explanation.

"I'll have a word with Hamilton, just the same." He decided.

His lack of concern and urgency in the matter was understandable. This was a farm; things died, things went missing. Generally, they were found later, or their remains were dragged off by foxes. A few years back, when his livelihood depended on his produce, he would have been more eager to resolve the mystery - a good milking cow was worth the effort. But now the small dairy herd was like a hobby for him, something to keep him occupied and active. He didn't even need the milk. He had no pasteurising plant on the farm, even that was done at the Cooperative Dairies, where he sold his surplus for a few shillings a day. All he kept was enough for himself, his cats and Jess. On reflection, he couldn't remember a year when they hadn't lost at least one beast. He shrugged his rounded shoulders, called on Jess, and began the climb back to his home.

ooo000ooo

Peter awoke from a disturbing dream, wondering why no one was paying attention to the fire alarm ringing at the coalface. It was a few seconds before he realized it was his alarm clock and another few moments before he remembered where he was.

He crawled out of bed, sauntered, eyes barely open, into the toilet, emptied his bladder and, slipping out of the shorts he wore for bed, stepped into the shower and let the water complete his waking process.

At 7.15 am he was showered and shaved and had changed into the clothes he had lain out the night before, a pair of dark blue

51

jeans and a casual sports shirt. In his bag were his coveralls, Wellington boots, thick socks, and a miner's safety hat. He wandered down and into the dining room. Although he knew he was the only guest, he noticed that all tables were set for breakfast. He was surprisingly hungry and had two eggs, bacon, a slice of flat, Scottish sausage, some button mushrooms and a couple of rounds of toast with butter and honey. Leaving the maid, waitress, barmaid and receptionist, he made his was to Easton Colliery. He jumped in his car and pulled out onto King Street.

Another car, going east, tooted its horn making Peter brake hard.

"My God," said Peter sarcastically, "another car. It must be rush hour."

At five minutes to eight, he was walking into the main reception to the colliery offices noting with relief that the crowds of yesterday were no longer massed at the gates. The full team was assembled in the meeting room as arranged the day before. Harry was already in coveralls, as were Hamish and Brian; Inspector Mathieson and Constable Phillips were in uniform, and another thickset man in red coveralls Peter hadn't met before.

"Good, we're all here then." The Manager said. "Peter, this is Charlie Peters, our Health and Safety Officer. Charlie, this is Peter Graham, our Consultant Geologist." Peter smiled at his new title, and shook hands with the safety officer.

"Right..." Continued Harry, looking at Peter and the Police, "You boys better get down to the locker room and get changed or geared up or whatever. We'll meet you in the elevator room when you're all ready."

Peter couldn't help noticing the change in the pit boss. The dark patches were no longer visible; his eyes were alive again and despite his build, he looked fit and dapper in his coveralls. In fact, they all looked well considering all, that is, except Alex Phillips who had gone to football training, which quickly had developed into a piss up. He was looking rather peaky. As they walked together to the changing rooms, Peter leaned over to Alex, out of earshot of his boss, and whispered, "Doo doo doo doo, doo doo doo doo!"

Alex groaned and covered his ears.

Peter whispered again, "Nice of them to bring Father Christmas along," referring to the safety officer in his red jumpsuit, "bet he doesn't get it dirty!"

Alex managed half a smile.

A few minutes later, they were all prepared; lamps, flashlights and power packs issued and slung on their belts. They boarded the shaft cage empty handed, except Peter who carried his aluminium equipment case. Jock let them down to Level 17.

As they alighted, Bob Mathieson told them to stay together, so that they could all progress as one. He wanted the area investigated inch by inch. Slowly, they worked their way round the loading area, and then began down the tunnel. When they got to the end of the lighting that Hamish had had reinstated, Harry suggested he run more extension cable through to the end. With Hamish and Peter's assistance, they had four electric lights rigged up around the cutting wheel in less than ten minutes. The search, as before, rendered no further clues.

53

The inspector rubbed the back of his hand over his forehead, leaving a black streak-

"OK guys, it's all yours. See what you can make of it, but keep me informed."

Hamish immediately headed for the mechanical mole, Harry close behind him. They needed to assess the damage and determine whether it could be salvaged. Brian, on the other hand, grabbed Peter's arm and urged-

"Come on! You have to see this."

He led the geologist to the coalface where the last cut had been made. Peter gasped in amazement as he stared at the smooth black wall before him. He had never seen anything like it. He ran the beam of his torch all around the perimeter of the shiny area - about six feet in diameter -similar to the circumference of the wheel, he estimated. He touched it, and gasped again at its smoothness and texture.

All he could say was, "Fascinating!"

He called Inspector Mathieson over.

"This is incredible, am I free to take samples? I have to examine this, take the specimens back up to the lab where I can set up my microscope and things."

"Yes, of course," conceded the policeman, "do what you have to do."

Peter opened his metal case and took out a small hammer and chisel. He tapped on the wall, merely scoring the surface.

"Shit!" He cursed, "It looks like coal, but it's a lot harder. I'll need to drill or cut."

He came back to where Harry was with Hamish and explained his predicament.

"OK." Said the Manager. "You'll find grinders and drills with the construction crew's equipment, use what you need. It's electrical, so we will need to run more cable extensions for you."

Twenty minutes later, and Peter was set up with power and a hand drill. He was about to start when Charlie Peters yelled-

"Wait! These shafts are tested each shift for gas seepage. It's been a few days now since this tunnel was checked out. The construction foreman keeps a gas detector with him for specific checks when they do 'hot work' like welding. Its possible there could be a build up or pocket of gas here. I'll go see if I can find a detector."

Within a few minutes he was back holding a black box, its strap hung over his shoulder. In his left hand, he held a plastic hollow wand attached by tube to the box, and in his other hand another tube with a bulb of rubber half way along.

Peter laughed. "I thought you had gone for a canary!"

"Fuck off!" Laughed Charlie. "We're not that backward here!"

He pumped the bulb with his hand as he waved the wand around the coalface, the pumping action sucking in the ambient air through the detector.

"Alex, in view of what you were drinking last night, I'd advise you to stand back. If you let one rip you'll set the alarm off!" Joked Peter.

"H-huh?" stuttered the young Policeman subconsciously stepping away from the safety officer.

There were knowing sniggers among the remainder of the

55

party. Bob Mathieson raised his eyes to the ceiling in mock disbelief. The dial on the monitor consistently read 20% oxygen, and there was no beeping to indicate gas.

"OK." Said Charlie. "It's fine." He continued.

Peter started the drill and the relative silence was filled with the whirr of the motor, then a screeching sound as he introduced it to the surface. It penetrated after a few seconds of purchase.

"Great!" Said Peter, "Now I need a different drill bit. Brian, can you reach my case? See if you can find my circular bit, I need to take core samples."

The surveyor located the two-inch diameter drill bit and passed it to Peter.

"Do me a favour?" he asked, "grab one of these sample bags, and hold it under the drill for me? Try to collect some dust as I drill."

They continued the operation four times, the geologist taking samples from different areas of the material. Peter scribbled a quick drawing on the notepad in his case, marked where the samples had been taken from, and numbered them one to four, labelling the dust particle bags Brian had collected in the same way.

He went back to where the others were milling around the giant machine.

"OK." He said to them all. "I've got what I want for now, I need to get back to the surface to have a look at this in daylight and under a microscope, run some tests. Can I be taken up now, or do I have to wait for you to finish?"

Harry looked over to Hamish, who shrugged. "Not a lot more we can do here, now. The cutter doesn't seem too badly damaged. We

56

do need lifting gear though to set it upright and give it a test run."

Inspector Mathieson agreed they had completed their search, and Charlie nodded assent, so Harry raised his hands and said, "Fine. Let's get out of here then."

On the way back to the lift Alex whispered to Peter, "You bastard! You had me going then!"

"Sorry?" asked Peter, his mind on other things.

"That gas detector - I thought you were serious!"

"Oh, that!" Laughed the Geologist, "Actually, it's not that far from the truth. That detector isn't as sensitive, it's only for oxygen and combustible gas, but there are others for specific gases. In Grangemouth at the chemical plant there, they have detectors for individual products. One of the by- products there is hydrogen cyanide- deadly. I had to laugh when I visited there as a student. All the operators were at great pains to tell me that one whiff from that would kill me in seconds! Then they told me it smelled like toasted almonds. I always wondered if one whiff killed you, how did they know what it smelt like. I had this vision of some poor chemist taking a sniff, collapsing on the floor, and in his last dying breath gasping, 'Toasted almonds!'"

Alex laughed, "You know, you're crazy!"

"So they tell me," agreed the geologist, "so they tell me."

ooo000ooo

Peter left the others at the lift exit and headed towards the little laboratory on the south side of the administration buildings. Harry

57

had told him to look for Debbie, the full time lab technician, who would give him all the assistance he required.

The geologist found the lab easily enough and entered a spacious room about six yards square. There was a long workbench down the centre of the room with space for a stool, and a passageway at each end. A further two stools stood on either side; the perimeter walls covered in shelving and cupboards with waist-high work surfaces. All, that is, except the wall at the entrance, which had two metal four-drawer filing cabinets flush against one corner, while the remainder was plastered with posters of rock identification pictures and level depth charts.

The shelves were filled with books, mainly reference, but here or there were notebooks or files. On the bench itself, were open folders and metal gas 'bomb' sample bottles, a few pieces of testing equipment, Draeger Tubes, litmus paper, note pads and pens.

There was no sign of the technician herself. Peter pulled up a stool at the far end of the bench, which was relatively free of debris, and opened his sample and tool case. He took out the plastic bags with the specimen from Level 17 along with some basic tools; his notepad, a jeweller's eyeglass and a few coloured pens. He was already looking at his first sample, turning it slowly in the overhead light when the door opened and Debbie walked in, her eyes glued to a clipboard she held in her hand. She was walking directly towards the geologist when he called out, "Hey!"

With a shriek, she jumped back and dropped her clipboard. Automatically, both bent to pick it up and...Crack! Their heads banged together.

"Ouch!" She yelped.

"Ouch! Twice!" He retorted, rubbing his forehead. "Sorry." He added. He bent down again to retrieve the clipboard just as Debbie was about to do the same.

"It's alright," he warned, holding up his hand, "I'll get it!"

Handing it to her, he introduced himself-

"I'm Peter Graham, the geologist Harry sent for. He said I should look for you. Hope you don't mind me making myself at home?"

"No, not at all," she said affably, "I've been expecting you. But, well, obviously...I hadn't expected you here, now!"

"Sorry again." He said. "I didn't realize you were from Glasgow?"

"I'm not!" She moaned with a hint of bruised pride. "What makes you say that?"

He winked and said, "Just that you greeted me with a 'Glasgow Death Kiss'!"

"A what?" she gasped, flushing slightly.

"You know, a head butt? From Glasgow ganglands, their trade mark?"

"Oh," she realized, giggling. "I'm so sorry; I don't normally see a lot of people down here. It's unusual for anyone to be waiting for me...you startled me."

He smiled back at her-

"Right! Now you can tell me what you have by way of facilities and apparatus, and show me where everything is."

"Ok, Mr. Graham, we..."

59

"Peter." He corrected kindly.

She smiled.

"Peter; it's a bit basic here, but I'm sure we can find some things to assist you with whatever you need. Mr. Grant, Harry, will authorize any requisition I make and it can be here same day if available locally or next day from Edinburgh Head Office."

He followed her round the lab as she opened and closed drawers and cupboards pointing out various types of equipment - microscope, over head lighted magnifying glass, precision scales, Bunsen burner, and a tool box with hammers, chisels, clippers, pincers, tongs, vice and other things he might need.

Debbie was a middle-aged lady, but was tall, slim and agile enough to flit around the room with ease. She had greying, reddish brown hair tied up in a bun, accentuating her slim neck; she also had pretty grey eyes behind half lens spectacles, the legs of which had cord attached and hung around her neck like a black necklace. The white lab coat over a navy skirt and white blouse polished off her professional demeanour.

She had begun her career many years ago, having trained as a pharmacist, but gave it up in favour of motherhood. Now, with her two daughters in their late teens, she had gone back to work where her certificates and experience, albeit almost twenty years old, had easily qualified her for this mundane position.

"Will you be alright for now, Mr. Gra...Peter? I have a few routine things I have to attend to, but just yell if you need anything."

"Yep! I'm fine thank you, just go ahead, ignore me!" He replied.

"I'll get us some tea first, if you like? How do you take it?"

"I prefer coffee, if you have any?" he asked.

"Well, we only have the vending machine stuff, if that'll do?"

"Good enough for me!" He laughed.

As she left, Peter was still trying to place her accent. It was definitely Scottish, but it was well spoken and without lazy colloquialisms. It was a bit like his own, nurtured by a few years of annunciating words in an endeavour to be understood by non-Scots.

By the time Debbie returned, the geologist was already immersed in his investigative work. Some of the dust particles they had collected were already caught between two glass slides ready for microscope examination, with the other core samples labelled and placed on the bench with notes scribbled beside them. He was busy looking at one sample through the mounted cantilever magnifying glass, whilst beside him was his jeweller's eyepiece and a small metal hammer resembling a miniature ice pick. He would move from magnifier, to eyepiece, to microscope, then to his note pad, scraping, hammering, scribbling and every now and then uttering a few words of disbelief. Debbie noticed with amusement that he hadn't touched the coffee she had brought him in the horrid little plastic cup.

He occasionally walked over to one of the rock and coal sample charts and compared his specimen with something pictured there. Sometimes he would forget he still had the jeweller's glass held in his eye and would step back cursing at the chart. Finally, he sat back on his stool and absent-mindedly picked up the plastic cup, taking a full swig.

"Yeuch!" He winced, wiping his mouth, "It's cold!"

Debbie giggled, "It's been there almost an hour! Anyway, I was just about to ask if you wanted to have lunch. It's almost 1:30 and I usually go at this time to get something at the canteen. It's relatively quiet there after the day shift has been fed."

"Good idea." He said. "Just let me make a quick phone call first. How do I get Harry?"

"Easiest way is dial zero. Lizzie will pick up and put you through."

Harry said he would have everyone assembled in an hour or so to hear the initial results or findings from the geologist's analysis. Peter followed Debbie to the canteen, and found she had been right about it not being busy.

Out of sheer nostalgia for his student days, he could not resist the temptation of the Scottish pie, chips and beans. The lab technician gave him a reproachful stare over the top of her spectacles as she chose some macaroni cheese and salad. He also grabbed a large mug of black coffee and, winking at Debbie, said, "At least it's hotter than yours!"

She smiled, rolling her eyes to the ceiling in mock exasperation, and went to find a free table – a relatively simple task since only one other was occupied.

They engaged in light conversation over lunch, Peter giving his dining companion an abridged version of his origins and career to date. Debbie, reciprocated, telling him about her Husband, Alistair MacDonald, a Local Government Officer working in Linlithgow, and her two daughters, Morag and Sheelagh; one in her first year at university studying accountancy, the other about to start her first year at Bathgate Technical College after the summer holidays and attempting to do something in interior design.

Debbie also inadvertently answered the question Peter had wanted to ask regarding her accent, when she explained how they had all come south from the Fort William area, shortly after the birth of their second daughter and as Alistair had been successful in gaining the

63

position of assistant treasurer at West Lothian County Council, based in Linlithgow. They had found a nice place to live on the outskirts of a little village called Torphichen, about half way between Bathgate and Linlithgow.

As to her soft-spoken Scottish accent, Peter recalled an unexplained phenomenon in the Highlands of Scotland. It seemed that as you travelled north and west, the accent thickened or broadened, even to the point where other Scots had difficulty understanding. In some cases, a distance as little as twenty miles could open up a new language. However, for some reason, in the area of Inverness, on the shores of Loch Ness, the inhabitants spoke the proper, Queen's English, albeit with a soft Scottish accent.

Theories abounded as to the reason for this, some say it was due to an influx of English teachers in the vicinity, or an English Kirk minister; or, going even further back, to an English Lord of the Manor exerting influence. Others again, say it is due to the tourism industry. That particular area being one of the most beautiful and most frequently visited areas in Scotland, with imposing mountains and the series of lochs, and not forgetting of course its most famous inhabitant; Nessie the Loch Ness Monster. It was believed the Highlanders in that region learned to temper their accents in order to be understood by Sassenachs (strangers) as a necessity; you can't extract a tour fee if they can't understand when you tell them the price!

Debbie interrupted his thoughts as she got up to leave and saying with a smile, "Ah well, back to the grind. And you, have your meeting to attend."

Peter accompanied her back to the lab where he picked up his notes and samples and headed for the meeting room. The usual quorum had gathered in the small office used for interviews and Board or Managerial Conferences. Harry, Brian, Hamish and Bob Mathieson and in addition was the rotund and red-faced Charlie Peters. Peter mused to himself that it always seemed that health officers invariably appeared the least healthy characters. There was another person in the room this time. Peter recognized his Uncle Tommy immediately and, after greeting everyone else, he strode directly over to him with his hand outstretched and a huge grin on his face.

His uncle grabbed his hand and pumped it.

"Good to see you, Peter!" He boomed, smiling affably, "It's been a long time!"

"Yes." Replied Peter, "Too long! Good to see you too, Unc. You're looking really well, lost some weight too?'

The area manager let go of his hand and waved his in the air.

"Let's not go there!" He urged in mock horror. "Your Aunt Linda is on one of her health food kicks, I'm surprised I don't have rabbit teeth by now. When you get time you must come over to dinner."

Then, in a stage whisper, he added, "But if I were you, I'd eat before I came!"

They both laughed and Peter promised he would drop by soon.

"Well," continued the area manager, changing the level of his voice to include the others, "we have business to attend to, so let's get right down to it. What have you got for us, Peter?"

His young nephew set up his effects on the boardroom table-

65

"I'm afraid, all I have is more questions rather than answers. What we have here is something new and, in my experience, unique. The microscopic analysis of the powder collected is simple enough; yes, it is coal, but of the highest purity. It has basic elements missing that we would expect to see in natural coal formation, gases and tars for example. If I didn't know where it came from, my initial opinion would have been that it was some form of coke; coal treated by heat to remove impurities and give clean burning for industries. Suffice to say, that is impossible in real terms here."

There were mutterings and nods around the table. The geologist continued-

"As to the solid samples we took..." He held up the four cylinders of the specimens taken and holding one in his hand, he passed the other three around the room for all to examine. "...they have a porous subsistence, but if you look at the end you will see it is practically smooth. Coal, as we all know, is formed from compression of fossil remains over millions of years - predominantly wood - layer upon layer of dead carbon based vegetation. The weight over the years causes it to crush on itself and compact into the solid matter we see as coal or, fossil fuel as we call it. That's what makes it relatively easy to mine; it cuts and breaks with little effort as our tools fractionate the compressed seams."

To demonstrate, he held up a normal sample of coal he had picked up from Level 17, about the size of a small cigar box. He traced the uneven surface of it, pointing out the seams within, and then he struck it with his small hammer. It shattered along compressed joints and fell on the table in five or six pieces. He then tried the same thing with the drilled sample he had. The hammer hardly dented the object after repeated blows.

"This..." he said, pausing for effect. "...is not compacted or compressed. This appears to be fused!"

His audience shifted in their chairs, muttering words of disbelief. Peter went on-

"As I said, this only leaves us with more questions than answers. I have never seen this before. The closest I can get to a theory is that it resembles rock I have seen when working with lava from volcanoes. It would take extraordinary heat to cause this fusion, and it still wouldn't explain why the surface was so smooth. We are aware that millions of years ago this area was volcanic; Edinburgh Castle rock and Arthur's Seat, the hill to its north east, are both extinct volcanoes. But no one is aware of any historical activity in this vicinity. It defies logic. And..."

Again he paused, making sure he had everyone's attention-

"What really scares me is that the power that would be required to accomplish this would not only have to be phenomenal, but it could not have been achieved without oxygen. Where did the oxygen come from at that depth?"

As Peter sat down, the muttering around the table grew with intensity each talking to his neighbour. Eventually they all fell silent, staring at the samples before them.

Tommy Graham spoke first.

"Well, well, well! One mystery follows another. Anyone got any comments or ideas?"

Bob Mathieson added his own question.

"Peter, is it possible this has just gone undetected and we are only finding it now?"

"Nothing would surprise me in geological terms, Bob." He replied. "I have seen some incredible things, and new discoveries are made each year; this, defies explanation for it to be so isolated from anything else. I have to do more work to confirm whether it is indeed isolated or if it has a source. We have to map the lode path."

"How do we do that?" Bob asked.

"Similar to tracing coal, diamond, gold seams; first we drill deeper into the face we already have and try to determine direction, then we hope we can drill down and take soundings from the levels 15 and 16 directly above. It may be difficult since they appear to be running parallel to the coal seam in Level 17, but this anomaly seems to be at a tangent."

"You know what?" Harry interjected, "I always had a bad feeling about this seam. I said so to Hamish before." Hamish nodded agreement. "There was nothing I could quite put my finger on, but something about the soundings just didn't ring true. I put it down to error tolerance on equipment and instrumentation. Maybe you could have another look at that data, Peter?"

"Sure." He nodded. "I'll look into everything."

Harry continued, "I don't know what equipment you need, but if we have it, it is all yours and if we don't have it, we'll get it. Hamish, why don't you get together with Peter after the meeting and draw up a list of requirements?"

"I'm on it, boss." Hamish replied enthusiastically.

"Fine," concluded Tommy, "looks like we have some action

68

we can get our teeth into. I can't see us doing anything more here for now. Shall we call it a day?"

"Hmmm." Bob murmured. "This is all very well, and sets your men on a road to explore the geology and technicalities of this strange business, but in my view, it goes no way to explaining the disappearance and re-appearance of twenty-four men!"

"You're right, Bob." Agreed Tommy. "But we're all out of theories there, this may or may not throw light on the whole situation, but we will have to wait and see. It's all we've got for the moment. Yet, like you, I fail to see how there can be any connection. Anyone else got any ideas?"

The assembled Managers looked at each other again, and then Brian suggested hesitantly-

"I had a thought the other night; it's a bit off the wall, but in the absence of any conventional pursuits...what about hypnotherapy? I have heard that it's worked with amnesia victims before. If we could get some of the men to agree to it, they can perhaps be regressed?"

There was silence around the room.

"Why not?" asked Tommy eventually, "nothing ventured and all that." He paused before continuing-

"Harry, can I leave that with you and Bob?" And Both men nodded affirmatively.

The meeting concluded and after Peter had made his farewells to his uncle, he went into Hamish's office and discussed the tools and equipment required. Peter was pleased to note that most were readily available on site and Hamish could obtain the rest fairly easily. The engineer told him he could have everything delivered to Level 17 by morning by leaving instructions for the night shift.

The geologist thanked his associate then, aware that he could do no more that night, said his Goodbyes and returned to the Fairway in time for a shower and change of clothes, before deciding to eat in again.

ooo000ooo

After dinner - he ate lightly having been still quite full from his large breakfast and heavy lunch - Peter decided to clear his mind of the events over the last two days. There was nothing he could do for now, and felt that chasing shadows without sufficient information was a total waste of time. A nostalgia trip seemed like a good idea; a drive round old haunts, maybe a beer in an old watering hole. He set off around 7:30 into a mild, balmy, Scottish, late spring evening, and was amazed to find just how quickly he got round everywhere. His memory (before he could afford a car) was of walking, or taking the bus; it always seemed to take forever, taking into consideration his size while walking with juvenile footsteps, or the waits at bus stops and the perpetual stopping en route.

Within just a few minutes of leaving the Fairway, he was already driving round the Marchwood suburb, past his old street and the house where he spent his formative years. How small his street seemed yet, when he was younger, he could remember it being longer and steeper. He knew everyone in every house then. How many were still there now, he wondered? He resisted the temptation to find out.

He drove along Kirkton Road until it became Marjoribanks

70

Street, passed the Academy and drove down Hopetoun Street, glancing at the shops as he passed through the main thoroughfare.

Wee Jock's' Café was unchanged, he had spent many nights there usually broke, but trying to look cool with one coffee or one coke lasting all night. Speedie's the Butchers was still there, as was the dance hall, Bathgate Palais, where he had first met Annie.

He drove on, up to Glenmavis and down to Belvedere, out to Falside and Windyknowe and back towards the town centre again. Realising just how little time it had taken him, he thought he would try further a field and, to his surprise, places he was familiar with but had taken the best part of a day to visit were suddenly well within reach. Within an hour in his car, he had gone south to Whitburn, then north east to Blackburn. That had always intrigued Peter as a kid; Whitburn and Blackburn were on the same small river, yet upstream it was white (Whitburn) and downstream it was black (Blackburn).

Controversy raged as to whether it turned black because of the hygiene of Blackburn residents, or whether it was Whitburn residents' effluent that turned it black for their downstream neighbours. The truth be known, it was neither black nor white, just muddy. He continued towards West Calder, another den of iniquity from his past, many a night being spent at the Polytech dance hall there. Then he turned north towards Broxburn, and back west along the A8 road to Boghall and Bathgate. He smiled at the memories it conjured up, and also at the speed in which he was now able to visit all these places of his past. He mused, the story of my youth in sixty minutes!

He stopped at Kaimpark Hotel on Edinburgh Road and had a half pint of beer. Not seeing anyone he recognized, he made his way

71

back west and returned to the Fairway. No one was there to welcome him home. There was a note in his key partition asking him to mark a box on a breakfast menu as to what time he would wish to eat in the morning. He ticked seven a.m, and after a nightcap of Drambuie from his mini-bar, and he slipped into bed knowing that tomorrow was going to be a busy day.

REUNION

True to the Scottish weather, Peter awoke to the pitter-patter of rain on his window, the 'heat wave' of three days seemingly over.

Hamish met the young geologist at 8 am with the news that everything was set up for further investigations. He and Peter went straight down to Level 17 to survey the equipment and the handpicked men (non-union volunteers) assigned to the tasks. Peter marked the areas where he wished bores taken, and the depth he required.

In addition, he and the engineer paced the levels approximately eighty feet above using Brian's drawings and plotted the direction at right angles to the Level 17 tunnel. They marked off a few spots for vertical bores to be taken after work was completed in the shaft below. That done, they returned to the surface for a coffee while waiting for the first bores to be drilled.

Hamish left to supervise the work, and Peter told him he would be in the Lab should he be required before the first cores were available for examination. It was less than half an hour later when the phone rang. Peter ignored it at first, thinking it might be a routine call for Debbie, but he left his mountain of blueprints and the soundings data Harry had sent him when the ringing became persistent. Obviously, Debbie had gone out somewhere. With a mutter, he picked up the receiver- "Peter Graham here."

"Peter!" Hamish's voice was urgent and excited. "Get down here quick! You've got to see this!"

"What is it?" Peter asked.

73

"We had only drilled in around six and a half inches, then...
nothing!" Hamish yelled into the mouthpiece. Peter's brow furrowed in
confusion.

"You mean you got to six and a half inches and could go no
further?"

"No!" Hamish now sounded on the verge of hysteria. "We
drilled in and...Nothing. We thought it might be an air pocket, so we
tried the other two areas you had marked. Same thing, nothing, hollow!
You'd better get down here, fast!"

Peter's mind was racing. He threw on some coveralls and
boots and was on his way in the cage within five minutes.

The engineer met him gibbering excitedly.

"It's a cave of some sorts. We shone a lamp in through one
hole and looked in the other. I can't explain or describe it; you have to
see this for yourself!"

Peter did just that and stepped back in amazement.

"See how much of this wall we can knock out." He said
decidedly.

Hamish picked up the drill, while Peter and one of the
volunteers picked up sledgehammers. They were amazed when the
whole thing gave way without too much effort. When the dust had
settled, Peter just gazed in awe at the opening. With the light
emanating from Level 17, he could see that the internal cave led back
at least twenty yards before the gloom prevented further visibility.

"Incredible!" Peter exclaimed, "You checked for gas?"

"Yep." Answered the crew foreman, a large man looking
ominous in his dark work clothes and features made angular from the

lighting and lamps on their helmets.

"It's air alright, 20% oxygen."

"Jesus!" Said Peter, "How?"

He made to start forward into the cavern but Hamish caught his arm. "You have to be crazy to go in there! Remember, twenty-four men went missing! I reckon that's where they were!"

"I remember," agreed Peter, "but someone has to investigate. Are you game?" The engineer groaned.

"Now how did I know you were going to say that? OK, but let me get some ropes. We don't know if the ground is safe, and if I disappear, I want someone to pull me back! I can't afford to disappear for forty eight hours - I'm on a promise tonight!"

Peter laughed. They both tied rope around their waists and set off like mountain climbers. They took lamps and torches with them and followed the tunnel for around eighty yards until they came to a dead end, similar to the one they had just broken through. Peter looked all around him and whistled as he took in the formation of the tunnel.

"This is the result of heat, Hamish, I'm sure of it. How it was formed, I haven't a clue. Call the others in with the drill and hammers and let's see if this is another entrance or a solid wall."

After twenty minutes, they had broken through the second barrier and found another tunnel, this time forking into two passageways with sealed entrances to each.

"What is this?" asked Hamish, an element of fear in his voice.

"I don't know, I just don't know. Look at the walls and the ceiling. This has been caused...or should I say, made - formed, by tremendous heat fusion. Look over there," he gestured, pointing at a

75

tunnel. "There has been sandy soil in this area. Look where it has fused; it's almost like glass in parts."

Hamish looked where the geologist was pointing, and, as he turned, the light from his lamp reflected off the glass like substance casting prismatic rainbows on the ceiling of the structure.

"I don't like this, Peter. Let's get out of here. At least let's get more men down here. Safety in numbers!"

"OK." Peter agreed and turned to make his way out. "Wait!" He called.

"What's that?"

Adjacent to one of the passage-blocked entrances, he had noticed some scrapings on the wall surface. He traced it with his forefinger.

"This looks like markings of some kind; purposeful, not random."

He was looking at a series of vertical lines with horizontal lines coming off the vertical at uneven intervals and at different angles.

"Bit like early hieroglyphics, perhaps a counting system of sorts?" He suggested.

"Beats me," said Hamish hurriedly, "But I want to be out of here before whoever, or whatever, comes back!"

With that, everyone headed back to the main seam face, the engineer practically dragging the geologist along by the umbilical rope. Peter asked the foreman to have the area lighted and guarded; no one was to be allowed in without his authority or accompaniment.

"Aye!" Said the foreman. "But if ye don't mind, after we light it, we'll guard it from the upper levels. I don't think my men'll be too comfortable down here for too long!"

"Fine," conceded Peter, "just as long as no-one gets down here, OK?"

ooo000ooo

A hasty meeting was convened to discuss this latest turn in events. Of course, Bob Mathieson insisted he be taken there right away; soon enough he and the manager, along with Peter, Brian and Hamish were making their way back down. Peter delayed them for five minutes while he ran to the lab for a Polaroid camera and some film. Peter wanted to knock down another entrance wall, but the police inspector forbade it, insisting he have more men there first, and reminding them this was still a police investigation. Instead, they all headed back for the surface and reconvened around the table, each one pouring over the eighteen snap shots Peter had taken with the self-developing film.

"What do you make of it, Peter?" asked Harry.

"I don't know; I have a hundred thoughts running through my brain right now! The first thought is just too wild for words and the rest are even worse! I would say someone, or something, is definitely down there, or has been, Lord knows when. I have no idea how the tunnels were executed; I wouldn't have a clue as to who may have the technology to do that. I would hazard a guess and say it was done relatively recently, but no-one can do that without high energy output and the equipment necessary would have to be so bulky...I can't see how they could have managed it at this level, nor did I see any

77

evidence of it."

"But what about these markings?" asked the policeman, holding up a photograph.

"I'm sorry, Bob, I'm a geologist. We did skim over some archaeological work in studies where the two factions had mutual interest, but I'm afraid it wasn't my forte. All I can say is it looks like very ancient Egyptian or Babylonian type script or count marks."

"Well, who can tell us?" asked Harry.

"I have a friend in the history faculty at Edinburgh University." Brian suggested.

"Perhaps he can throw some light on it?"

"Fine," said Inspector Mathieson. "This is urgent, I'll get one of my men to courier the photographs to him. I'd rather we did it so we can keep this under wraps for now. We have a bad enough rapport with the Media at present - I don't want this to leak out."

ooo000ooo

Professor Douglas Dalyell (D.D. to friends) shifted his thin frame uncomfortably in the large, leather armchair in the university reception lounge. He scratched thoughtfully at the grey whiskers on his chin as he scrutinized the photographs before him one by one; his mouth appeared to form words, but no sound came out, as he tried to decipher the context. Finally, he gasped and sat back, sinking into the plush upholstery and crossing his legs. Constable Phillips could not help observing that one of the lecturer's socks was on inside out.

"Where on earth did these come from?" he asked after

clasping and unclasping his fingers a few times, an expression of animated excitement, "they are truly remarkable." He continued without waiting for an answer.

"Finest examples of script of this age I have ever seen; very early Celtic writing. No! Earlier even than that, Runic I would say... yes indeed! Runic! Magnificent!"

"Writing you say?" asked the Policeman, "Can you tell what it says?"

"I wish I knew, my boy, I really wish I knew, but not my field I'm afraid; sort of thing old Dr. McCabe was into, but he's dead now, heart attack..." His voice trailed off as he picked one of the pictures up and examined it yet again.

"Is there anyone else you know who might be able to assist us?" Encouraged the young constable.

"What's that? Hmmm? Oh yes...sorry...ummm...there is someone, very competent, over in the west, lectures at Strathclyde University in Glasgow from time to time. Did some work for us last year. I think I may still have a card." He leaned over the arm of the lounge chair and rummaged in his briefcase. A few minutes later, he sat upright, his thin face now red from the effort of bending.

Alex Phillips couldn't help thinking and smiling that it appeared that the old man's head was upside down, no hair on top, but ample whiskers below.

"Ah!" Gasped the Professor, "Here it is!"

Alex took it from him.

"Thank you Sir, you have been most helpful." Alex said politely.

"Hmmm yes, well, let me know what you come up with, can you? I am so intrigued by this, amazing, truly amazing. Where did you say you found this?"

The lecturer was still examining the photographs.

"Bathgate, West Lothian." This was all the information Alex divulged.

"Now, if I could just have the Polaroids back?"

"Oh yes, yes. Of course." The Professor scooped them all off the glass coffee table before him and handed them to the policeman.

"Thank you, we'll be in touch." Concluded Alex, as he left the elderly gentleman still muttering to himself.

Two hours later, the young policeman was back in Harry's office at Easton Colliery, and the manager was already finishing his call.

"Great." He said, "Doctor Fraser will be with us around 2 pm tomorrow. Can you let everyone know please, Alex? I want a full quorum so we can collate all the information for the doctor."

"No problem, Harry. I'll get right onto it."

ooo000ooo

In her neat apartment, overlooking the Gairloch on the Firth of Clyde, Doctor Annie Fraser's mind was racing as she packed her clothes for a few days travel. Three aspects were competing for attention in her brain, and she had difficulty with each. First and foremostly, was what she should take with her, how long would she be staying away from home? The second thing was the amazing find that

80

had been uncovered in Bathgate. And last, but not least, was Peter. Peter Graham, after all these years she thought.

"Focus." She willed herself, "First things first!"

She lived on the top floor of a three-storey block of apartments with a commanding view of the River Clyde estuary and the Naval Base on the north shore. It was small but comfortable, as much as she needed since her divorce from Richard Fisher, Dick to his friends, 'Dickhead' to her. She chose the flat, not only for its view, but also for its spaciousness. It had a large lounge, which she had furnished after her divorce settlement.

It featured a cream, short pile carpet and five-piece Lounge suite; including matching coffee table, TV, music centre, desk, a glass fronted cupboard, a folding table and a few scattered wine tables supporting either vases or antique lamps. Her kitchen was basic, with a table, chairs and assorted cupboards. Her bedroom contained fully fitted wardrobes, drawers and a vanity table with mirror. A large, double bed featured in the centre of the room, tastefully covered with a bright sun and moon motif duvet and an array of multicoloured cushions.

Her favourite room, however, was the second smaller bedroom that had been converted into her own 'romper' room. It was filled with her books and files. She spent more time in this room than any other.

"What to take, what to take?" she muttered to herself as she surveyed her wardrobes.

She needed to look professional, since she wanted to be taken seriously, yet she could not ignore her urge to dress provocatively for

Peter. Her mind drifted yet again in his direction. She shook her head abruptly. Finally, she decided on six outfits; three working suits and three casual, evening wear outfits, along with a couple of sets of coveralls and boots suitable for working down the mine. She filled the remaining available space left in her suit bag with an array of lingerie from her underwear drawer.

Annie finished packing, satisfied that she had outfits for all occasions for at least three days and nights. It was 9:30 pm, and she felt tired. Although she did a lot of travel in her work, she always found the preparation taxing. She sat on the end of her bed wearing only her nightshirt; a white, satin, oversized shirt with an open neck, the hem reaching her knees. Sipping on her gin and tonic, she now felt she was relaxed enough to deal with the other matters on her mind. First, there was the find at Bathgate. She was amazed and excited by it all – twelve hundred feet deep! She had difficulty coming to terms with that, most of her digs were superficial by comparison, usually ten feet deep, perhaps twenty at a stretch.

Annie had gone to university in Glasgow after her return to Helensburgh all those years ago. She was Annie Wilde then. A lot had happened over that time; first, there was Peter. She was always upset that he had not replied to her last letter. She supposed, to an extent, she was as much to blame; the promises made so long ago had quickly dissipated. She remembered her last letter to Peter was in reply to his from a month before. Maybe he never received it. Students at that time and age were, by nature transient; either by choice, moving in with others, or, it was forced upon them by lack of funds, bills, evictions, rent and so on.

She had first of all thought about pursuing history, and had initially plotted a career path in that field encompassing archaeology. But, during the course of her studies, she had become enthralled by culture and mythical legends from beyond history, and became obsessed with putting credence to the fables, if not proof, at least basis in fact. She continued with her prime objective in her historical vocation, but concentrated on her labour of love, both as field studies and theses and with Anthropology, thrown in for good measure. It was in her final year she had met Richard Fraser. She had had a few boyfriends before then, but nothing serious. She always had Peter at the back of her mind - he was hard to forget. Even now, she couldn't recall how her relationship with Dick escalated so quickly. At one time, they were dating; they had slept together on a few occasions and saw each other most days at university where he was studying civil engineering.

Suddenly, she found he was moving in; and there he stayed. Since they were both in their final years and had so much studying to do, they seemed to be able to keep out of each other's way.   The arrangement appeared to be working; then, five months after graduation, they were married. Annie still couldn't understand why she accepted his proposal. Was it convenience? Family pressure? She was still unsure. All she knew was that very soon after, she began to see a different Richard. Gone was the bright young engineering student with potential and ambition. Instead, here was the lazy, balding, drinking womaniser. She forgave his first indiscretion, putting it down to a drunken one-night stand, but separated from him immediately after the second time. One year later, they were divorced. She moved back home then and bought her own apartment looking out over the Clyde.

So, now she was going back to West Lothian where she had spent a year or more of her younger years, when her father had been transferred there in the sixties and where she had met Peter. She had told the manager of the colliery when she received his call that she wanted to keep her involvement secret for now; she wanted to surprise Mr. Graham.

Harry had told her who the other members of the team were whom she would be working with. Her heart skipped at the mention of his name. At first, a darkness came over her, then the pleasant thought of having the advantage and springing her surprise. She sat for a while at work, playing the meeting scene over and over in her mind; be pleasant? Be sarcastic? Be aloof? Pretend she didn't know him? Had forgotten him? In the end, she decided to play it by ear. She retired to bed and drifted off to sleep thinking about that time so many years ago. Could it have worked had they not been separated by her parent's return to the west? What would life have been like with Peter instead of Richard? She wondered if he had changed, put on weight, still had his hair, long, short? Maybe he was married, engaged or seeing someone.

"Stop it." She told herself. "What do you care anyway? It was a long time ago, people change. Go with the flow."

In spite of herself, she fell asleep with warm thoughts of the night of her eighteenth birthday in an old Morris Minor under the shadow of the Knock Hill.

ooo000ooo

84

Annie had not had time to cancel her first class, so the next day she held her morning lecture as usual; her class was small, so she gave them a spot test ignoring their wails of protest, and dismissed them early so that she could get a head start on her journey across the country. Thoughts of Peter had been relegated to the back of her mind now that she was metaphorically wearing her professional hat. She hadn't been able to see the photographs Harry described, but she could picture what they might look like and even more so, when she heard that dear old D.D. had thought them Runic.

She went into the varsity library to withdraw a few tomes on her employee card then threw them into the back of her little Volkswagen car along with all her other notes and reference books she had brought from home. She set off from Glasgow around 12:30 pm, and two hours later, was driving into Easton Colliery. Approaching from the west, she had almost missed it, having only lived in the vicinity for about a year so long ago.

Lizzie met her and showed her straight into Harry's office. Annie was wearing a navy trouser suit with faint pin stripes, the jacket covering a white linen blouse with a frill neck. She wore matching navy high heel shoes, and carried a navy purse along with her black brief case. Her chestnut hair was tied in a neat French twist at the nape of her neck. Harry was stunned and he stammered a welcome, trying not to be blatantly obvious in his admiration.

"I know you said you were at school with Peter but, when it comes to historians, and experts in fields, one always anticipates someone…elderly." He smiled at her.

85

She giggled politely, she had heard this so often in the past.

"Take a seat, please." Harry rushed round from his desk to pull up a chair for her.

"I'll rustle up a cup of tea for you, and then bring the others in."

"Thanks," she replied, "I'm dying of thirst."

Peter and Hamish were heading for Brian's Office when they passed the manager's room.

"Mmm," said Peter, sniffing the air, "Harry's changed his after shave! We'd better keep an eye on him; he may be coming out of the closet!"

Hamish laughed, and said it smelt like perfume.

"Without a doubt!" Agreed Peter, "And expensive too!" He recognized the scent, but couldn't put a name to it. They were just about to enter Brian's office when the manager's door opened.

"Ah! There you are, good. That saves me some running around." He said.

"Can someone find the police inspector and the safety officer? I have Doctor Fraser with me now, so we can all have a chat about what we have found."

"Hmm." Said Peter. "Would it be the good doctor we are smelling then? I had expected an old fogey, but I think we got female company?"

"Never you mind, just get your arses in here, OK?" Laughed Harry.

He returned to his office and, one by one, the others trailed in. Annie was sat with her back to them.

"Doctor Fraser? This is Mr. Graham, Peter Graham. Peter, I believe you know Doctor Fraser?"

"Please," said Annie, still sitting facing across the desk, "since my divorce, I am reverting to my maiden name. I'm Annie, Annie Wilde. And with that, she turned towards the young geologist.

"Hello, Peter." She smiled, and extended her hand to him. Peter took her hand and smiled, "No, I don't think I've had the pleasure of meet... Annie?"

He stopped, abruptly dropping her hand as the realization hit him.

"Annie Wilde! My God! Let me look at you!" He stepped back and looked her up and down, much to her embarrassment. She too gave Peter the once over but much more demurely and discreetly.

As they stood there, facing each other in silence, Harry interrupted-

"Yes, well, I'm sure you two have a lot to catch up on, but that will have to wait. We've got a lot of work to do." He continued with the introductions, until they were all seated.

ooo000ooo

The rest of that day was a blur for Peter. His mind was swimming with memories of Annie. This chance meeting was incredible and too coincidental. He found it very difficult to focus and went through the motions of normality on autopilot. Annie, on the other hand, seemed to relish in his bemusement.

The meeting continued with further introductions, briefing

87

and other updates. It was agreed that they should all re-visit Level 17 so that those who had been there could re-familiarize themselves with the circumstances, while Dr. Wilde might have an opportunity to see all that had been talked about. They all went to change into 'mining' gear. Peter couldn't help observing that Annie looked just as becoming in her tight fitting, tan-coloured coveralls as she had looked in her business suit. He wondered if her hair was as long and silky as he remembered it.

She carried a small case together with a large artists pad for drawing. Annie, like Peter's first descent into a mine, was overcome at the size of the underground operation. She felt heady in the synthetic atmosphere, polluted by the old, musty smell of water-saturated earth. Her discomfort dissipated somehow when she first saw the ancient Celtic markings. She immediately began work on the already uncovered ones, placing artist paper over them and extracting precise facsimiles of them by means of charcoal rubbings on her paper. All others rendered assistance by clearing debris or simply holding the paper in place while she charcoaled. When she had concluded, they returned to the surface, and she and the Geologist retired to the lab to analyse the findings. Debbie had cleared space for them and remained to observe their work, offering assistance where necessary. It didn't take her long to notice that the two young scientists were something more than professional acquaintances.

There was obviously a history between them borne, out by cutting remarks and hidden innuendos; for example, when the geologist was explaining the telephone procedures for internal, external communications, Annie commented-

"Communication? Hmmm...I didn't think you were into things like that."

And again, with reference to the Celtic writing, Annie commented, "Strange how our ancestors devised the means for writing, yet somehow some of us forget how to use it."

Peter jumped at that remark.

"What do you mean?" he retorted feeling somewhat insulted.

"Ahem," coughed Debbie, "I think I'll make myself scarce for a while."

Neither of them paid any attention to her nor even noticed that she was leaving the room.

"Oh, nothing, really." Annie voiced innocently enough, but with such an under current of sarcasm that Peter couldn't ignore.

"You're the one who ceased our communication!" He accused.

"You're the one who didn't respond to my last two letters! I gave you the benefit of the doubt with the first one, but after the second one, I got the message." She countered, with a trace of anger.

"Me?" he asked incredulously. "I wrote to say I was going to the Grand Canyon on a geological survey for six months but you didn't respond! I told you not to write to my current address as I would be leaving in a few days, but I would send my new address when I had one. I sent you a post card from USA with my new address on it and heard nothing since!"

This caught Annie off guard since she had received neither the letter nor the card and had continued writing to his old address. Obviously a communications breakdown neither of them were to blame for.

"You did?" she looked confused. "I never got them."

After an embarrassing silence, Annie pipped up-

"Looks like we have both been the victims of the vagaries of postal services. After all, it's neither here nor there; we each got on with our lives, didn't we?"

"So it would seem." Replied the young man. "Truce?" he held out his hand to her. She shook it and said, "Best get on with this, yes?"

"OK, but maybe we should catch up with each other- Dinner later?" he offered hopefully.

"Well," she thought for a second or two, "I have no other plans, so, you're on. I'm staying at the Golden Circle. We could eat there?"

"Sounds good to me, it's a date!" He said, slightly too enthusiastically.

The rest of the day passed mundanely with discussion restricted to the work on hand with views and theories, all far fetched at this stage and banded back and fore. They left for the car park together, agreeing to meet at 7:30 for dinner.

A CLUE

Peter ought to have felt tired, but had a light step instead as he entered his lodgings. Annie Wilde...he kept saying to himself. He felt like a teenager again, going out on a first date.

"Good evening."

The voice brought him back to earth with a bump. He turned to see Mrs. Tait sat behind the reception desk.

"Hello," he replied, "didn't see you then, but it saves me having to find you." He smiled. "I won't be eating in tonight, got a dinner engagement out of town."

"Oh," she said, sounding disappointed. "I'd got some fine steak for tonight, but I suppose it'll keep. Do you think you could give us some notice to let us know whether you'll be eating here or not?"

"Of course!" He exclaimed, with a suspicion of guilt. "Sorry about that, short notice for me too I'm afraid, but I will try to let you know earlier in the future." With that, he bounded up the stairs, glancing quickly at his watch.

In his room, he stripped quickly, and rushed into the shower, too quickly; having forgotten to let the shower run for a few minutes, he gasped as a deluge of ice-cold water flooded over him. He thought about what he might wear then, having decided on a white turtle-neck jumper, cream slacks and light tan jacket, his mind wandered as to how the conversation might go. He ran possible scenarios over in his imagination, but then gave up.

"It's impossible to have a two way conversation alone." He

91

concluded.

By seven, he was showered, shaved and dressed. He knew it was only 10 minutes drive to Blackburn Road, but nevertheless, he made his way down stairs and set off in his Capri. It was a beautiful evening as he drove along Edinburgh Road and turned right towards Blackburn at the Toll crossing near Kaimpark Hotel. It was a few years since he had been down this road, but he noticed nothing much had changed since.

However, that was not the case prior to his departure as this was the most changed area of Bathgate in his adolescence. He remembered how he and his friends used to take walks down this avenue, with nothing but fields either side. The minuscule river Almond, on the east side, offered many opportunities for adventure, fishing, paddling, (never deep enough, nor clean enough for swimming), building dams, catching frogs or collecting frog spawn in jars. On the west side, was just field after field of Rolling Meadows.

That was until the early sixties, when the whole of Bathgate became excited by the news that the BMC (British Motoring Corporation) had taken advantage of government subsidies and decided to build a car and truck manufacturing Plant on Blackburn Road. The whole area was enthused by the prospect of employment opportunities. The plant took almost two years to complete, and for many months, the site became a quagmire of mud and sludge as huge earthmoving machinery scraped grass and topsoil into huge mounds to level foundation areas, changing the whole topography of the area.

He recalled with a smile how his gym master at school, Big Dan Markie, had sent them on a cross-country run close to the site. He was joking as they left the school grounds-

"And keep away from those bulldozers! I don't want any of you gobbled up by these big machines, it generates too much paper work for me."

On completion, what was previously a green expanse of agricultural land became a series of roads with huge brick and glass edifices in the middle of man-made hillocks and mounds, landscaped with trees and shrubbery. Since then, other companies had followed to capitalize on the subsidies, making both sides of the road into a huge industrial estate.

Now, as Peter drove by, he felt as if he was passing a mini city with its own road system, buildings and lighting, eerily soft against the twilight. He snapped out of his reverie as he came upon the unmistakable landmark of the Golden Circle Hotel tower emblazoned with a huge neon lit golden circle.

He drove in and parked his car as close as he could to the hotel entrance (which wasn't too difficult since there were only a few cars parked). Annie's Beetle was already there. He strolled into Reception and asked for Annie's room number. This caused a bit of confusion at first, as he wasn't sure whether she had registered as Fraser or Wilde, but was pleased to see she was Ms A. Wilde, room 24.

He checked his watch again as he went into the bar: 7.20. Time for a glass of Dutch courage, he thought. He toyed with calling Annie to let her know he was in the bar, but decided to wait until 7:30.

Peter took in his surroundings and noted that, even though it had been years since he had last been at the Hotel, nothing much seemed to have changed. The foyer had a nondescript, oatmeal carpet and cane and glass coffee tables with matching armchairs. There were hallways either side of reception, one leading to the restaurant, the other, to the guest rooms, stairs and an elevator to an upper level, which boasted a coffee shop and more bedrooms. The hallway to the main dining room had an entrance to the right into the main bar; to the left was the entrance to the cocktail bar where he had decided to wait for Annie. The cocktail bar was simple but pleasantly decorated, with seating for around fifty persons. It was pretty quiet tonight. Peter noticed whilst looking beyond the bar, that the dining room was as sparsely occupied as the cocktail lounge was. He chose to wait at the bar and sat on a bamboo barstool.

At precisely 7:30, Annie walked into the cocktail lounge. His heart skipped a beat as he saw her. He was right about her hair; she had combed it out and it fell around her shoulders, soft and smooth with inward curls at the ends. She was dressed in a soft, light blue dress with thin shoulder straps, cut low to show a subtle hint of cleavage, figure hugging to accentuate the fact that she still retained curves in all the right places. The dress was a little above her knees, highlighting her perfect legs. She carried a white cashmere sweater on her arm and a light blue clutch bag in her hand to match her dress and high heel shoes.

She looked incredible. Peter took all this in within the time it took Annie to walk the few yards from the entrance to where he was sitting. He rose from his chair at the bar, took her hand and kissed her cheek, his heart soaring as he inhaled her perfume and noticed her glossy pink lipstick.

She smiled at him, eyes sparkling, and sat beside him. His

eyes automatically dropped to watch her climb onto her stool, exposing a little more of her leg as she did so. Annie noticed his glance and felt inwardly pleased at her inadvertent tease. She asked him what he was drinking, and when he said gin and tonic, she asked for one too. He found it difficult to take his eyes off her and she felt the same way, albeit disguising it better than he could.

When they both had drinks, Peter said Cheers, and they clinked glasses.

"To old times." He toasted.

"To old and new times." She returned.

"So," he enquired, "I want to hear all about what you have been doing since we last chatted."

"Well," she said with a glint in her eye, "I drove back here, had a shower, changed and came down for a drink."

He laughed, "Still as cheeky as ever!"

She smiled then added, "Well, how long do we have before dinner? Do you want the essay version or the abridged?"

"We can go in any time we want to apparently; they're not too busy, as you can see."

Annie looked around. There were perhaps half a dozen people in the bar, and so far as she could see into the adjoining restaurant, only four or five of the twenty tables were occupied.

"Let's go eat then, I'm starving. I suppose we can take our drinks with us?" Peter picked up both drinks as he slipped down from the bar stool and, holding his arm out, ushered Annie towards the dining room.

ooo000ooo

They met the head-waiter at the door; he was a thin, middle-aged man who looked like he had taken his wine tasting too seriously over many years. They were shown to a table near an unlit log fireplace at the far end of the room. Peter sat as the waiter pulled Annie's seat out for her. They were presented with menus, the big sort that requires two hands to manipulate. Peter gave it a quick glance, chose automatically and laid his menu down on the table.

"That was quick!" Annie remarked. "What did you pick?"

"Well, I'm partial to pâté and, if I'd stayed for dinner at the Fairway, I'd have been given steak, so I saw peppered steak and thought, that'll do me!"

"Well," she said, "sounds good to me! I do enjoy a good steak, but I'll go for the prawn cocktail to start with." She smiled at him.

"Ok, done!"

Due to the lack of clientèle, their order was taken very quickly and Peter chose a nice Château Neuf Du Pape to complement the steak.

Having small-talked their way through the first course, Annie finally asked-

"Peter, what have you been doing over the last few years?"

He smiled, waving his index finger.

"Oh no you don't: I asked you first! You were going to give me chapter and verse!"

His little finger waggled making Annie laugh, and with a hint of embarrassment she quipped-

"OK...I'll be brief - the edited highlights from the life of

96

Annie Wilde, a.k.a. Mrs. Fraser!" And for the next hour or so, through the main course and coffee to follow, they exchanged histories, each interrupting the other for more details, names, places and feelings. Annie was upset at the accidental death of Peter's parents whom she had met many times and still had affection for.

When asked if they would like another coffee or liqueur, Annie suggested they have a nightcap in her room where they could have more privacy. Peter's eyes must have lit up, prompting Annie to add the qualifying remark that it was for a *professional* discussion.

The geologist tried to mask his disappointment then smiled as he declined the waiter's offer and asked for the bill.

"Since we are both here on expenses, just charge it to my room." Annie interjected, "It is much simpler that way, and, after all," she added, eyes twinkling, "we are going to discuss business aren't we?"

They headed for Annie's room, choosing to use the stairs rather than the lift, perhaps subconsciously thinking of the huge elevator at Easton Colliery. They entered her room, and Peter inhaled the aroma, still fresh from her shower and toiletry a few hours before.

Peter sat on the sofa - or rather sprawled over it - while Annie made for the mini bar.

"What's your poison?" She asked.

"Hmmm…Any Drambuie there?"

"Yep, got a miniature bottle here and mmm Grand Marnier too! Well, that was easy!"

She poured the drinks and ambled over to the sofa.

"Shove over, you big lout!" She said playfully, nudging his

thigh with her knee.

Peter made way for her, inwardly pleased that she had decided to sit by him and not on the armchair. He smiled at the flash of thigh as she tucked her legs up under her when she squatted down on the other end of the settee.

"So," she began, between sips of her liqueur, "what do you make of all this, really?"

Peter sighed. "I don't know for sure. Weird is perhaps an understatement."

"I know," she agreed.

"What I do know," added the geologist, "is that it is going to be very interesting. And I am particularly favoured in that, not only am I to work with the country's leading authority on runic script, but she also happens to be the most beautiful too!"

"Hmm," said Annie, "bearing in mind the country does not have too many leading authorities, and the top five are all decrepit, retired university lecturers…I don't take that as much of a compliment!"

Peter laughed. "Anyway, is there any value in discussing this at the moment? We are both tired; have little or nothing to go on, all our research and files are at the colliery…anything we do consider can only be hypothetical at this stage."

"I know," she said, "but I can't get those drawings out of my mind. They must mean something. There has to be a key, a clue, something to give us some form of a lead. We are groping in the dark without some direction to go in."

Peter mumbled-

"Groping in the dark is fine by me..."

"I heard that!" Annie scolded in mock severity. "Stay focused!"

However, the point had got across to Annie that discussion on the mystery was futile, and so she began to reminisce.

"Remember our trip to England? 20 times!" She laughed.

Peter laughed heartily too, confessing he had only just recently thought of the same incident on his way north.

"Really," she asked, "and what other 'incidents' have you been thinking of?"

"Oh, that would be telling now, wouldn't it?" Peter teased.

"Aw, do tell." She coaxed seductively.

"Well, from time to time, I think about our first meeting; about the fun we had, the laughs in the old car, your birthday..." He paused. Annie's heart flickered in memory of that night, but she hid it well.

"Yes," she agreed, "we had some moments." She laughed as she had her own recollections.

"Remember the time you were so mad at me when we were out in the boon-docks somewhere, we had a small map and it was summer so we had all the windows open and I let the map blow out the car window at sixty miles an hour?"

"Oh yes!" He exclaimed, the memory flooding back and he teased, "It wouldn't have made much difference anyway, the way you read maps!"

She picked up a scatter cushion from the armchair and thumped his chest with it-

"Cheeky bastard!" She yelled. "You weren't much better; you were always getting us lost!"

Peter's arms were flailing protecting himself from the blows raining on him.

"At least I could...OH MY GOD!" He yelled suddenly and jumped up off the sofa. "That's IT!" He screamed.

Annie was still in shock from his loud reaction and then piped up.

"What is it?" she asked in bemusement.

"What the numbers are!" Peter was still shouting. "You've cracked it, you little, wonderful, brilliant..." Suddenly, he grabbed her face and kissed her on the lips.

Taken aback, Annie was speechless for a few seconds. She composed herself quickly.

"Peter, you're not making sense. What numbers? What have I cracked? And why did you kiss me?"

Peter sighed as if in exasperation.

"The numbers in the tunnels; the clue to the direction and... because I wanted too!"

Annie still sat looking bemused. The geologist sat down beside her, took her hand and looked her full in the eyes.

"Don't you see? The map, the roads, the grid reference numbers. What if the numbers and letters you have found are not script, but just numbers? Grid references, directions!"

Peter could see the dawning on Annie's features, the bemusement lifting, and the frown of concentration changing to a smile of realization.

"Yes!" She blurted excitedly. "Yes, yes...they could well be!"

"We have to get on to this right away." Peter urged as he threw on his jacket.

"Um, Peter?" Annie said matter-of-factly, "It's almost midnight."

"Good lord!" He exclaimed, checking his watch. "So it is. Well, first thing in the morning then. You driving? Or do you want me to pick you up?"

"I'll manage." She said, bemusement now overtaken with amusement at Peter's urgency.

"OK, fine." The young man said, "See you there around eight?" And, without waiting for an answer, he rushed out the door; only to immediately open it again, run back in and give her another kiss, but for longer this time before saying-

"That was a great night, thanks. We must do it again sometime. Tomorrow night?" without waiting for reply however, he was gone, and this time did not return, leaving Annie stunned but amused by his exit.

"Hmmm," she mused, "the last of the great lovers!"

Her mind was still spinning at the course the evening had taken over the last few minutes as she began undressing for bed. She slid out of her dress and let it fall to her feet. She looked at herself in her expensive underwear, stockings and suspender belt, and suggested to herself with a wry smile-

"Well, a fat lot of good you guys were!"

She unfastened them and walked naked to the bathroom to take off her make up. As she brushed her teeth, she played back the

101

evening in her mind. Seeing Peter in the bar, God he was handsome! she thought and his eyes...how they twinkled, especially when he laughed. She could still taste him on her lips. She knew he still had feelings for her. She knew then she still loved him,

but, she decided to play it cool. He needn't know for now. She smiled to herself as she snuggled up in bed, feeling more comfortable and safe than she had been in a long, long, time.

CAIRNPAPPLE REVISITED

Martin Preston did not like people getting one over on him. Ever since his experience at the Knock Hill, he had come in for ridicule from his friends intimating near lunacy in sightings of apparitions. He regretted going to the police, since their attitude implied the same degree of scepticism as his buddies. He thought as to how he could turn this around; stopping short, of revisiting the area at night. He considered going there with some hand picked mates, but how would he persuade them? Alcohol or pot perhaps, he deduced.

While Peter Graham was whining and dining the anthropologist, Martin was treating his mates to pints of beer. By ten o'clock, he and three friends; Frank Burns (a burly, no-brain guy); Chic McAlister (an unemployed waster); and Mick Malone (the local hard nut), had found themselves in the car park of the Dreadnought Hotel, and ready for adventure. Martin had convinced them that there was indeed some unexplained manifestation at the Knock Hill. Because of the beer, or as gratitude for the free-loading, they had all agreed to go with him to check it out. By 10:30 and in pitch-blackness, save of course, for the old Cortina's headlights that Martin had left on full beam, they were standing at the base of the County's highest point.

"So, what now?" asked Frank.

"I don't know." Confessed Martin. "I guess we look around?"

"Look for what..." Moaned Mick questioningly, "this is just stupid, you know that?"

"I don't know, but, we're here so what's the harm?" protested

Martin.

"I got to go take a leak." Was Chic's contribution to the matter in hand, as he disappeared into the shadows with a hiccup.

"Well, I can't see nothin." Whined Frank sounding bored.

"Just give it a minute or two, will you?" Martin snapped back, his desperation leaking into his speech. "It was right there, I tell you-big as anything, an' movin' real fast."

"Was your imagination, kid." Offered Mick. "Night time can play tricks with shadows."

"Aye! And it was her imagination too, I suppose?" retorted Martin.

"Ach! Ye know what women are like! She probably just said it tae stop you getting into her pants!" Laughed Frank. Martin glared at him.

"I tell ye, what's that? Listen!" Martin cut himself short, hearing a rustle behind him.

"It'll just be Chic. You're spooked man, I tell ye! Chic? Chic? Is that you there?" yelled Frank.

Chic stumbled out of the darkness.

"See? I told you!" Yelled Frank, somewhat relieved himself.

But Chic did not look well at all. In the glow from the headlights, all three could see he was white as a ghost.

"Th…there's something back there…!" He stammered.

"Like what? There's lots o' sheep an' cattle up here on the hills, you probably woke one." Said Mick, convincing no one, not even himself.

"It's not a sheep," argued the ashen-faced Chic, "it was like a

104

shadow…just a shadow, it made no sound, just seemed to…drift."

Before any could argue they all jumped in fright as a whooshing sound caught them unawares passing behind them. They all turned towards the noise in time to have a fleeting glimpse of a dark shadow.

"Jesus Christ! What was that?" Mick uttered in a whisper, the hairs on the back of his neck standing up.

"Fucked if I know!" Frank whispered urgently. "And I don't care either. Let's get the fuck outta here!" As he made for the car door.

Another noise, this time in front of them, stopped him in his tracks. And this time, they all saw the crooked shape of a manlike creature pass before the car headlights not more than ten feet from them.

In fear and panic, Mick threw the bottle he was drinking from at the thing, or at least, where he had last seen it. Urged on by hysteria or alcohol, the others took his lead and began throwing rocks from the car park in the direction of the recent sighting; followed by jeering and yelling, "Take that you fucker!"

As the panic subsided, they looked at one another, wide-eyed and gasping for breath.

"Let's go!" Encouraged Chic, his voice a few octaves higher than he intended.

They dived for the car, Frank and Mick in the back, Chic in the passenger seat and Martin driving.

"GO!" Yelled Chic. "Come on, GO!" Echoed Frank as Martin fussed with the ignition key.

"Holy Shit!" Screamed Chic as he saw the ball of flame

appear out of nowhere about thirty feet away, steadily flying towards them. It struck the windscreen of the old car and seemed to splatter into a hundred individual flames to engulf the vehicle, just as Martin got the engine to fire. The Ford took off in a screech of tires and a maelstrom of dirt and small rocks, careening onto the road.

The bonnet was still alight as they sped forward. Mick looked out the back window and saw a black figure begin to glow in its own light as a second ball of fire headed towards them.

"Jesus!" He screamed, "Turn left, quick!"

The alcohol would normally have dulled Martin's reactions, but somehow the adrenalin had honed his reflexes to sharpness as he threw the vehicle onto the left verge of the road. The missile missed the rear of the car, but scraped by the passenger side with a series of mini explosions and a myriad of flames to the tune of the screams from within the now flame engulfed potential coffin.

Martin's instincts told him to flee and his body responded automatically. The accelerator to the floor, the old car groaned into life and sped off down the hill back towards Bathgate like a flaming chariot.

Despite the rising temperature inside the hulk, he didn't take his foot off the pedal until the engine finally succumbed to the heat and died in a gasp and a shudder. All four scrambled for the doors and fell out on top of each other in a heap, quickly sorting themselves out and galloping away on foot. They did not stop until exhaustion set in and they collapsed on the road, chests heaving and panting. As they caught their breath, they looked behind them; there was nothing to be seen except the glow from their car as it burned itself to a shell.

106

"What the fuck was that?" Frank was the first to have breath enough to speak.

"Fucked if I know," Martin panted, "but I'm not waiting to find out."

With that, he was on his feet again and trotting down the road. The others looked first at each other, at the burning wreck, then at Martins' disappearing image. They got to their feet and followed at a steady pace all the way through Glenmavis and into Bathgate itself. When they reached the centre of town, in the safety of the street lights, and the last dregs of people making their way home, their courage seemed to return, or rather their fear dissipated somewhat.

They stood in the main street and looked at each other. Martin was the first to speak.

"Well? Did I not tell you there was something there?"

"Aye, you did!" Confessed Mick. "But what the heck was it? I've never seen the likes!"

"Me neither," admitted Frank, "but what do we do about it?"

"I don't know," whined Martin, "all I know is that my motor's wrecked!"

"We'd better tell the Police." Suggested Chic, "It's not safe for anyone up there!"

"Aye and they're likely to believe us?" said Mick cynically.

"Who knows," said Martin, "but I'll have to report it. It's my car, it can be traced!"

"Well, leave me out of it." Demanded Mick. "I wasn't there, right? I want no doings with the Police."

"Nor me!" Agreed Frank.

107

"Thanks guys!" Said Martin in disgust. "What about you, Chic?"

"I'll go with you, Martin, but don't expect any favours from them. They won't believe a word. They'll think you're up to something."

"Well, I have to say something." Martin was whining again. "I have to report it else I can be done for leaving an accident or something."

"Ok, but just remember, neither Frank nor I was with you, OK?" Mick reminded him.

"Fair enough. Let's go Chic, I've got work tomorrow and I need to get some sleep."

ooo000ooo

Peter hardly slept that night, tired as he was. His rest was interrupted by feverish dreams of runic symbols, dark cave entrances, laboratories and Annie. He felt he could kick himself, the way he had acted. He had set out that night to be aloof and mature, but he had succeeded in making a fool of himself. He knew he had always harboured feelings for her long after they had last met, but didn't realize, until he saw her again, just how deep rooted those feelings were. He woke before his alarm rang and jumped out of bed, his brain immediately active with planning a method to check out their hunch.

He was in the shower, wondering how many more tunnels had been discovered, when his alarm went off.

"Bugger!" He said to himself as he grabbed a towel. As he

108

hurriedly made his way out of the bathroom to stop the ringing. He slipped and slid in the process and stubbed his toe.

"Bugger!" He cried out again.

He was dressed and had a quick breakfast, to the chagrin of the hostess, of toast and coffee, and was on his way to Easton by 7:35. Brian Sharp was the only one in the office at that time.

"You're early...Thought you had a big date last night?" He teased.

"Yup." Said the geologist. "Had an interesting discussion, too. Lot's to do. That my coffee? Cheers!" He grabbed the mug from Brian's desk and made for the door.

"Hey!" Howled the engineer. "That's mine!" But he was talking to himself.

Peter made his way to the laboratory, and was pleased to find it open. He settled his coffee on a bench, his brief case on another. He opened the brief case and pulled out a writing pad and a few pens and took a swig of coffee-

"Yeuch!" He grimaced. "No sugar!" Then put it down quickly.

"Now," he muttered to himself, "where, where, where?" as he opened and closed drawers.

"Looking for these?" the soft voice came from the doorway.

There stood Annie in a white blouse and fawn colored tight slacks, waving in her hand the rubbings they had taken the day before. He smiled sheepishly.

"Good morning Peter, sleep well?" she asked, walking to the bench and laying her drawings out.

"I thought we might start with trying to..." Peter's reply was cut short.

"And good morning to you too, Doctor Wilde." She said, sarcastically.

"What? Oh, yes. I'm sorry; good morning Annie...Was way ahead of myself then." He smiled genuinely.

"So, what have you come up with? Got a plan of attack?" she asked.

"I'm thinking that we need to look at what we've got, then see if they fall into a likely pattern...And by the way, you look lovely." He added casually.

"And do you greet all your colleagues like that?" she teased, raising an eyebrow. "I bet you didn't say that to Brian!"

"Brian didn't look lovely." Answered Peter, keeping a straight face.

Annie giggled softly, shook her head and gave a theatrical sigh.

"OK, let's get on with it. But first - where did you get the coffee?"

"Stole it." He said with no contrition.

She shook her head again, and went into the lab tech's anti room.

"Two sugars please - this one doesn't have any - and black." He yelled.

There was a pause...

"Alright, but this is the first and last time!"

When Annie returned with the drinks, Peter was already pouring over her charcoal rubbings, four in all.

110

"I don't think we have sufficient data, nor can we get much further without a point of reference." She stated.

"I was just thinking that." He said, lifting his cup and sipping the hot tea. "Mmm, nice. Thanks."

Annie lifted her cup in a 'cheers' gesture and sat beside the young geologist. She could smell his after-shave.

"Nice." She smiled to herself, "Wonder what it is? Uh oh, careful, your professionalism is slipping."

"OK," said Peter, "I suggest you continue deciphering what you have here, whether it makes sense as yet, or not. I'll get ready and go down to Level 17 and see how far they've progressed with other finds." He continued in this dominant vein-

"If you let me have your pad and charcoal, I can do some more rubbings so as to get a better feel for what we have. I'll also get some tunnel plan drawings on the way back, and we can plot our finds and the translations on the grids, and see if they make any sense by cross referencing."

He looked at her questioningly, soliciting agreement. She replied by hauling up her artist sketch bag and pulling her pad and crayons from it.

"Be sure to get every mark; even the smallest, insignificant indentation could bear some relevance."

"Yes, Doctor." He said with an air of sarcasm and left immediately for the locker rooms.

ooo000ooo

111

Annie smiled at the closed door. She couldn't believe how quickly she felt comfortable again with Peter, a handsome mature man, but still same little boy. She smiled again. With a shake of her head, she banished all thoughts of him and resigned herself to her task, carefully spreading out each drawing and clipping notepaper to the tops where she could scribble thoughts and ideas.

In the meantime, Peter had donned his coveralls quickly and was on the telephone to the lift operator asking for authority to descend to Level 17. Since it wasn't Jock on shift, he had to wait a moment until his identity had been verified, but soon he was exiting the gate to be met by Constable Phillips.

"Good morning, Alex. Don't you have a home?" Joked the geologist.

"Don't!" The young policeman grimaced. "That's two nights on the trot I've drawn the short straw! I'm bored out of my mind!"

"You have my sympathies, anything interesting to report?"

"Nope, nothing. They're still finding and opening entrances, but all they seem to do is lead into new passages with new blocked exits. It's a veritable labyrinth in there."

"Who's about? Anyone I know?" asked Peter.

"The shift foreman, Dan, I think you know?" Alex phrased it as a question. Peter shook his head.

"Well, Charlie Peters is here, been down there since 6 am, early starter. Mind you, he's an ex miner, so old habits die hard."

"Ah, Santa!" Peter half whispered. Alex smiled in acknowledgement.

"Good." Said Peter. "I'll go reintroduce myself then carry on

112

with some rubbings from the recently opened tunnels. I take it there are more marks on the walls at each entrance?"

"As far as I know, yes. What is this all about, really, Peter? Does anyone have a clue?"

Peter stopped in his tracks, turned back to the constable and answered with a serious tone-

"I haven't a clue yet, Alex. And I don't know who does, or might. But I do know, we are going to get to the bottom of all this."

He walked off, spoke briefly with the safety officer, and then disappeared into the maze of tunnels and passageways. He whistled at the sight before him; labyrinth was an understatement. There were tunnels leading off in all directions, each perfectly formed and of uniform size. He went to each new entrance in turn; followed it to the blind end, then took rubbings of the markings adjacent to each unsealed access, carefully logging each sheet of paper with an identity he could easily cross-reference with mine drawings later. It took him three hours to catch up with the latest openings. By then he had around sixteen more sketches and had walked almost four miles tracking the tunnels.

Dan Drummond, the shift foreman, met him on his way out. The burly man introduced himself, saying he knew who Peter was, then went on to say he thought all this work was thankless and fruitless.

"We have no idea where we're going or where it will all end; just one tunnel after another!"

"I know," said Peter. "I'll see what I can do."

"Wait," said Dan, "my relief is here, I'll come up with you."

113

They made their way to the surface and were met by a considerably more active foyer than when the geologist had descended. The manager and the police inspector were both there, and asked himself and Alex to report to a meeting as soon as they had cleaned up.

On returning, he was shown into the meeting room by Lizzie and found Annie, Brian, Harry, Hamish, Bob and Alex already deep in discussion.

"Ah!" Exclaimed Harry. "The prodigal returns! Dr. Wilde has briefed us on your possible theory. Are we any further forward?"

"It's a bit early to say Harry, still collating data; anything from your experts' end?"

"Not a sausage! Stumped! Every one of 'em." Harry admitted dejectedly.

"And the police?" Peter looked directly at the inspector.

"Well, we're a bit like you, still collecting evidence, reports, etc."

"Hmm, so nothing either, huh?" Peter concluded.

"Nope, nothing." Bob agreed reluctantly.

"There was one weird report last night, Sir." Offered Alex.

They all turned enquiringly towards the young Officer who blanched slightly at their attention.

"Late last night as I was leaving the station to come here, there was a strange report by two youngsters about being chased near the Knock Hill. They reported that something threw fire bombs at their car and made it catch fire..."

"Goodness, Phillips! That's hardly relevant, hoodlums dreaming up a cock and bull story to cover a drunken night escapade.

Probably set fire to it themselves as some sort of insurance scam!"

The inspector shuffled his papers impatiently.

"Well," said Peter, "I suppose we all ought to get back to our respective drawing boards? Annie and I have a lot of work to do, trying to establish or understand some form of pattern in these tunnels we are finding.

"Speaking of which, until we find any logic in this, I see no need to waste manpower opening more and more caverns. We have no means of knowing how many there are, or where they are leading. I suggest we call a halt until we have at least analysed what we have to date and perhaps offer some direction?"

Bob again sucked in a breath-

"It's all part of the investigation. But, I take your point. It would be nice to have some general guidance for us to focus on a clear direction. I'll get them to stop for forty-eight hours until we see whether we are progressing on any other initiative."

"Good." Said the geologist. "We can't promise anything, but we'll give it our best."

He smiled in Annie's direction. She returned the smile and nodded in agreement.

On the way back to the Laboratory, Peter suddenly felt very hungry and asked Annie if she wanted to have some lunch. She said that as she had coerced the assistance of Debbie, they had a sandwich together earlier. He gave her the file of rubbings he had finished, and said with a smile-

"That should keep you busy for a while then."

"Wow, thanks!" She replied sarcastically, and headed off for the temporary office as he made his way to the canteen. Debbie had reorganized her lab moving all her samples, equipment and stationery to one side to leave ample space for Annie's work to be spread out before them. She was busying herself with rearranging benches and chairs when Annie returned. She smiled as the anthropologist entered.

"More data!" Annie said as she waved the new drawings at her. "Let's get them recorded and placed in sequence."

Debbie helped sort them out according to Peter's scribbled location plan, then sat watching as Annie lost herself in her analysis of them.

After a while the lab tech asked, "So, you and Mr. Graham?"

"Yes?" Annie muttered questioningly; startled by the sudden break in silence as well as by the question. "What about it?"

"Oh, nothing." Debbie went on, "It's just that I've seen you two together, and I get the feeling there's more to it than just mutual professional interest." She added with a twinkle in her eye, which did not go unnoticed by Annie.

116

"Ah, yes," she managed, "well, Peter and I go back a long time. I guess it's fair to say there's some, shall we say, unfinished business?" She concluded cautiously.

Debbie replied, "You ought to finish it then! He's a good looking guy, and I hear he has no attachments?"

Annie did not reply, but smiled inwardly as she examined a fresh rubbing.

"Speak of the devil...!" Debbie said, looking up at the opening door.

Annie flushed slightly, aware of Debbie's presence as she too looked up to see Peter enter clumsily, pushing the door with his hip, a tray of coffees in his hands.

"Thought you ladies could use one of these." He offered, smiling, "How's it going?"

"I suppose I could say getting there, if I knew where it was we were trying to get." Annie replied.

"Hmm, let's have a look." He said, walking behind Annie and leaning over her shoulder. He could smell her perfume and smiled a little as she squirmed almost imperceptibly at the proximity. She moved slightly aside and gestured with her hand over to the other bench.

"Your mine plans have arrived. Hamish brought them, just before the meeting."

"Oh Good. I was hoping they might be here."

He stood up, squeezing her shoulders in his hands as he walked around her yet again. Annie looked at Debbie, who had her head bowed over her work, trying to hide a knowing smile. Annie

117

shook her head, sighed, and got back to work.

They each studied their respective material for half an hour or more, Peter pouring over his plans while Annie examined each drawing, wrote a few notes, then handed them to Debbie who carefully placed them back in order.

Annie sat back in her chair and stretched. Peter caught the movement and looked up.

"Found anything?" He asked.

"Don't know for sure." She said, finishing her stretch.

"There definitely seems to be a pattern, but I'm getting conflicting information. Seems it's not just one definitive set of rules I'm working to. I see ancient Celtic, Runes and Ogham characters which implies to me they were either written over a long period of time, or more recently by someone who knew, or knows, all those scripts."

Peter raised a questioning eyebrow.

"Who would know such things? And how did they come to be twelve hundred feet below ground and... YoYum? What's that?"

"Oh yum. It's spelt O-g-h-a-m, pronounced Oh yum." Explained Annie. "An ancient script similar to old Runes, but developed much more recently. See..." She pulled over a sheet of rubbings; the markings appearing in negative white against the charcoal etching.

"Here," she pointed to a series of scoring marks meeting a vertical central line, "I was confused at first, since I had been looking at the previous one." She pulled another rubbing over the first one.

Peter saw no significant difference between the two examples.

118

Annie continued-

"This one, as you can see, has three distinct tangents and two dots. But this one..." she pulled the top sheet away, "has much smaller tangents, four in all, and only one dot. The first one meant something to me in Ancient Celtic script, but the second one made no sense at all. It wasn't until I saw runic hieroglyphics creep into another one, somewhere here."

She rummaged through the other drawings until she found what she was looking for.

"Yes! Here, do you see?" from Peter's expression, obviously he didn't.

"The lines are wavy." She explained, tracing them with her pencil. "It was then I realized it was not all script from the same era, so I looked again at this one and discovered it was Ogham."

"Umm, right." Peter conceded tentatively. "Er, so?"

"So? So, nothing." She sighed. "Just that it makes it all the more curious, not to mention more difficult to decipher!"

"But you can handle it, yes?" Peter smiled.

"Given time, I suppose, but making sense of the literal into the practical may take more than one brain."

"Well, we've got three here!" Peter exclaimed enthusiastically.

Humph, Was Annie's response, echoed quickly by another, humph, from Debbie.

"OK." Peter suggested. "You two work on the literal, I'll concentrate on the tangible."

Debbie and Annie exchanged glances. "Good luck!" Said Debbie.

119

"I think we have to be a bit more systematic and scientific than that, Peter. What we have means absolutely nothing, individually, we have to look at it as a whole." Annie felt she needed to take control.

"We considered the numbers might be reference points. Let's go with that hypothesis, since it's the only theory we have at present. I suggest we pin up a sketch of the underground layout, then overlay the translated script on the tunnel entrances they were found and try to form any link; numbers, letters, similarities, any semblance of a pattern, correlation whatsoever. That should be our starting point. Can you handle the draft layout sketch Peter?"

"As good as done!" He volunteered with an elaborate salute. He was so glad he now had something he could act on productively, and felt a welling of pride for Annie's professionalism and logic; pride and relief, in fact, because at this point he had no idea at as to what he was doing. He set to work.

He pinned large sheets of Annie's artist paper side by side on the wall of the Lab and, with the aid of the mine plans and his notes of the tunnels and entrances, plotted them with the same reference as the drawings. In less than an hour he was finished. He stood back and admired his work. He was still admiring it when Annie and Debbie crossed his line of vision, each holding notepad and crayon. He stepped back to give them room, then changed stance from hands in pockets to folded arms, simply observing them at work.

They consulted their pads, found the reference, then jotted down the numbers and letters Annie had translated, placing beside each note a 'C', 'R', or 'O' depicting Celtic, Rune or Ogham. It took the ladies the best part of an hour to complete the inscription, each starting from opposite ends, giggling and playfully pushing each another as one impeded the other towards the centre of the display.

When the last entry was made on the makeshift chart, they joined Peter six feet back from the plan and each stared mystified at its portent. There was a pregnant pause for at least two minutes as they each tried to absorb the whole picture.

"Right," began Peter, "what we've got is a plan, with markings, and things scrawled around the markings."

"Well done, Sherlock! Glad you are here to advise us." Annie applauded sarcastically.

"Elementary, my dear. So, what do we have?" he looked at Annie and Debbie.

Debbie shrugged; Annie was deep in concentration, standing with one arm across her midriff, the elbow of the other resting on it, her hand holding her chin as her index finger gently stroked her lips in contemplation. She moved slowly back and forth to and from the map, then slightly sideways, her head cocked from time to time to left, then right, as she read and re-read the translated scripts.

Peter had to ask-

"What are you thinking?"

"Mmm?" she murmured abstractly without taking her eyes of the sheets of paper.

"Oh, nothing, nothing really. In fact, I'm being totally unscientific and letting my imagination wander."

"And where is it wandering to?" asked Debbie.

Annie sighed. "I'm just trying to imagine who would spend so much time writing all this. It's like something a scientist would do;

121

someone intelligent, someone trying to tell us something, or keeping a record of something for himself. I'm trying to imagine what type of person would want to do that in this day and age, and then my mind drifts off on tangents as to who, or what, might have wanted to do this hundreds, maybe thousands of years ago."

"Very romantic." Peter observed. "But where is it getting us? Is there anything tangible at all? This one here, you've written G.E. and 200, and this one here," he pointed to another tunnel marker, "G.A. with 400. What are these G's and A's?"

"I was hoping they might offer simple clues, like North, South - but I suppose that was going to be too easy." Annie confessed.

"Well," Peter offered, "the only significant pattern I can see is on your C's R's and O's; they at least seem to be grouped. What do they refer to again?"

"Here, let me show you." Annie replied and, walking back to the bench, pulled over a couple of hefty books lying open there. "This here is Old Celtic script, and this here is a much later adaptation - perhaps a thousand years between them."

Peter was looking at a drawing that, to him, looked like an intricate pattern woven on cloth or moulded into jewellery.

"That's writing? Is this what you have been translating?" he asked.

"Yes," said Annie, "but once you have the basic principle in mind, it's not all that difficult. You are looking at an intricate way of putting words on parchment or rock, a bit like how the Japanese write back to front. Once you understand the alphabet, the flow of the language becomes much simpler. Here, let me show you it in linear form, more like what we have been seeing on these tunnel walls."

"OK, I get what you mean. And I bow to your knowledge." He conceded with a smile.

"So, next step, I would say, is to take them in pairs: start at the most recent, work back to the next one opened, then compare second with third, third with fourth, and so on. What do you think?"

"Ah," said Annie in mock surprise, "you are a scientist after all!"

He stuck his tongue out and she smiled wryly as Debbie giggled.

They each scribbled down couples of data, working systematically from the tunnel entrance formed by the mining on Level 17. After a while, Annie observed and commented-

"It seems the most recent and the ones adjoining, appear to have similar lettering and similar script - although the numbers vary -and the ones spreading outward seem older and have different lettering, although there is repetition of numbering."

"Right!" Agreed Peter. "I'm finding something similar. I've also noticed that on the plan, the numbers reflect closely, but not definitively, the distances between entrances. See here, the distance is one-hundred-and-eighty yards, where the numbers say '200'. And here, between these two points, the actual distance is three hundred and seventy yards, where the numbers read '400'. Do you think these numbers represent paces?"

"Hmmm. Could be," Debbie countered, "but then what do you make of these numbers I've found at multi converging tunnels? The figures run into thousands. I have five thousand and four thousand-five hundred if Annie's translation is correct."

"Yes," agreed Annie, "and the letters are different at these points. We have prefixes G followed by either A or E, and we have D as well with varied small numbers, but the letter prefixing the large numbers is always A on it's own."

"So," concluded Peter, "we just go through the alphabet and see what we can make of them? A equals abode? Apple? Adder? We could be here a long time!"

"Longer than you might think, Mr. Geologist." Annie added cynically. "You forget this is Celtic, Gaelic, you would be looking for old Irish words beginning with the letters!"

"Damn!" Cursed Peter, "I hadn't even thought of that! So, we're in your hands again, Dr. Wilde?"

"What if we follow the hunch of directions, map references, grids?" Suggested Debbie.

"OK," agreed Peter, "as good a place as any to start. What's Gaelic for...?"

"Ogham!" Annie corrected.

"Alright, what's Ogham for north, south, east and west?"

"*Deas* comes to mind for south as I recall." Annie squinted as she racked her brain. "Fraid I don't know the others off-hand, if there are, or were, specific literal translations for them."

"Well, we have some D's. That's a start. How about G? That seems to feature often?"

Annie considered this. "Doesn't seem to ring bells for north, east or west."

"What about with the A or E?" Debbie offered. Suddenly she

noticed the time by the beautifully setting sun.

"Goodness! Look at the time! It's well after six, I'd better be off, don't want to be driving after dark."

Annie followed her gaze, "Grian alach." She said, almost in a whisper.

"What was that?" Debbie asked.

"Oh," Annie smiled, "just old Celtic; grian alach - sunset."

"Nice," Debbie commented, then, "well, I best be off. See you tomorrow, same time?"

"Yes, of course. Take care Debbie." Annie said with a smile.

"Goodnight, Debbie." Peter added.

The Lab Tech slipped out of her white Lab coat and shucked into a light overcoat, struggling into it as she opened the door and left. Peter stood looking absently at the door slowly closing on its spring, and jumped when Annie yelled his name.

"Peter! Grian alach!" She enthused.

"Pardon?"

"Grian alach!" She yelled again.

Peter's expression showed he was still none the wiser.

"Grian alach!" She repeated yet again, frustrated. "Grian alach -G.A! Sunset, west!"

The discovery slowly dawned on the geologist, his expression changing from bewilderment to acknowledgement, then to a broad smile. "And east? Sunrise?"

"Ummm, ooooh, let me think...Grian...eirigh I think, yes...I'm sure, eirigh. G.E!"

Peter was as enthused as she was now, and he moved round

the table to take her hands in his. She did not resist this time.

"Cracked it! I'm sure!" He said, pulling her towards him in a hug. Again, she did not resist, seeming to enjoy the sensation of his bulk wrapped around her slender frame. He pulled away, holding her shoulders and looked into her eyes. He saw in there more than he had expected, and it threw his train of thought momentarily.

"I…erm...so, let's recapitulate." He managed to blurt out.

"Mmmm," she smiled, "let's. That sounds like a lot of fun!" And they both laughed. Peter did so nervously, with just a hint of embarrassment.

He regained his composure quickly, "So, what have we got? Deas, or 'D', is south, west is Green Ally, or whatever you said, G.A., and east is G.E. right?"

She nodded.

"Then," he continued, "can we assume the other reference is north? What was the other reference? A on it's own?"

Annie screwed her face up, looking nonetheless pretty.

"Seems logical, but I can't think of anything relative to north beginning with A."

"OK." said Peter, now mimicking Annie's ponderous stance with his hand on his chin.

"So what other possible words are there beginning with A?"

Annie gasped and laughed cynically, "What am I, a dictionary? There are hundreds!"

"Great idea!" He yelled.

"What is?"

"Dictionary! You have a Gaelic/English one?"

126

"Sure, right here." She rummaged in her bag, producing a small paperback. "It's not the best, but the most convenient I could find to bring with me."

"OK, let's take a look." Peter pulled up a stool beside Annie as she sat at the bench and opened the book between them so both could read.

Annie chuckled to herself at Peter's phonetic pronunciation of the foreign words before him, before he gave up and stuck to the English versions.

"Abairt, adhair, agair, airgead...nothing." He said as they reached the end of the A section.

"Hmmm," Annie agreed, "Me neither. Mind you, I was concentrating on 'north' or anything similar - even obscure synonyms."

"Me too. Let's look again, but just keep an open mind for anything that could be relevant, not necessarily compass or directionally focused."

They began again, from the end of the A's, Peter reading.

"Athscriobh," (which sounded even more foreign to Annie the way he said it) "Athair, anam."

Suddenly he stopped muttering and put his finger on the word Abhaile.

"That's it!" He said dramatically. "Abhaile! Home! It's the origin of everything; Base Camp!"

He almost jumped from his stool and said, "Let's look at the plotted marks on the map."

Annie followed him over to the wall.

Peter was enthused again as he pointed to specific markings

127

and plotted translations. He spoke almost to himself as he traced imaginary lines with his finger.

"Now, let me see; if this means west, and that means east, then we could assume for theory that this point is two hundred paces, or yards, east of that point, that would make this point two hundred yards north of this point. Yes! That checks out. Then this would have to be two hundred yards west of there."

He strained to read the scribbled mark, which was high on the chart, "Eureka!" He yelled, clapping his hands. "So, if all that rings true, that would make this point here - let's see – five thousand paces from 'home', and here, four thousand-four hundred paces from 'home' but due west, and here." He almost had to leap to point to it high on the wall to the right, "Is the last point we opened and that is, if I can read your writing, three thousand-six hundred paces from home."

He stood back, completely satisfied with himself.

"OK, Einstein. So what's the relativity theory here?" Annie chided.

"We need a map." He said.

"We've got one!" She said, pointing to the one behind him.

"No, a bigger map."

"Peter, we don't have a bigger wall!"

"No, no, sorry - a smaller map. I mean, a bigger area, but smaller scale. I mean, of the area, outside, the County. Call the manager; see what he has in his records."

"Peter, it's almost eight!"

"What? Oh, yes, so it is." He said, glancing at his watch. "No wonder I feel so hungry! How about a bite to eat? We can follow this

128

through in the morning."

Annie was tempted, but remembered her strategy. She rolled her neck on her shoulders, nursing the back of her head with her hand and, almost yawning, replied tiredly.

"Thanks, but no thanks, not tonight. I'm bushed. I just want to get back, have a snack, languish in a hot bath and get some quality shut-eye."

Peter almost let slip his disappointment, but recovered in time to say,

"Good idea. I think I need some of that languishing too. Early start?" she nodded.

"Here at eight?" asked Peter and she nodded again, still rubbing the back of her neck. Peter was tempted to offer a neck massage, but thought better of it.

"OK. I'll see you to your car." Peter offered.

He picked up his jacket and threw it over one shoulder, picking up his bag in the other. Annie threw a few things into her briefcase including a small scale drawing of the map before them, grabbed her coat, and followed him outside.

She opened the door of her car and threw in her bag and wrap. Peter held the door for her as she slipped into the driving seat, then he leaned in and kissed her cheek softly.

"Have a good night. Get some quality rest. I'll see you tomorrow." He smiled and closed the door for her. Annie waved through the window and blew him a kiss.

Peter, following Annie along King Street, flashed his headlights at the disappearing Volkswagen in a final goodbye, as he turned into the Fairway parking lot, leaving Annie to continue on to the Blackburn Road.

His mind was still buzzing with the day's revelations when he was interrupted by the harshness of a voice from the dining room.

"I thought you weren't coming tonight, I've put all the dinner things away. Were you wanting any supper?" it was his illustrious hostess.

"No thanks, really. Sorry I'm so late. Would a sandwich of some sort be out of the question?" he said apologetically.

"Well, I suppose, if that's all you want? I've got some roast beef, if that's OK?"

"That'll do fine. Could you bring it up when it's ready?" Peter acknowledged her sigh and nod, as an affirmative and carried on upstairs to his room.

He had only just undressed and was about to go into the shower when his sandwiches arrived. He slipped his trousers back on, and took the plate from the landlady.

"You'll be sure to bring the plate down with you in the morning?" Peter took this as a command masquerading as a request.

"Yes, of course. Thank you." He took the tray, laid it down on his coffee table, and headed back to the shower. Refreshed, he sat down to eat his snack, while his mind digested the day's events.

As before, he seemed to oscillate mentally between the enthusiasm of their success and the emotional tug-of-war so far as Annie was concerned. She was indeed stunning, intelligent, witty, thorough and...distant? He finished his light meal and lay down on the bed, still mulling over everything that had been said and done during the last few days. Eventually, he fell asleep on top of the quilt.

Annie arrived back at the Golden Circle Hotel and, after dumping all her gear in her room, opted for the coffee shop rather than the Dining Room. She had a simple cheese omelette washed down with a glass of house white wine. She didn't know, or care what it was.

Her bath and bed beckoned, but after her bath, she felt revitalized and, instead of retiring immediately, she dragged out the papers she had retrieved from the Lab before leaving. She studied their findings again, then went down to the car park where she found a large fold-up map of Central Scotland amongst other paraphernalia in her glove compartment. She spent the next hour or so drawing and pencilling in markings from her records, using her ruler for scale measurements.

She fell into bed around 11 pm exhausted, mentally and physically.

ooo000ooo

"Cairnpapple!" A voice shouted behind him.

"Huh?" said Peter, turning abruptly as he locked his car door in the colliery car park.

"Bathgate Hills!" Yelled Annie from the entrance to the admin

131

buildings.

"I worked it out using the data we had and a map of the area, I plotted the info. It all points to an area around Cairnpapple!"

Peter wasn't sure he was hearing correctly and walked up the few steps to join her.

"Good morning." He said. "I think I heard you correctly, but my hearing isn't too good until I've had some coffee. You want to set it up and I'll meet you in the lab?"

"Get your own damn coffee!" She replied in mock hostility. "And get your ass into the lab! You have to see this."

"OK," said Peter, backing off, "I'll see you in five minutes."

Ten minutes later, coffee still warm in his hands, he was pouring over Annie's calculations and conclusions. They could not be faulted.

"When did you do all this? I thought you were exhausted?"

"After my bath," she said, "it had a rejuvenating effect on me."

"You work well when you're tired." He smiled. "Hey! Just a minute. Wasn't there something yesterday, or the day before, I've lost track, about some police report on something strange going on up there?"

"Yes, I think you're right. Knock Hill area." She agreed.

"Best get the others in on this, seems we finally have something to go on." Peter helped Annie to gather up her files and maps before telephoning Harry Grant and arranging an impromptu meeting.

"Well." Concluded the police inspector, having absorbed

Annie's evidence.

"That's all very well, but it's a monumental uphill task to get to the bottom of this." Peter smiled, he was sure there was a figure of speech in there somewhere, but he couldn't place it.

Bob continued. "It's taken us about three days to get to where we are now. It'll take us weeks to follow all the leads some four or five miles! Can we up the ante, Harry? More resources? More machinery?"

Harry looked over to Hamish the engineer, who was slowly shaking his head.

"Not a chance I'm afraid. Assuming resources and equipment were limitless, which they're not, there just isn't enough space to throw more bodies at it."

"We'll just have to make do, then." Bob Mathieson conceded reluctantly.

"But perhaps with this new information, we can exclude all tunnels leading off from what we discern as the Prime Route to home, as you call it, and concentrate all our people there. That should narrow it down a bit and save a lot of time?"

"Yes, that might help." Agreed the engineer. "Let's see." He started scribbling on his note pad before continuing-

"It seems there is an entrance approximately every two hundred/three hundred yards or so, so that's...maybe seven or eight per mile - and we estimate five/six miles - so that's...theoretically, all things being equal..."

"Bottom line!" Interrupted Harry.

"About six or seven days, and if we work two shifts, we could be there in three and a half days." He finished his arithmetic and looked up with a beaming face.

"Fine," said the police inspector. Let's see if we can't manage it in two days, working round the clock."

Hamish's beam left his face.

"OK. We'll give it our best shot."

Bob Mathieson wasn't finished yet.

"Good! But that still leaves too many questions unanswered. Like, what might we find when we get home? We have to be prepared for something, but what? Any ideas?" His eyes surveyed the rest of the occupants. There were murmurs, but unworthy of submission.

"Well, Dr. Wilde? There's something for you and young Graham to get your teeth into! For the others, let's concentrate on the practical side, but keep your ears and eyes open. I want to be informed of anything - and I mean anything -relevant as soon as you hear of it."

Bob began picking up his papers, and the others did too, realizing the meeting had terminated, they began shuffling towards the door of the conference room.

"Come on, young Graham!" Teased Annie, slapping Peter on the back. "Let's get our teeth into something!"

ooo000ooo

Annie was looking through books of Ogham script and reference books on Celtic and pre-Celtic writing, trying to find some clue or lead as to their conundrum. Every now and again, she looked up from her research, interrupted by the geologist - pacing the length of the Lab; hands held behind his back, head bowed as he stared at his feet in concentration.

Finally she asked him. "Bored are we? Got nothing to do?"

"Eh…Uh, no, as a matter of fact, not at all. I've got an idea."

"Oh, poor thing! Shall I send for a doctor? They can be quite painful, if you're not used to them." She pouted patronizingly.

Peter completely ignored the jibe. "I was just thinking if it's going to take them a few days to follow underground routes, why don't we explore the possibility of an alternative strategy?"

Annie was interested now. "Like what?" She encouraged, spinning round on her stool.

"Like, why don't we go to the source itself? Go to Cairnpapple, but above ground? See if there is any way down from there? There has to be another way in, and out, for whatever it is that's doing this. Can't be underground forever; and there are those weird sightings?"

"Don't you think that's a matter for the police to investigate?"

"You heard what the inspector said; they are using all resources available trying to break through from the tunnels."

"Let me get this straight." Annie summarized, "You want me to go with you on a wild goose chase, whilst there is so much research to be done here?"

"That's the idea."

"You really mean it, don't you? You want me to leave all these interesting reference books and just jump in a car and drive around remote countryside. OK Let's go!"

Before Peter got a chance to realize what she had said, she had her jacket on, her map crushed roughly under her arm, and was on

135

her way out the door.

Annie was in the car park in seconds. She began to put on her short denim jacket, but after looking around at the clear expanse of blue sky, and feeling the warmth of the sun on her upturned face, she felt her pale blue cashmere turtle-neck sweater was sufficient covering.

Peter caught up with her quickly, and he too decided against wearing his burgundy blazer, loosened his burgundy and grey striped tie and undid the top button on his light grey shirt.

They automatically went for their own cars, then looked over to each other and laughed.

"Your car or mine?" said Peter, mimicking Sean Connery.

Annie thought for a second, and then replied-

"Yours has a sun roof."

Peter unlocked his side and, getting in, leaned over to open the passenger door. He couldn't help notice the flash of flesh when Annie's tight beige skirt rode up her leg as she struggled into the low bucket seat. What he didn't know was that Annie had elaborated her movement to produce just that effect. Both were now smiling for different, but essentially the same, reasons.

Within minutes, they were speeding through the town centre, up Hopetoun Street, and passing Glenmavis district beyond the fringes of the Burgh. Annie was looking out the window and, when they passed the old reservoir on their left, the countryside became all too familiar. With a tinge of nostalgic pain and an air of excitement at the same time, she remembered as if it were yesterday, the last time she had taken this drive to the Knock Hill with Peter Graham. Peter too was fighting mixed emotions as the car turned onto the minor road on the way the back way to Linlithgow, but was also the only route from the south to the Knock Hill and Cairnpapple.

He pulled the Ford into the car parking area for sightseers to the Knock Hill, and brought it to rest facing down the hill back towards the pine forest they had just driven by. Annie took in the view and sighed. She remembered this from her walks, in what now seemed like a previous lifetime, but her most potent thought was of the last time she was parked here, at night, with Peter. In spite of herself, she turned to look at him, only to find he was watching her.

Their eyes met, and each smiled at the other. Her resolve having been depleted by the nostalgia, she leaned over and kissed him softly on the cheek; his hand shot up and held her head, and he softly kissed her mouth. She closed her eyes and savoured the embrace. He released her, and they just sat for a while, smiling.

Then Peter remembered why they were there.

"Let's walk the rest of the way."

She nodded, then opened the door and extracted herself from the car. Peter also got out, and walked round to her side, took her hand and led her out of the car park onto the narrow road.

"Where to first?" she asked.

"Let's start at the beginning, or end; Cairnpapple Hill."

They began walking, past the base of Knock Hill and round the corner towards the valley of the old silver mines. The geologist loved this walk, having done it numerous times in his youth. The views were not as spectacular from ground level as they were from the hill summit but, nonetheless, they took in the vista of hills, green fields, forests and valleys; the most picturesque vale being the almost sheer drop from the roadway to the small lake nestled in high green banks about three hundred feet below them. They rounded another bend then up a hill where they saw the National Trust sign for Cairnpapple Hill. Peter helped Annie through the stile.

"Not the best attire for countryside romps!" Annie apologised, referring to her short skirt and high-heeled shoes.

"It'll do for me." He replied saucily and she smacked his arm playfully.

"Just get on with it!" She added.

The access began with a few wooden railway sleeper steps set into the hill, but, near the summit, the steps petered out to a grass track. They followed the track up another incline and finally reached the distinctive hillock that was Cairnpapple.

Being a weekday, there was not a soul about, giving the solitude an eerie feeling. They strolled round the mound, looking at the old circular stone filled depressions in the ground, which formed a circle around the hill, then crossed a grass grown ditch, which surrounded the burial ground like an old moat or remains of a rampart. Inside the ditch were some boulders, placed there thousands of years ago. At the south end of the henge, they found more wooden steps leading up to the summit, where Peter stopped to read the National Trust plaque.

"You know," he said absently, "this place has always fascinated me, even as a kid. I think its importance was never fully explained or understood by history teachers. How they can simply 'mention' it in passing, as a one-sentence reference, is beyond me. It's like...this is where it all began. Look!"

He ushered Annie over to the plaque, pointing out as he read extracts from it.

"2,800 years B.C - that makes it more than five thousand years old! Here there were artefacts found from as far away as Wales. This place was a focal point for Britain, not just local. And here, look…"

He spread his arms out and continued-

"It's a henge like Stonehenge in England, but probably older. It covers eras of Beaker people through Iron and Bronze Ages. I just can't imagine five thousand years ago, and yet here is evidence, burials, in our own back yard!"

"I know what you mean," Annie smiled. "I find this all the time in my work. So much history, so much information, heritage, origins; yet they're met with lack of interest."

They looked in the plate glass top of the mound and could see the extracted interior, but the entrance to the access ladder was closed and padlocked. Peter cursed softly.

"Bugger! We will have to get the authorities to let us in, but from what I can see, there is nothing untoward here. Shall we go on?"

"Where to? And just what exactly are we looking for?" Annie needed some form of direction as to Peter's intent.

"Hmmm. Good question." He conceded. "I'm not entirely sure. I guess I'm hoping to find something, anything that seems out of the ordinary. I was hoping you might see something of interest, maybe some script similar to that in the mine…a shot in the dark, really. Maybe even some form of access, an entrance that might lead to that labyrinth at Easton."

"OK I'm with you so far. So, where now?" Annie looked around her, they were surrounded by green; green fields, hills, shrubbery, forest, with Cockle Roi hill overshadowing them like a sentinel.

"Let's split up and wander round here for a bit. Humour me!" He said, smiling.

After an hour of aimless wandering, they met up again at the closed information hut at the base of the mound.

"Nothing?" Peter raised his eyebrows.

"Nope. I was looking at the boulders, searching for writing." Annie shrugged.

"Let's head back to car, then, maybe we can search further a field."

They began their trek back to the Knock Hill, holding hands.

Annie felt secure and comfortable as they progressed in silence. As they passed the valley to the silver mines, Peter stood on the edge of the road, leaning over the fenced railings looking down onto the miniature loch.

"Fancy a ramble?" he asked.

"In these shoes? You've got to be kidding!" She laughed.

"I suppose." He smiled back at her.

They turned away from the fence and almost jumped out of their skins as they found themselves staring into a pair of sunken eyes set within an ancient, wrinkled face. Jamie Wardrope seemed to have appeared from nowhere. The Farmer ignored their surprised expressions.

"Fine day to be walking." He asked distantly.

"Ummm, yes, yes it is." Peter recovered first, looking around automatically to see where the old man had come from. They stood in silence for a moment, the couple watching the farmer as he, almost ignoring their presence now, looked wistfully over the valley before them.

Annie and Peter exchanged glances questioningly. Finally, Annie asked the farmer a question.

"Do you live around here, Mr...?" Jamie's dog Jess was sniffing around the strangers and Annie squatted to pat the collie.

"Wardrope, Miss, Jamie Wardrope. And, aye, I've lived around these parts all my life, me and my Father's afore me. Seen some changes in that time too, I can tell you." He answered, still staring off into the distance as if he were talking to himself.

"I was born around here - Bathgate," Peter countered, "and I haven't seen much change up in this neck of the woods since I was a kid."

"Aye," retorted the Farmer, "that may be, that may be. But I'm talking farm talk; different folks, different crops, different beasts." His brow furrowed and his eyes squinted as he thought of Hamilton's sheep.

"Takes all sorts, I say. For instance, take yon valley..." He gestured with his walking stick.

"Times was, there was people working there. Afore my time, mind ye. Peoples reckon'd it were silver they was after, I thinks it were tin meself. Now, there's just the old pond, a few bits o' fencing props and a couple of wee caves."

"A couple of caves?" Peter was curious. "I have been up here

141

so many times, we only knew of one, and that was sealed off."

"Aye, well, they're all sealed and overgrown now, just become part of the rocks, saving the big one, that is. And I have my doubts as to whether that's still sealed."

"How so?" Asked Annie.

"Well," Jamie gave a big sigh, screwed up his face and shifted his grimy cloth cap to scratch the top of his forehead.

"I haven't had the chance tae get down there recently, but I've had a few wee beasties go missing over the last few years, and thought it might be yon Hamilton, Ken." Again, a general flourish with his stick towards the north before he went on.

"But, the most recent instance, just the other day, I followed a trail and it led down yonder." Another flourish with the home-made, gnarly, wood stick which Annie now considered an extension of his arm whilst Peter followed the direction of the stick and saw he was pointing towards the north bank of a pond. There was only room for a small, steep path, between the water's edge and the cliff face. Jamie continued-

"I was going to have a look inside yon cave, but I didn't have a light with me, and when I got home, I got sidetracked with some other business."

Peter thought for a minute then asked, "How far is your farmhouse from here? If we could borrow a torch, we could have a look for you?" Annie dug him in the ribs and glared at him. He ignored her.

"Oh, it's just round that bend, behind The Knock, if you'd like?" He turned and began walking without waiting for a reply. Jess immediately followed him.

Peter started to follow, Annie tugging on his shirtsleeve.

"What?" He whispered.

"You must be crazy! There's a mystery here, dubious sightings of weird night creatures, and you want to grope around in dark caves without any sort of back up or protection? What's more, I expect you want me to come with you. In these clothes?"

"It'll be OK." He smiled. "The cave is a dead end, has been for years. I just want to see if there is anything abnormal about it."

"I think the only abnormality here is you!" She whispered, exasperated.

They followed the old Farmer back to his home, around a quarter of a mile down the hill and up a gravel driveway. He led them directly to the front door of the Farmhouse; a large, solid, wooden door painted dark brown and opening on to a small hall with a stone-flagged floor.

He ushered them into the Kitchen, which Annie considered huge by comparison with modern homes. The place was surprisingly tidy, with a large double sink and work surface occupying a whole wall. Cupboards made of natural, real wood, a large pine kitchen table and six spindle backed, wooden chairs. There were dozens of jars of all sorts of sizes, shapes and material all over the worktops; containing anything from sugar; tea or biscuits; to spoons, tools and papers. The only other 'furniture' of note in the room was a battered dog basket shoved in one corner with a water bowl and another dish next to it.

Jess made straight for the water, lapped up a considerable fill, and then scoffed the remains of her meal as if to show that she didn't fully trust these strangers yet, most certainly not with her food.

"Make yourselves comfortable." Invited Jamie. "I'm not used to guests, so I'll just have tae make do. I'll go see if I can find a flashlight."

Annie looked round the room, and sat on one of the wooden chairs.

"What have you got us into?" she accused.

"Who, me?" Peter said innocently. "Aw, come on! Where's your spirit of adventure?"

"Back in a safe, cosy office, if you must know!" She chided.

Peter was about to say something, but the old Farmer returned with a large hand held battery lamp. "This is the best I have and I checked the battery; she'll do you."

"Thanks," said Peter, "just the job. Oh, by the way, you wouldn't have any gumboots around? It's a bit muddy looking down there, and we're not particularly well attired for exploration."

"Gum boots, you say? You mean wellies? Aye, there's plenty of them about, but I'm not sure any will fit."

He showed them back to the entrance hall where there were half a dozen pairs of Wellingtons, all dirty, and all black.

Peter found some pretty close to his size. Annie had more difficulty, but eventually settled for a pair at least two sizes too large, being the smallest available. They took off their shoes and climbed into the gumboots. Peter looked at Annie in her knee-high black boots and short skirt.

"Cute." He said which earned him another dig in the ribs.

"We'll return them later, if that's OK with you?" Peter said.

144

"No worries," replied Jamie, "No rush, I only have one pair of feet."

They picked up their shoes and the torch and left. He laughed as they left the farmhouse, watching Annie flip-flop along in her oversized Wellingtons.

"Piss off!" She rasped. "I don't know why I let you talk me into this. I still think we should go back and get the police or someone to do this!"

"And what if there is nothing? Wouldn't we look like fools?"

"Oh, so it's we now?" she said, hands on her hips. Peter ignored her.

Within minutes, he had dumped their footwear in the boot of his car and was rummaging through a metal box of tools. Eventually he found what he was after, a small compass. He also grabbed a large screwdriver and a small hammer and slipped them into his trouser pocket. "Just in case." He said.

"In case of what?" Annie cried, alarmed.

"In case I need them!" He replied simplistically.

They reached the fence surrounding the rim of the valley. Peter helped Annie climb over, then, standing back; he ran and vaulted over the three-foot high wires.

"Smart arse!" Annie said under her breath, and they made their way down to the lake, following the course of natural grass terraces. At the base, they skirted round the pond, and headed up the north bank following the outcrop of cliff until they came across the entrance to the cave or tunnel. Peter switched on the torch and aimed the beam of light into the darkness; there was nothing to see other than the rocky cave sides.

"I didn't know there were caves here." Remarked Annie.

"There are caves all over central Scotland, if you know where to look." Advised the geologist.

"Robert the Bruce was said to roam these parts, anywhere from Ayrshire to Edinburgh to Bannockburn. History says he hid up in a cave when pursued by the English. Remember the story of Bruce and the spider? Watching it spin its web inspired him to have another crack at the Auld Enemy. It could have been this very cave, around the year 1310, for all we know."

"Oooh." Annie shivered elaborately. "I hope not! I can't stand spiders!" Peter laughed.

"OK, here's the plan - we are hunting some mythical entity that slips out in the hours of darkness, steals cows and shoots fire bombs at passing teenagers. You go find it; I'll keep my eye out for any seven hundred year old spiders!" He tried to push Annie into the entrance. She evaded his shove and swivelled round behind his back.

"No way! You first!" She pushed Peter forward. Still laughing, he carefully picked his way through the entrance by the light of the torch, watching his footing on the loose stones and rocks covering the floor of the tunnel. Annie followed, gripping his hand tightly.

Following the beam of light, they moved slowly and cautiously into the nether regions of the cavern. Their progress was chorused with a series of ouches from Annie as she grazed an elbow, lost her balance or slipped on a rock.

Peter was completely unsympathetic towards her-

"What's the matter? Just walk where I walk!"

146

"It's alright for you." She complained in a loud whisper. "Have you ever tried walking in clown's shoes?"

Suddenly Peter stopped abruptly having just rounded a sharp bend.

"What the...?"

"What? What is it?" Annie was feeling more and more insecure by the second.

"Bingo!" Peter replied.

Annie grabbed on his shirt and pulled herself round him to see what he was looking at. The torchlight was illuminating a large blockage, similar to, but considerably lighter in colour than the entrances, they had found in the mine.

"This is not natural, nor is it man-made." Peter stated, running the beam from top to bottom of the eight-foot wall.

"Don't be ridiculous!" Said Annie, "It has to be one or the other! Doesn't it?"

"Well, it's too smooth to be natural, and I don't know of any man-made process that could do that." The geologist responded, approaching the wall. He ran his hand over the surface and pulled it back immediately as if something had bitten him. Annie gave a muted shriek.

"Don't do that!" Her whisper was almost a shout.

"Jesus Christ!" He placed his hand back on the surface, tentatively this time.

"Jesus Christ." He swore again. "It's warm!"

"Warm, as in warmer than the other walls? Or warm as in shouldn't be warm?" She enquired.

"Warm as in, recent!" He said.

"Right! Fine! That's it! I'm outta here!" Annie let go Peter's arm and turned back on herself.

"Wait!" Peter's voice had become urgent now. "It's getting warmer! Here, feel. This part here is…ouch! Fuck! That's hot!"

Annie looked on, filled with panic, but her eyes fixed on the wall. There seemed to be wisps of smoke coming from the edges; then she discerned a faint red glow emanating from the centre.

"What is it Peter? I don't like this one bit!"

Peter was transfixed. The wall, impossible as it seemed, was melting before his eyes in a halo of smoke and gas. Within seconds, a gap had formed and the geologist gasped audibly as he saw a figure appear on the other side of the conflagration, either grotesquely disfigured or distorted by the radiated heat of the melting rock. Annie was mesmerized, caught like a rabbit in a car's headlights. She too could see the shadow of a figure. She stood behind Peter, gripping his arm tightly.

From the misty orifice a voice cold and malevolent, old and menacing, rasped-

"Welcome, I have been expecting you!"

THE CAVERNS

As the air cleared in the cave, Peter could not believe what he had seen and heard. He shone the torch into the hole created in the tunnel wall and saw the figure of a man throw the wing (of what can only be described as a cape) over his face; at the same time an unearthly noise, sounding like the release of steam from an engine, emanated from the vicinity.

The figure moved back inwardly beyond the range of his lamp. Again, they heard that malevolent rasping voice.

"Extinguish your light! You have no need of it here!"

It was a command, not a request. Peter turned the light back onto Annie, who was standing frozen behind him. She was as white as a sheet, the paleness accentuated by the light on her face. He looked back into the recess of the exposed tunnel and found the creature was correct. There was now a visible reddish glow from the interior, somewhat akin to the light of a low wattage bulb in a large, dark room. He looked at Annie.

"What do you think?" He whispered. "Try to run, or stand and fight?"

Annie was trembling now. "Do you really think we have a choice?"

The voice spoke again. "You're lady friend is quite correct. You have no choice. Come in, step carefully over the entrance, the ground is not yet cool."

Peter shrugged resignedly and switching the light off, took

Annie's arm and guided her through the newly formed entrance. They followed their host along a corridor walled in the same way as the tunnels at Easton; fused rock. Peter searched in his pocket and brought out the screwdriver and compass. The screwdriver he held in one hand as a weapon; he gave the now useless flashlight to Annie, and opened the compass with his other hand, checking direction as the tunnel guided them left or right. But Peter's feeling was that whichever direction they were going compass wise, without a doubt, they were going downhill.

After a few hundred yards they passed through another unsealed entrance, then another. Peter was still trying to memorize distance and direction. He had calculated they were a little more than half a mile from the original cave entrance when the entity turned and gestured.

"Welcome to my humble abode." An unseen dark curtain was swept away to reveal a much larger entrance, to a marginally better-lit inner cave of enormous proportions. Peter estimated it was around twelve feet high and circular with a diameter of around thirty-five feet. Annie gasped as she saw the interior; there were artefacts, trinkets, furniture and tools perhaps spanning centuries. And there were books, hundreds of books; lining the walls, in piles on the floor, on shelves, everywhere.

Peter sniffed the air.

"I smell a barbecue." he whispered to Annie. "If you see a large cooking pot, run for it!"

"You are not on my menu; there is no need for alarm." The voice said.

Peter was surprised. "You have good hearing."

"What makes you think I hear at all?" The voice quizzed.

Peter looked at Annie, eyebrow raised. Annie answered with a shrug. She felt a little more at ease in the knowledge that their captor appeared to have a sense of humour.

"You say you were expecting us? How so?" Peter ventured.

"All in good time, my young adversary, all in good time. Firstly, my manners; please be seated."

The couple looked around and sat side by side on two antique carver chairs in the centre of the room. Their host turned to face them for the first time. They both winced slightly at the wrinkled pallid face of a withered old man who might have been a hundred years old.

"Oh much, much older than that." He said, with a grimace that might have been a smile.

They looked at each other in bewilderment, for although they were both thinking the same thing, neither had spoken.

"I can read your minds and converse telepathically. Mr. Graham, you may put away your weapon, it is of no use to you whatever."

Peter embarrassedly put the screwdriver back in his pocket.

The voice continued-

"I have not had much use for conversation over the years. However, though it tires me, I will speak with you, as you are unfamiliar with telepathic thought. But do excuse my vocal chords, they're a bit rusty, I'm sure." It said, again with a sort of cackle.

"How do you know my name?" Asked Peter.

"I have been watching you both, you and Dr. Wilde. You

151

intrigue me. You work well together, you found me quicker than I would have given you credit for. It comforts me to know there is yet intelligence in the human race."

"By implication, you are not?" Annie was becoming bolder now, and a little chagrined to know that she was being watched.

"Ah, the impatience! Very well, let me explain." The figure threw back its cape in a flamboyant gesture and sat opposite the enthralled audience. Annie saw he was wearing tight, almost Tudor style trousers, black and threadbare; a white lace collared shirt, which had seen better days, shoes, black again, but scuffed and pointed, and a three-quarter length black cape. His hands were old and gnarled like Jamie Wardrope's walking stick, yet his frame, although crooked and bent with age, gave the impression of a previously well-built, tall man. He literally filled the wing-backed armchair he had sunk into.

"This is my home." He gestured round the room with his long arm. "The tunnels you see here, and the ones in the mines, are my country. Not by choice, I hasten to add, but that is neither here nor there as far as you are concerned."

He sensed the question on their minds and held up a hand.

"No. You have no need to know. Your function here is to provide me with information, there is no vice versa."

"Information?" asked Peter.

"It's how I survive and learn things. In the many, many years, I have been imprisoned here; it is the only way I have been able to keep up with events. I abduct those who stray too near, absorb their knowledge, erase their memory of our encounter and send them back into their own world of light."

"The miners!" Peter gasped. "You kidnapped them? Read their minds? They remembered nothing!"

"Yes, the miners; that took so long, so many. Normally it is individuals, or couples, small groups of travellers, perhaps. But the miners, I had no option but to take them all, they had all seen me, you understand? They dug into my tunnel. I had kept away from them for centuries, burrowing deeper as their technology advanced. I had not realized they had progressed to that depth."

"But the tunnels... it was just a question of time before you were discovered?" Annie suggested.

"No, my dear. You are incredibly beautiful, if I may say, you remind me of someone I knew long ago." Annie blushed. "No, it is not a question of time. Time is mine. It would simply be a matter of abductions and erasing minds. Time consuming, perhaps, but I have lots of it."

"You mentioned imprisonment, and centuries?" Peter was curious now.

"Imprisoned, by whom? And surely you mean years, not centuries?" He added.

"Imprisonment, yes. Who would choose to live like a burrowing animal?"

There was hatred and disgust in his rasping now.

"And centuries? Yes, centuries. Too many! More than your minds can comprehend."

"Are you an alien? From this planet or another?" asked Annie.

He gave a rasping cackle-

"Well that depends on who was here first, don't you think?

153

Perhaps you are the alien?" he pointed directly at Annie and cackled some more.

"But how did you get here?"

"And when?"

"How do you speak our language?"

"And the books, where are they from?"

"Your power? How can you melt rocks?"

"Who are you?"

"Enough! Enough!" The creature held up both hands. "As I said, you are here to feed me, not the other way around!" Then another cackle, "Such curious children! Very well: I have learned most of your languages from travelers and books over many years. The books? Let's say I 'borrow' from your libraries. Who am I? I am the fiend, the man in black, the ghost, the devil - I am whomever you wish to call me. When and how I got here and the source of my power is of no consequence."

Peter tried another tack-

"You say you have so much time? We too have time, as much time as we are at your mercy, so where's the harm?"

"Yes," agreed Annie, "we have time, and we are curious. Indulge us." She smiled.

Their host sat for a moment contemplating his answer. Then, finally he continued.

"As I will erase your recollection before you leave, I would hardly be indulging you, but I may indulge myself, it's a long time since I have visited the past. Prepare yourselves then, for this is a long tale."

154

Peter and Annie exchanged glances and sat back in their chairs.

"I should explain that what you see before you is a shadow of a being that once was, ruined by innumerable years underground. But that is not as it once was. You are human, and as such cannot grasp the concepts of eternity and immortality. Therefore, do not question me on time. How do you measure infinity? Suffice that these things did pass. Think not of time, but chronology. I will enter your minds, now, and I will let you see, because it pleases me to discuss these things but, after, I must erase the memory."

Annie and Peter both opened their mouths in protest, but were silenced by the raising of his hand.

"When you hear my story, you will understand the danger I would be in - hunted, hounded, a freak, a circus act - if my existence were known. I must maintain the secrecy. I must hope that one day I will be released from all this. Perhaps even to die. Yes, we are immortal in man's terms, but we die and can be killed, either naturally in our own determination of old age, which could be eons in your world, or in battle, or if murdered either by other Gods or weapons made by Gods.

"Even then, we do not *die*, we *crossover* to other worlds where eventually, when we are ready, we are reborn.

"I see incredulity on your faces, questions already on your lips. Save them, hear my story; it will answer all. Now, I am about to enter your minds, and in so doing, you may enter mine. You will 'witness' the story as well as hear it. Watch and listen!"

156

The couple sat and looked at each other, then at the creature before them. Before they could speak, they felt a tiredness descend on them like a cloak; first, a shadow, then blackness, turning to misty greyness, then it cleared as they attached to the being's memory. The pictures were sharp and clear, and the commentating voice was still their host's, but not the rasping gruffness of before. Now it was strong yet serene, cultured and soft, with a hint of accent resembling the brogue of Southern Ireland.

"I am Lugh, Sun God of the Danaan, a race of Gods and demi-Gods from beyond your concept of time. Eons ago, we left our shores as a result of a defeat in battle with gods of the dark side and found a new home in the land you now refer to as Ireland.

"The land of the Tuatha De Danaan was beautiful. Forests, hills, meadows, lush fields in every shade of green, rolling countryside tumbling down from wooded mountains, the landscape broken here and there by silvery streams and flowing rivers, meandering or cascading into crystal clear lakes. The shores of the lakes and the banks of the rivers were abundant with flora of all nature, colour and perfume, gifts from Aine, goddess of love and fertility. Intermingled with nature's beauty were the homesteads and villages of the humans who tended the crops; neat hamlets, quaint cottages and municipal buildings, supply stores alongside produce warehouses and stock enclosures.

"The Tuatha de Danaan had their own domains, four major cities to the north, Falias, Gorias, Finias and Murias - the capital, Tara, in the centre of the country. Cities like you have not seen on earth since, magnificent edifices of marble and stone, brightly coloured roofs

157

and awnings, clean cobbled streets; buildings of one, two, three, and more levels high, parks and rivers and boats and lawns and orchards. The Egyptians, Greeks and the Romans all tried to emulate what we had, but even their magnificence fell short. And the people; laughing, smiling, friendly; each with a purpose, but never in a rush.

"I wish I could have told you I was born into this Utopia, yet I was not. I was born under strange circumstances.

"My Father was Cian, son of Dian Cecht, the god of healing. He was of a particular ilk of roaming god; neither the city life nor the harmony of the countryside was appealing to him. He loved adventure. A major part of his life was spent furthering that adventure, his escapades being a volume in their own right, seafaring tales of islands and monsters and witches, beautiful islands too of pleasure beyond your dreams. Strange lands, dark lands, islands of storms as the west coast of what you now refer to as Scotland, islands covered in ice.

"Father never cared. He had no idea where he was headed when he set out anywhere, his destination being wherever the winds blew. But I wish only to concentrate on one such expedition, when Cian came across the island of the sea gods and their watchdog, Balor.

"The Hierarchy of the sea gods; Lir and his son Manannan Mac Lir, were, for the most part, fine and fair entities, but always held enmity against the Tuatha over an escapade where one of their Fimorii minions stole Dagda's (our god king) magic harp. The harp escaped, but the incident was never forgotten. In addition, the Fimorii had at one time insulted one of the wives of a higher god with a detrimental comment as to the beauty of her son. In revenge, the senior goddess cursed their race and henceforth, all male Fimorii were born disfigured and hideous with arms or legs or eyes missing, deformed and dwarfish or grotesque and ogre size, the ugliness accentuated by their proportions. Their ugly features distorted their hearts and they became the feared terrors of the seas, pirates, murderers, abductors and rapists, all of them.

"Worst of all the Fimorii was Balor, their demi-god. He was the epitome of evil, huge, ugly and heartless. His skin was like that of a reptile, his hands like claws and he had one eye in the centre of his forehead, an eye bewitched by Calatin his nefarious druid sorcerer of Fomorian descent. The eye, under a spell from the dark side, could paralyse anyone - god, man or beast - who came within range, the paralysis leading ultimately to death.

"My father's interest here at this godforsaken island, was Balor's daughter, said to be the fairest in the universe; obviously, she had to have been the offspring of one of Balor's rapes, since she was certainly no pedigree Fimorii.

"Being female, she was not afflicted by the Fimorii Curse, but Balor had learned from Calatin's witch daughters that they had seen the future (probably in the entrails of a fetid pig) and Balor was seen to be slain by his own grandson! To prevent this coming to pass, Balor had a crystal prison constructed in the highest tower of his stronghold, and there he had confined Ethlinn, his own daughter, so that she knew naught of man.

"This was my father's quest, not to rescue Ethlinn, (that was impossible) but just to set eyes upon her.

"With the assistance of a druid ally and his sleeping spells, Cian was smuggled into the foul castle and with the aid of a stolen plan

159

of the edifice; he made his way to the crystal tower. Cian easily fooled the eunuch on guard as to his identity, and, using the druid's draft, the sentry was immobilised. He entered the Crystal Dome and fell in love with his first sight of Ethlinn, who was indeed a beauty to behold. Over time, my father visited his love as often as he could, and she became pregnant. Fortunately, Balor visited his daughter rarely, and she duped him into believing the rich foods he sent her as accountable for her weight gain. Soon, I was born...not in the halls or chambers of beauty and harmony of Tara, but in a crystal prison in a foul smelling castle on an island of evil.

"My father made plans to smuggle us out, but something went wrong that night, whether Balor became suspicious or Calatin and his familiars saw something, no one knows. All that is clear is that they became separated, and Cian escaped with me in his arms while Ethlinn was betrayed and her escape foiled.

"The wrath of Balor was relentless. He slew the guards one by one, ripping them apart with his bare hands, and it is said my mother died under torture by her own father, in his endeavours to ascertain the identify of her lover.

"My father was grief stricken and held himself responsible for the death of his Ethlinn. He was also committed to a quest that was to take many years, and so he could not take care of me, thus, he fostered me out to his brother, Goibhniu, god of armoury and smithing. There I grew up and was a young man before I ever saw my father.

"On attaining maturity, I was conferred the deity of Sun God, there having been a long outstanding "vacancy" you might say; since that role was common to all races it therefore required an entity of mixed blood. Being half Tuatha and half Fimorii, I qualified. Powers were bestowed upon me in what can only be described as a 'graduation ceremony', which went on for seven days. The power of the sun channelling energy through me giving the gift of heat and flame and fiery thunderbolts as one weapon, and of course, the usual godly traits; hypnosis, bending minds, reading minds, telepathy, kinetics and entry and passage to the other worlds.

"My foster father, by nature of his skills and duties, had taught me well in the ways of battle weaponry, the sling shot, the use of fire and heat, so that by the time of my transition to manhood, I was well versed in all matters militia. It was then I heard that since my rank of sun god was senior in deity hierarch, I was to receive one of the four ancient Tuatha Talismans, a magic slingshot that hurled pebbles at tremendous velocity and never missed their target. The other Talismans, gifts of the higher divinities, and protected by the Tuatha from time immemorial, were, a Magic Sword, worn and used by Nuada, our leader. One slight nick or graze from that sword meant death. There was also The Cauldron of Plenty, a gift from Dagda, our god king, which was never depleted, providing us with food and wine.

"The fourth, being the Stone of Fal, the test for the true kings of Ireland. The stone remained mute when stood on by anyone undeserving, but would scream aloud only when stepped on by the rightful heir to that throne.

"With my gifts, my teachings, and my newly found status, I took my place in the society of Tara. You cannot imagine our life in your wildest dreams. Our existence was wonderful, a mixture of youthful and older gods. We had other things to learn, the arts, history,

161

music, magic. We had tutors and lecturers and we teased them as all students do, - especially Abarta! -And we laughed and had fun in our learning.

"We worked hard, and we played hard, dancing, feasts, parties, dinners, plays, concerts, relaxing by the lakes, the rivers, fishing, swimming, sports, games. Life was full, never a boring minute. My friends were too numerous to relate here, save a few who are pertinent to this story: - Badb, the goddess of battle, sweetness itself in society, but fierce in her domain. Cliodhana, goddess of beauty, ruler of the Land of Promise: stunning to look at but such a personality and fun attitude! Creidhne and Luchtar, my other uncles: the goldsmith and the weapon maker. Older and younger friends, Abarta, heart of gold but soul full of mischief, the bane of those with no humour! Life was fun when he was around, always getting into trouble with his seniors. Aoifa, Warrior Princess of the Land of Shadows, Boann, goddess of water and rivers, so many, Etain, Midir, Scathach, Iubdan and Aonghus, god of love, - I think he had most fun, especially in arranging some dubious matches!

"Then there was Aine, goddess of love and fertility, Sister to Aonghus. The most beautiful creature I ever set eyes upon. A match, I am told, even for the construed beauty of Blodeuedd, conjured out of petals and blossoms! She had a mass of strong yet soft to the touch dark hair, the colour of chestnuts. A slim and athletic body beautifully curved as if sculpted by an artist; skin so smooth and glistening, softly tanned and without a blemish; hazel eyes that smiled at you more than her mouth, that perfect mouth sweet tasting and full lipped.

"We were in love from the minute we met, we were meant for

one another; we said so, as did all our friends and families. We were to be married. A marriage truly made in heaven! I have no idea how that inevitability came about; it was simply known, presumed.

"Prior to the nuptials, as was our custom, there was a period of separation, a semester of cleansing, and learning, sowing wild oats. The groom and his friends went to the Land of Wonders while the bride and her entourage went off to the Land of Promise, there to learn the skills and duties of womanhood.

"Our essence is built on many planes and levels of existence, each phase having it's own hierarchy and structure, but also, parallel to our world, exist other worlds, each with it's own function: be it transition to other levels of existence, or merely holding patterns in voids or places to escape to or for pure pleasure and recreational purpose.

"The Land of Wonders was just such a place. Such beauty and harmony, hills, valleys, fields, ocean, beaches, rivers, lakes, trees, shrubs, flowers, bees humming, birds singing, equal day and night, never too warm never too cold, garments were optional here. The sun shone all day, and each night there was a full moon, sitting high in the heavens, reflecting on the calm waters of the lake, it's reflection like a silver path leading you to even more wondrous sights. The main stream had a fountain at its head, which gave off wine of the best vintage. Here, you did what you willed - meditate, lose yourself in the sheer beauty of the environment, relax, do nothing, or engage and live in a fantasy of your own imagination. There are no limits to harmony, peace and pleasure in the Land of Wonders.

"The Land of Promise held equal delights, but of a different

163

genre. Here, the location was a huge edifice of innumerable rooms, innumerable in that it varies as to how many are required. The building is massive and magnificent in marble and granite, huge doorways leading in from fabulous ornate gardens. Inside cannot be described. Why? Because it changes! Every day it changes, by the nature of the people using it. It is the home of the arts. The students and visitors are encouraged to learn from and work with each other and the mentors, and they use the surrounding structure not only as their venue, but also as their tools and canvas.

"It is the foundation for the builder, the structure for the architect, the canvas for the artist, the material for the sculptor. The walls are covered in masterpieces, only to be covered with new ones the next day: the decor changes with the whim of the planner, the shape changes with the instruction of the architect and the skills of the builder, all who inhabit the ground floor of the Land of Promise.

"On the second floor are the composers, the writers and the poets: sounds and words can be heard from every room.

"On the third floor are all the musicians and singers, each room emanating sweet sounds of solos, duets, sung or being played on every musical instrument even to full orchestras and choirs. Yet there is no cacophony of sound, the magic of the place allows you to hear each one clearly without corrupting another.

"The top floor I can't speak of, as it is forbidden to man; it is the Promise of Pleasure and Harmony in Marriage. Here all things marital are taught and experienced from cooking, dancing, massage, sexual pleasures, even to the experience of pregnancy and childbirth.

"The Otherworld least visited by choice, is the Land of

Shadows. Here people go to grieve lost ones, or to atone sins or repent grievances, or simply, having passed the current existence are not yet ready to move on to the Cauldron of Rebirth. It is a Land of Loneliness, so made by its visitors, as that is their main purpose, to be alone, to reflect, to grieve, and to repent. Hence it's name, since, as you walk through it's grey corridors and grey buildings, you see grey people skulking in corners hiding themselves in the grey shadows. But, I digress.

"It was while I was in the Land of Wonders and Aine in the Land of Promise that the news reached us. Word had come to Nuada from reliable sources that the Fimorii had amassed an army under the leadership of Balor and were, as we spoke, setting sail to invade our world. We men were required to return home with all due haste, while those in the Land of Promise, our ladies and the non militia scholars and musicians were to remain there until sent for." With a long sigh amidst a fading image of the beautiful Aine, Lugh's voice broke as he murmured

"Little was I to know I would never see my love again."

"I thirst." Lugh's voice was harsh and hoarse again.

Annie and Peter jumped at the change in voice as the visions faded and they reverted to normalcy inside the sun god's underground domain. Annie's immediate emotion was pain and sorrow for Lugh. As she looked at this wizened creature before her, she thought back to the scenes she had just witnessed, as in them, she had seen him as he had been; tall, golden hair, golden skin, muscular and handsome.

Peter was still stunned by all that was appearing before him. He watched Lugh pour from a large cask into three stone goblets, offering them one each. They sniffed at the fluid, which was clear but rather viscous: an aroma of alcohol with a hint of fruit. They looked at each other. Peter raised an eyebrow, and then drank from the stone goblet. He coughed and choked as the liquid hit his larynx. Lugh smiled. Annie had a taste, but on seeing the reaction from Peter, she sipped slowly.

She too felt the alcohol attack her throat, but felt and appreciated the warmth rather than the harshness.

"I guess that's the way to go, easy does it." Coughed Peter. Then he asked, "What is this?"

"Hahaha." Roared the creature. "It's my own concoction; you don't really want to know. Suffice to say, it's nectar of the gods! Hahaha...!" He laughed.

There was a long silence broken by a long, drawn-out breath from Lugh. Within the sigh, Annie heard, or perhaps felt, the words,

"Magh Tuireadh."

"Sorry?" she said, "did you say something?"

"Magh Tuireadh." Lugh repeated, louder this time. Peter recognised the bitterness in his expression.

"The battle field." Continued the sun god. "I had hoped I would never have to go near that accursed place again. I wasn't born at the time of the first battle there, against the Firbolg, but I was there in a previous incarnation. I died there! So many good men fell that day, even though we were victorious. Even our great leader Nuada lost a hand there. I was bodyguard to him, yet I was unable to prevent the attack. I went to his assistance and was binding his wound when I was set upon by a Firbolg. I had no weapon, having laid them down to tend Nuada. I had no defence. I felt the sword enter my gut and sear my heart. My last memory was of Nuada severing the head of my assailant with the magic sword held in his good hand. It was some time after this battle that I was reborn as I am today.

"Goibhniu had brought me there again as part of my training, to explain and practice tactics on battle soil. I could still envisage the scenes of carnage, the death, the pain, the screams, the stench of copper-scented blood, the stifling odour of eviscerated bodies, the smell of the fires and the sickly sweet burning of human flesh.

"The place has an atmosphere all of its own - just about the only place in our world that isn't green. Dull grey, mixed black with peat; misty, forlorn, undulating hills and plateaus, barren stretches of sloping mire running off into the distance and ducking down into hidden valleys as if they were ashamed of their appearance. It was forever desolate and cold: not even my sun power could penetrate the ambience.

"Now, here I was, ready to do battle once again in a new incarnation. Waiting to kill...or be killed. We could hear them already. We had just enough time to muster as many men, gods and humans mixed, as we possibly could at such short notice. No sooner had we assembled than the ships began to amass on our doorstep. Now the Fimorii were here. An army of hideous monstrosities, disfigured, dismembered; a grotesque horde. The war cries in the distance, the jeers, the taunting, the tramp of thousands of feet, the clashing of swords on shields as they came, outnumbering us three to one. And there, leading them with his giant stride was the beast Balor!"

Lugh paused then realised he was talking mostly to himself, having almost forgotten his audience in his thoughts.

"You seem tired. Is this too much for you?" he asked them.

"No. Please, go on!" Urged Annie. Peter nodded eagerly. "We are just a bit bemused going in and out of your mind control, but your drink has certainly revived us!"

"Very well." Sighed Lugh. "Relax then, watch, and stand beside me at Magh Tuireadh."

ooo000ooo

The historian and the geologist once again felt the overbearing tiredness as the dream sequences of Lugh's mind invaded and swamped their psyche; emerging from the darkness into the greyness of fog and out of focus images. But this time, the mist did not clear, and they realised they were witnessing the battle ground as it had been

168

that morning; dull and grey, cold and damp, a watery sun desperately trying to pervade the morning fog swirling over the countryside like a huge veil.

"The horrors of that battle are imprinted on my memory for ever, as if it were yesterday. We and our captains had war council the day before and had drawn up plans and strategy to make full, economic use of the scant resources we had at our disposal. While my friends and I were returning from the Land of Wonders, Nuada had been busy sending his messengers far and wide to recruit able bodies for the confrontation. Many had been successful, others had not. Among the unsuccessful ones, was my father, Cian. His mission was to the north, but the traitors and cowards of Tuireann waylaid him.

"His Sons, Brian, Luchar and Luchara intercepted Cian and under a false greeting of friendship, murdered him as he slept using some weapon fashioned by the dark gods. I received the news when I arrived at Tara; the first casualty of this war, my own father. How many more would there be before this day was over? I swore vengeance on Tuireann and his family, but the greater more pressing need was here, on the battlefield. I made a pact with my uncles, that whomsoever should survive this day, would exact revenge for us all, and we devised a suitable punishment for the perpetrators of the dastardly crime.

"The second casualty was my Uncle Giobniu; he was working in the foundry putting finishing touches to weapons, when Ruadan, son of the dreaded Princess Brigid, attacked him. Ruadan was the infamous Fimorii spy and assassin and had been tasked with stealing the secrets of our weapon production and to kill the producers in so doing. Two

169

nights before the battle, he had eluded our security and had found his way into the great iron foundry, but my Uncle discovered him and although Ruadan wounded Goibhan with one of his own spears, my uncle was able to overcome him and slay him there and then; first blood to the Fimorii, then, but first victory to the Tuatha. Goibhniu, although wounded, still managed to attend the battle scene, and played a hero's part in the outcome.

"So, there we were, dawn of the second battle of Magh Tuireadh; two armies facing each other across the great divide that was the barren desolation of those historic plains.

"The gods, the heroes, the human minions of Ireland, all preparing for the assault of a larger horde of subhuman lesser gods, champions and creatures of the accursed Fimorii. Thousands upon thousands of beings, men and monstrosities each cheering, jeering, taunting while we prayed.

"On the Tuatha side, resplendent in armour, was Nuada of the silver arm, fashioned in my uncle's furnaces to replace the arm the Firbolg had taken at the previous battle and on his waist belt, still sheathed for now, his enchanted sword. On his left was Macha, his wife and one of the four goddesses of battle, behind her stood her three associates, Badb, Morrigan and Nemain.

"I took up position on Nuada's right flank with Aoifa, Warrior Princess of the Land of Shadows and Abarta, god of mischief, who despite his tomfoolery, was trustworthy and a force to be reckoned with in battle.

"On the left flank were Scathach and her entourage, another warrior princess, and to the rear were the non-combatants, my three uncles, Creidne, Luchtar and the brave Giobhniu, tending weapons and preparing equipment for replacements and repairs. Behind them were Dian Cecht, the god of healing, and his son, Miach, with their cohorts of attendants preparing their tables and medicines to treat the wounded. In front of us, were our limited legions of minions lined up or formed in squares depending on our strategies as to whether we attacked or defended.

"Opposing us were the battalions and regiments of one eyed, one legged, one-armed disfigured and deformed monstrosities of the Fimori, their chiefs on a rise to their rear, surveying our strengths and weaknesses. In the centre, almost twice the size of any of we Tuatha, stood Balor, the Fimorii champion and my grandfather. The most foul and grotesque creature one can imagine. He required no armour, his skin being thicker almost than any metal plate, ridged and knotted like a crocodile's. He carried only a huge shield on his left arm and an enormous club in his right hand. He took in all before him, his one great eye roving the battlefield; that one eye, with the power to stop men dead in their tracks, if they were within range and met his gaze.

"No one knew for certain the extent of his power. We were about to find out. On his left, was Calatin, the deformed sorcerer, the druid who was Balor's servant, following him like a faithful dog, waiting for scraps to fall from his table. Alongside Calatin were his three nightmarish children, the one eyed witches spawned from the depths of hell. They were the support for Balor with spells and incantations gained from books written in blood. On his right, were Delbaeth, son of Elatha, the sea god king, and the wicked Searbhan whose deeds defy even the concept of evil.

171

"The hordes not only outnumbered us, but wielded weapons we were not accustomed to. Serrated sword blades hacked from swordfish, clubs imbedded with shark's teeth, arrows tipped with poison from jellyfish and other deadly sea creatures, spears charged with the energy of thousands of electric eels.

"We too had our weaponry, the finest iron and steel forged by my uncles, swords, spears, daggers and arrows. We also had our powers and gifts, my slingshot and fireballs, Nuada's sword, and the goddess of battle and her associates had the power to change shape and transform into any creature of land, sea or air. Against us, Balor and his cycloptic eye backed by the sorcery of Calatin and his familiars.

"War was waged differently in our world. The mortal minions fight one another in conventional combat, as humans cannot harm gods, unless with weapons fashioned by gods. Gods can kill deities however, and can easily slaughter humans. Thus normal warfare was for man and gods to attempt to destroy the legions of the adversary then challenge each other. However, we had an advantage, our troops being armed with the weapons of my uncles; fashioned by gods, they could in fact attack the lesser gods and wreak havoc while we could concentrate our efforts on all out attack against the hierarchy of the enemy , thus leaving their army leaderless. This was our main strategy of the day.

"Observing everything were our god kings who by culture, tradition and chivalry, were not allowed to interfere. In our 'corner', so to speak, were Dagda and Dana, founders of the Tuatha de Danaan, children of Dana. On the side of the Fimorii were Lir, sea god king, and his son Manannan Mac Lir.

"In addition, there was a further passive observer. Lurking in the shadows was Donn, god of the dead, waiting to transport all who fell to the Netherworlds. Yeah, indeed! 'Twould be an easy wager to say that Donn was going to be kept busy that day!"

oooOOOooo

"And so it began. On a signal sounded on sea-shells like so many horns, the hordes advanced. Our captains took up their positions and mustered their battalions around them, bracing themselves for the first onslaught. Within minutes from the first blow to be struck, it was obvious we had underestimated the power of Balor. We had considered him staring at individuals one by one from very close range, yet he was immobilising men by the dozens in huge sections with a sweep of his eye from twenty paces or more. As soon as they returned his gaze, and who could fault them in their terror, they became motionless and were hacked to pieces by the advancing scum, chopping and slashing at the defenceless infantrymen. We kept filling the breaches with reserve soldiers on instructions to look down, never up, but this, of course, impaired their fighting ability.

"I tried to distract Balor by letting fly a series of fireballs, but I was too distant to cause damage, and he swatted them away like pesky insects with his huge shield.

"Nuada said something above the din of battle to the effect of magic needs magic and despatched his wife Macha and her comrades to distract the giant. They immediately transformed into crows and flew into his face, carefully avoiding eye contact, circling, diving,

173

swooping and pecking. This had the desired effect as Balor concentrated on trying to pluck the birds out of the air and looked quite foolish in the midst of battle, waving his huge arms and club and shield all around his head in an effort to rid himself of this unexpected annoyance.

"While Balor was not wreaking havoc with our army, the captains rallied the men and reformed in offensive positions; we began to push the Fimorii back somewhat, they being no match for our well trained soldiers and superior weapons, despite the advantage of their numbers. Besides, the Fimorii are generally cowards and only fight if they think they can win. Resistance, and violent retaliation at that, soon had them in retreat. Scathach had taught her soldiers well, as they scythed and jabbed through the Fimorrii advance foot soldiers, (well named for the Fimorii, since many only had one foot), herself in the forefront driving the opposition backwards. The noise became almost a tangible thing like the air and the weather, it was all around, banging and crashing and clanging and screaming in agony and fear, the shouting of orders, the battle cries, collision of shields. There was nowhere within miles you could communicate without yelling. Soon the stench of battle too began to permeate the air itself, smoke from fires ignited by my projectiles, the thick metallic odour of blood, the stench of entrails and rotting fish from the gutted Fimorii and the wet earthy smell as the ground became a quagmire saturated with blood.

"Calatin and Delbaeth watched in horror as they saw the tide of war turn against them and quickly realised the cost to them of the distraction to their champion. The sorcerer saw the cause of Balor's distress and also realised magic was at work. He immediately called his daughters to him and between the four of them, quickly prepared a counter spell. Suddenly the crows around the Cyclops's head began to drop and soar again as they flitted in and out of transition, first crow, then goddess in hazy transformation. Calatin's power supported by the hellish hags was all too powerful for them, and one by one, they dropped to the ground.

"Badb, Morrigan and Nemain scrambled to their feet immediately, and with heads bowed against Balor's gaze, they ran back to safety, but Macha had injured herself in the fall and stumbled in her flight. Balor seized her in his great claw hand and with one swipe decapitated her with his huge club.

"Nuada let out a fearful howl of pain and torment as he witnessed the death of his beloved, slain and cast aside like a slaughtered chicken. Before I could prevent him, with a shriek of rage, he had unsheathed his sword and was racing towards the monster. Oblivious to the carnage in his path, he slashed his way through the throngs of fighting soldiers until he broke free of them and confronted their champion.

"I can only imagine in the furore of his rage and grief, he was unmindful of the power of Balor's gaze, for as he was about to strike the Fimorii leader, the monster met his eyes full on and Nuada froze in mid stroke. With a cry of triumph, Balor lifted him up above his head so all could see, and then dashed him to the ground in a cloud of dust and spattering of mire. Nuada was already on his way to join Macha as guests of Donn.

"The three other goddesses witnessed all this as they arrived back beside me and despite their exhaustion, were about to rush back

175

into the melee to avenge their sister. They were already attempting transformation yet again, (Calatin's counter spell, though powerful, being short lived) when I yelled, "NO! It is too dangerous. Wait!"

"I called upon Abarta and Aoifa for counsel and we six withdrew to reconsider our position, our troops now back peddling with the power of Balor again focused on them and the Fimorii encouraged by the sight of the death of Nuada. Our captains had formed defensive squares and were endeavouring to hold their positions. As a parting gesture, I fired off another volley of fireballs at Balor, and though they did no real damage, one caught his shield and set fire to it, his attention diverted to releasing his shield giving temporary respite to our officers.

"On the death of Nuada, I was now leader...All depended on me. I had to kill my grandfather, and I had to move fast. But how? Then it came to me. Balor is protected by Calatin. My distractions have been directed at the wrong foe! Hurriedly, I spoke to the three battle goddesses.

"We have seen the power of the monster's gaze, he must be stopped. He must be distracted long enough for me to slay him. It is too dangerous for you to attack him as before; sooner or later you will fall foul of his stare. This time, you must become bats! They are blind and manoeuvre by sound. Can you distract him in that form?"

All three nodded vehemently. "Yes! That will work, but what about Calatin and his counter spells?"

"That is my concern, I will keep him busy. Spread the word, my friends, encourage our soldiers. Balor is to be slain. I am his grandson. Let it be known! The prophecy will be fulfilled!"

"As the three Goddesses prepared for their transformation, Abarta and Aoifa set off among the army and the captains, while I began to flank the masses and made my way down the ridge towards Balor, but as I went, I unleashed a rain of fireballs at Calatin and his entourage. They found their marks causing panic among his throng as they ran hither and thither trying to escape my fire. The projectiles landed all around them and there was chaos as they ran from the fires, some with their cloaks ablaze. I kept up my barrage until I saw Abarta and Aoifa with a troop of experienced men outflank the infantry and position themselves between Calatin and Balor where they were keeping the druid busy under a hail of arrows. This was my chance. I headed straight for the giant.

"To add potency to my magic, I was required to slay Balor in the manor of Fimorii, and the ritual involved my emulating their deformed nature, so, while Balor was busy swatting at three vicious, biting, clawing bats, I stood on one leg, covered one eye, and hopped round my foe in a large circle. On completion of the circle, I took out my Talisman, loaded it with a huge pebble of hard granite rock, spun the sling shot round three times and fired it directly at his one eye. As is true to the magic of our Talisman, the pebble found its target and struck the offending eyeball with such power it forced the eye right through the back of the creature's head propelling it into the melee around Calatin and his spawned hags. It was never seen again.

"The Fimorii leader was motionless for a few seconds, then like an almighty oak tree, he began to topple then fell with such a crash as to make all cease fighting to determine the cause. Within seconds, all had realised the source and with a mighty cheer, our army rushed

177

the invaders with renewed vigour. Whatever heart the Fimorii had before, now forsook them and they turned tail and fled, Calatin leading the exodus.

"Our men gave chase, slashing and stabbing at any stragglers, and did not give up the chase until every last Fimorii yet alive was back in his boat or swimming in the sea.

"The day was ours! The battle won! The Fimorii routed and put to flight!

"I have no idea how many men fell that day. We had many both dead and wounded. Dian Cecht and his staff would be busy for days as would Donn, endlessly ferrying souls to his kingdom.

"Yet, such is the nature of things and people, amidst all this carnage and grief and loss yet we celebrate victory. And celebrate we did. Tara was alight with torches and feasts and fireworks that night, and despite our exhaustion, victory coursed in our veins and would not let us sleep until we had exorcised the elation.

"In the early hours of the next morning, wine and exhaustion having satiated the euphoria, loss and grief set in, and we began wordlessly wandering off to our homes. Dawn was breaking as I collapsed into bed.

"I recall a smile as I thought how different the dawn is today as opposed to the mist and fog of yesterday. How beautiful the sky looked shrouded in pink and gold. I saluted the rising sun, my patriarch, a greeting from the god of light.

"That was the last time I was ever to see the sun. I woke up in this infernal underground prison."

Peter blinked a few times as the visions faded and felt a bit light-headed as the mental contact was terminated. He looked over at Annie and saw she too appeared slightly disorientated. His first thought was that she did resemble Aine, whom he had now seen through Lugh's memory. She was blinking now, but still seemed in a trance, as if she didn't want to let go. There were tears in her eyes.

The sun god was sat opposite them, head in his hands. Peter went to Annie and began massaging the back of her neck. She blinked again and looked up at him, then smiled as if just recognising him that second.

"Lugh? Are you OK?" asked Peter softly.

He got no response.

Peter looked at Annie.

"Lugh?" Annie called to him.

The creature looked up at them. Tears welled in Annie's eyes again as she saw what he had become; a mere shell of a being. Gone was the handsome god she had been watching, yet, in his sunken eyes, she discerned a shadow of the sparkle that once was there, a fleeting glimpse of fire, of love and life.

"Lugh." She tried again. "We have to go, soon. We will already have been missed. People will be searching for us." She lied.

The sun god turned in their direction. At first it appeared he was looking through them, then his eyes focused on man and woman. He simply nodded very slowly as if he were contemplating something else, something far, far away in time and dimension.

Peter asked if he would like a drink, ugh waved his hand in reply. The two humans exchanged glances again, Peter raising his eyebrows in question, Annie full of concern.

"Are you alright?" she asked. Lugh took a deep breath and sighed, then continued as if they weren't there.

"Calatin!" He rasped as if in answer to a question.

"Calatin's sorcery; Black Magic of the most foul. He had evoked the powers of Darkness, enlisting them to assist as revenge upon me for the death of their evil champion. What sweeter punishment could he exact on the god of sun and light than to banish him to an eternity of darkness! He tried to use all four elements against me - earth, air, fire and water - confining me to the earth to live underground. He made my skin sensitive to the sunlight so I was restricted to the night. And he chose his site well for water containment. Natural water became my prison bars. The extent of my prison containing me within boundaries I cannot cross, rivers to the north, east and west, lakes and pools to the south. I cannot traverse any of them on land or burrow beneath. His only failure was by fire. Even he and his hellish assistants could not take away my god-given powers.

"Fire and energy are mine to have and can only be taken away by those who bestowed them. But by that same token, I am trapped here for all time for none can break this spell save the one who cast it! I am doomed to eternity, or death! How I long for death! I cannot take my own life; else I would have done so long ago." He sighed again.

"Lugh?" Annie whispered after a long silence.

The sun god looked at her. "Please don't erase this from our minds. You must let us retain this. You must let us try to help you." Her voice was full of pleading and compassion.

After another silent pause he answered.

"To what end? Eventually you will disclose to another, he to others - ultimately I will become an 'attraction', a curio. I cannot allow that. As for help, what can two humans do that I, a god, cannot? I sense sincerity in your voice and read compassion in your heart, but though it is well meant, it is futile."

Peter interjected, "At least we can leave here Lugh, while you are restricted. We can go places you cannot."

Lugh's face contorted in that grimace smile they had witnessed before-

"Indeed! And do what?"

"Right now, I have no idea." Admitted the young man. "My brain is full of images and impossibilities. My head hurts and I feel exhausted, please, give us time. We will keep this between only the two of us, we give you our word."

He looked at Annie, and she nodded, pleading with her eyes.

"Let us rest, and think on this. You have nothing to lose." Peter insisted.

"Obviously we can promise no solution, but let us try."

Lugh rose and shuffled around his cave, head bowed in deep thought, weighing up the pros and cons of the situation. Peter and Annie looked at each other their eyes conveying hope as if they were telepathically trying to convince the creature of their determination and integrity.

Finally, Lugh spoke.

181

"Very well, as you rightfully say, Peter, I have nothing to lose provided you retain discretion. I feel your honesty. I will trust you. But this cannot be indefinite, eventually you will convey something to someone albeit indirectly or inadvertently. You must return here within two suns and you must convey nothing to paper or to those voice machines. These are my conditions."

Annie smiled in relief, almost clapping her hands.

"Now you must leave." Lugh dismissed them and walked over to where he had sealed the entrance. With a flourish, he waved his hand over the solid rock door and, closing his eyes, he concentrated his energy. The rock grew hot, then began to glow red. Within seconds, it melted away. Peter looked on in astonishment. He could feel the temperature rise in the cave, the radiated heat warming his face and stinging his eyes. He took Annie's hand as they crossed to the now open doorway.

"Two suns." Reminded Lugh. "Now go, I look forward to your return, Peter. Take care, Aine."

ooo000ooo

The couple followed the entrance passageway back to the main tunnel.

Disorientated at first, Peter looked both ways, took the flashlight from his belt, pulled his compass from his pocket then turned right, heading south according to the needle. After a few minutes' uphill walk, they came back to a cross section he recognized, checked his compass again for confirmation, then continued east. They travelled in silence, each lost within their own thoughts, the rising tunnel making walking an effort and their breath conserved for movement. Soon they reached the entrance at the site of the old silver mine, and two minutes later, they came out squinting their eyes at the bright sunlight. A short walk across the field brought them back to Peter's Capri.

It wasn't until they had caught their breath and were sitting in the car that Peter spoke.

"Wow! I still don't believe all this! It is too much to take in."

"Hmmm me too." Agreed Annie.

"You know he called you Aine, don't you?" Peter remarked casually as he started up the engine.

"He didn't! When?" Annie asked incredulously.

"When we were leaving; he said, take care, Aine. Didn't you notice?"

"He said, Annie." She retorted, but there was doubt in her voice.

"Didn't he?"

Peter said nothing, but smiled as he put the machine in gear and drove off.

Half an hour later, he was pulling into the car park at the Golden Circle.

"Night cap?" Annie offered.

"Sure." He smiled back at her.

In her room, he flopped on her sofa while she headed for the drinks fridge, took out a miniature bottle of gin and shared the contents between two glasses, topped up with tonic water and ice. She walked over and, handing one to Peter, she sat beside him on the three-seater divan.

"Cheers." He said, clinking her glass. "Here's to our Sun God." He took a swig of his drink, placed it on the table to his left and, lowering his head, began rubbing his temples.

"Headache?" she asked. He nodded into his hands.

She placed her glass on her table, put her hand on his neck and dragged him over so that he had his head in her lap.

"Looks like you could do with some pampering, you big baby!" She laughed, and began massaging his forehead and temples.

"Mmmm." He responded.

With one hand continuing the head massage, her other hand slipped into his open shirt and began rubbing his chest, her fingers playing with the hair there. He sighed in contentment. Then her hand found a nipple and began playing with it, rolling it under her index finger, flicking it with her fingernail then finally tweaking it between her fingers, tugging on it, coaxing it erect. With his head in her lap, he only had to turn his head to sink his face into her breasts. He kissed them through her T-shirt.

As usual for Annie, she wasn't wearing a bra. With his left hand, he raised her top over her left breast and began sucking on her nipple. She withdrew her hand from his shirt and traced his body down to his crotch, there she gently stroked his penis and smiled when she felt it was already beginning to respond.

"I thought we were beat?" she teased.

"Mmmm, later." He mumbled through a mouthful of breast.

The foreplay now in full motion, they elaborated into full love

184

making with a passion making up for lost years. When they had regained their breath, he stroked her hair-

"Let's shower." He whispered.

Then slowly they got up, made their way arm in arm to the shower where they caressingly sponged each other in the warm flow of cascading water. They also dried each other, and then walked hand in hand to the bed. Peter lay on his back and Annie lifted his arm and tucked it round her neck his hand on her breast as she rested her head on his expansive chest. There they fell asleep within minutes of each other.

While Peter and Annie slept, a figure was at work stealthily creeping around the hotel. It seemed to find what it was looking for, and gained entrance through an open rear doorway to the Kitchens on the ground floor. Seemingly able to drift from shadow to shadow, it entered the building and, sniffing the air, followed a scent upstairs and along the corridor to Annie's doorway. There it stood, a final sniff of recognition, as if contemplating whether to enter or not. Annie stirred in her sleep as if disturbed by an unpleasant dream. The figure decided not to encroach on the slumbering couple, and pulling some paper and crayon from within its cape, it scribbled a note, slid it under the door, and disappeared again back into the shadows.

Peter awoke first, unsure of his surroundings, but then remembering where he was. He looked at Annie lying comfortably beside him. He smiled at her soft sleeping noises and sighed within himself as the memory of the previous night came flooding back. She was beautiful, then and now. He knew he had again fallen in love with her, or, had he ever really stopped loving her? He leaned over to the bedside table, and picked up his watch, which he had taken off and left there the night before.

"Holy shit!" He hissed. Annie stirred. He turned back and kissed her forehead, shaking her naked shoulder gently. "Annie?" He whispered. "Mmmmm?" she murmured.

"Annie, it's almost eight." Annie's eyes shot open. She lay there staring at nothing for a few seconds, trying to arrange her thoughts, dreams, recollection, and reality into some form of meaningful context in her head.

"What did you say?" she asked absently.

"It's quarter to eight."

"Oh my God!" Weren't we meant to be at the colliery for eight?"

"Yep! But don't worry. I'll call them while you get ready. Give them some sort of excuse."

She accepted his offer and reluctantly slipped out of bed, stood and stretched. Immediately, she folded her arms around herself and sat quickly on the bed curled up in the realization that she was completely naked. She looked over at her lover and saw that he was sitting on his end of the bed, dialling the hotel telephone. Oblivious to her state. She giggled to herself at her own embarrassment, considering her lack of modesty a mere few hours ago and, glad that Peter had not seen it, stood up with an air of confidence, and strolled to the en-suite bathroom. Peter sensed the movement and looked up, his eyes following her to the door. He sighed, smiled in appreciation, and went back to his task.

"Hello!" The gruff voice said on the other end of the line.

"Uh, Hullo! Harry? Is that you? Peter, here. I was expecting Liz."

"She's not in yet, doesn't start till eight. Where are you?"

"Ummm, something's come up. I'm at Annie...Dr. Wilde's hotel, picking her up. We spoke to a few people at Cairnpapple yesterday, and we have to follow up on something this morning. I won't bother you with details, as it might not amount to anything, I'll

187

keep you posted."

"Cairnpapple! What the hell were you doing up there? Debbie said yesterday you had gone on a 'field trip'. I assumed it was research of some sort?"

"Well, yes, it was, in a way. Anyway, we should only be an hour or so, catch you later." Peter hung up before the manager could reply or protest.

The geologist lay back on the pillows; he could still sense Annie's presence there - a residual warmth, a lingering aroma of perfume. He closed his eyes and savoured it.

Annie meanwhile, was in the shower, eyes closed, letting the hot water caress her body. She was smiling and thinking to herself, "Well, the cat's out of the bag now!"

She finished her shower, dried off, and went back into the bedroom, a towel draped over her head as she used the end of it to dry her wet hair. Peter couldn't take his eyes off her; all he wanted was to take her straight back to bed and make love again and again. She felt his eyes on her, but she did not let on to him she was even aware of his presence. Instead, she continued her toilette in a subtle tease as if she were alone in the room.

She sat at the dressing table, plugged in her hair-dryer and proceeded to dry her hair, combing it as she did so. Peter watched her, then rose and walked up behind her. She silently appreciated his nakedness in the reflection of the mirror. He stroked her shoulders and kissed her on the top of her wet head.

Her reflection smiled at him. "We have to go." She said softly. "What did you tell them, by the way?"

Peter turned and walked towards the bathroom, over his shoulder he said casually-

"Oh, nothing much. Just said you got drunk last night and I had the devil of a job waking you this morning."

"Bastard!" She cried, and he ducked into the toilet just before her comb hit the door.

Fifteen minutes later, they were both dressed and ready to go.

"I have to go back to The Fairway." Peter said, "I need a shave and a change of clothes. You look lovely, by the way, but I do prefer you in short skirts."

Annie had chosen a pair of tight fitting navy blue slacks to wear with a white blouse and casual navy jacket to match the trousers.

"Well, considering where you took me yesterday, I thought I'd better be prepared for anything."

Peter led towards the door, and as he went to open it, he stooped to pick up what looked like an old piece of parchment off the floor.

"Messy bugger, aren't you?" he teased as he went to throw it in the bin.

"Wait!" She said, grabbing his arm and taking the paper from him. "That's not mine!"

She looked at the message. Written in fine copperplate handwriting, was just one line- *I need to speak with you both. Lugh.*

Annie showed the note to Peter. He looked at her, eyebrow raised.

"I guess that determines our schedule for today then." Was all he said as he ushered her out the door and down the stairs. They each suppressed giggles as they passed the reception desk overshadowed by a scowling, disapproving night porter.

Outside, referring to the porter, Peter said, "That's nothing! Wait till you see the reception I get when we go to the Fairway!"

At the geologist's motel, the proprietor gave them a steely stare, opened her mouth to say something, but thought better of it.

"Good morning." Said Peter.

"Hello." Replied Annie. But each salutation was greeted with a shallow smile.

"I'd better wait down here while you change." Annie whispered. "If I follow you to your room, I think we may have a hostile reception of hotel clerks waiting to stone us to death!"

Peter smiled and said, "OK, I won't be long." He squeezed her hand and bounded up the stairs three at a time.

When he returned, he looked much fresher, and had sensibly changed into jeans and grey sweatshirt for their escapade. They set off for The Knock Hill, the car seeming to keep pace with drifting white clouds driven by a light breeze in a blue sky.

Annie said, "Glad you came back when you did, I was getting the third degree from your landlady. I was expecting the reading lamp in my face any minute!"

"I bet!" Peter laughed. "Nothing changes here, huh? Everybody needs to know everything about everyone else."

He had driven up Academy Street, turned left onto Marjoribanks Street and was now turning right onto Drumcross Road heading towards the Bathgate Hills.

"I wonder what Lugh wants?" Annie thought out loud. "I hope

he hasn't changed his mind and wants to erase our memories."

"As long as he doesn't erase my memory of last night." Peter said, smiling. "That was just incredible." He reached over with his free hand and gently squeezed Annie's knee.

"Hmmm, it was, wasn't it?" she agreed.

In a few minutes, Peter was once again parking at the foot of West Lothian's highest point.

"Need the wellies?" he asked Annie.

"No! Thank you very much! I'm wearing 'sensible' shoes today." He smiled as he saw she was wearing flat-heeled town shoes.

"Me neither." He said, as he raised his foot to show her his sneakers.

They walked up the hill and climbed the fence, Annie needing no assistance this time, and made their way back to the cave entrance in the silver mine valley. They tiptoed over the rocks in the poor light until they saw the faint glow ahead of them. Lugh had either not bothered to seal the entrance after their last visit, or had re-opened it, anticipating their arrival. As they approached the entrance, they felt rather than heard the welcome, "Come. I have been waiting."

ooo000ooo

Once more, they entered the home of the sun god, and Peter noticed the air was yet again filled with the smell of cooking. His stomach growled as he realized they had neither dinner last night, nor breakfast this morning.

"You have not breakfasted." Rasped Lugh, "I have some steak

191

prepared. Even after all these years, I have not mastered culinary skills, but you are welcome to partake. My diet here consisted of steak, mutton, chicken (which I 'borrow' from my neighbours) garnished with vegetables and herbs which I, shall we say, happen to come across in my nocturnal travels."

"I don't mind if I do." Said Peter. "I'm starving!"

Annie was more cautious and reserved her right only after she had seen the bill of fare.

Lugh presented a platter of thinly cut meat, a bit overdone, but innocent looking and appearing palatable. They both ate, tentatively at first, then hungrily. The meat was cooked well enough, but wanted seasoning.

While they ate, Lugh sat opposite them at the large table and began-

"I have been reflecting on your comments from yesterday, and I see merit where perhaps you have not. You mentioned you could travel where I cannot. This is of interest to me. There is one way in which I might escape this torture. But before I lay out my plan, I must warn you of the perils before you agree to assist. Dangers exist, not only to the physical, but also to your very sanity. You have to understand my world is so very different from yours. I shared with you yesterday some of my memories. They may seem already too much for your mortal minds to accept. But accept you must, if you are to assist me." He paused for breath and a sip of water.

"You will learn much, and see things that dreams could not imagine. You must be prepared."

"That sounds very melodramatic." Peter observed.

"Yes." Interjected Lugh, almost impatiently. "And that is an understatement. You have no idea of the power and possibilities we consider common and acceptable. They are long since lost in time and unknown to man save in fiction and nightmares!"

"What would you have us do?" Annie asked seriously.

Lugh smiled at her. "First, you must believe! Believe what I have shown you, believe the impossible and believe the fantasy; most of all, believe the peril you would be placing yourselves in."

"Go on." Peter encouraged.

Lugh stood up and began pacing, contemplating how best to explain his plan.

"You remember I told you," he said eventually, "that the only person capable of removing this spell was the one who cast it in the first place?"

"Catalin?" ventured Peter.

Lugh smiled, "Calatin." He corrected. "Yes, Calatin." He spat the name out, and was silent for a few seconds as if he was remembering some distant event.

"Suppose I were to tell you that I have the power to reincarnate that wretch?"

Annie and Peter exchanged glances.

"Yes, it is possible." The God continued. "But I need certain things to be able to perform the ritual."

"You don't want us fetching rat's tails and snake venom do you?" exclaimed Peter.

Lugh made a cackling sound, which may have been a chuckle. "Nothing so crude, and yet, nothing that easy. I don't even know for sure if the items I require are still in existence. The last I heard of them was from a travelling Druid many hundreds of years ago. I am hoping they are still interred and unfound."

"Lugh?" Annie was curious. "Just how old are you?"

The shadow figure stared off into oblivion. "How old is the earth, the universe? How can one measure eternity? We did not measure time as you know it - in days, weeks and months, we had no need. We existed, and we died, and when we died, we were re-born. We measured time in life times and each lifetime was timeless. I think perhaps the nearest I can give you is by reference to your eras of history, in which terms my current lifespan would be around twenty-five thousand of your years."

Annie was flabbergasted. "You mean you have been living underground here for twenty-five thousand years?"

"Not quite." Smiled Lugh. "Remember I had lived part of this life before the war."

"Still, that is an incredibly long time!" Peter was just as awestruck.

"Yes indeed, an incredibly long time. But I have made use of it; learning, exploring my domain, tunnelling, avenues to places within my confine I could safely go in darkness. I was starved of information for many years. No one inhabited this forlorn wasteland. There were the trees, the animals, the hills and the infernal weather. Then people started arriving. The area began to be populated. I tried to converse with them at first, but their language was different from mine and crude; they saw me as a spirit since I was restricted to nocturnal activities. They shunned me but revered me at the same time. They saw this hill here as holy. I believe that is why the cursed druid chose this location rather than somewhere closer to home. Religion and legend developed around me and about me. This hill became Holy Ground dedicated to the Ageless One, me.

They used it for burials. I gleaned as much from them as I could, but it was minimal. They were simple people, yet I learned from them about their forebears, the tribes, the Picts. Then your history began, the Romans, the Danes, Vikings, the Scots and the Angles, all had history, mythology, folklore. I learned all from those who passed this way. Then you developed, and there was education, books, ahhh books, wonderful information, knowledge, entertainment, wit, poetry. My love in all this time was reading."

"So, what do you want us to do?" Peter asked bluntly, snapping Lugh out of his reflections.

"Ah yes, your mission, so to speak." Lugh smiled and continued-

"As you now know, we made our home in the land you now call Ireland: that name will suffice for our purposes. My information gained over the years, vast as it is, is perhaps incomplete, so you will have to bear with me and assist in translating to modern day nomenclature. Aine, I know you are educated in this field, so we will rely on your knowledge. We had gifts from the hierarchy of the gods as I explained before. They were kept safe under guard, secured on an island, protected by spells and sentinels. I am assuming that, whatever happened to our Race, and subsequent history, at some time all those artefacts would have been secreted away for safekeeping. I have heard nothing of the contrary in all my time here, therefore I can only assume, hope, that they are still in existence in our secret vault."

The sun god stopped again for a drink of water, and offered the others goblets. Peter accepted, and tasted the water. He found it cool and refreshing, bringing back memories of the water they drank as kids from the natural spring that fed the silver mine loch. He wondered if it had come from that same spring.

Lugh continued.

"We had four main cities as I explained previously; primarily, my life was spent in the principal city which was in the south west of the island, in an area which has changed names frequently over the millennia. At one time, it was called Lughaid's Corner, which I would like to think was named after me, but the true origin escapes me.

"Later, it was to be known as Erainn, later still as Corla Loigde, and now as Munster. In the central plains was the battlefield we called Magh Tuireadh, which is now referred to as The Black Valley. It was entered through a pass we called the Valley of Death, but now it is more innocuously named The Gap of Dunloe. Some years ago, this was populated and the peasants tried to grow crops there, potatoes principally; the crop was blighted, and the people starved. Little wonder, had they known the history and were planting on ground tainted with the blood of thousands of their ancestors. But, I digress again. We roamed areas which now have towns, Rath Luirl , Beal Atha, An Ghaorfthaidh and An Dainlean, the latter being known to us as Corla Dibhne. It was from this promontory that we sailed to our island haven to bury our treasures. We knew it by another name, but I believe it now to be An Blascaod Mor."

Lugh leaned closer to Annie. "Does anything of what I say

mean something to you?"

Annie had been trying to follow all he said; some did make sense, but other parts escaped her.

"Yes." She said. "I am familiar with some of what you say, but I will have to research bits I do not understand. Your knowledge is expansive, but it drifts over differing linguistics, from ancient, medieval to current. I have to try to think in broad terms. It is a little confusing, but I'm sure I have the gist. I know of the Munster area, and I have been to the peninsular town you call Corla Duibhne - it is called Dingle in present day. It is famous in historical, archaeological circles as the centre for very early Ogham carvings, a Druid retreat of some sort."

Lugh continued-

"Good. On the Island, I mentioned you will find a pathway up the barren mountain. I have a map drawn here." He produced a parchment type scroll, which he unrolled before them.

"Here." He pointed a long bony finger. "You will find another little used path. Well, I trust it is still little used, for it appears to lead nowhere. Follow this path to its end. You will find what looks just like another cairn, a pile of stones. It will have a mark on it, thus." He drew a symbol on the map with an old piece of crayon.

"I don't recognize that." Annie confessed.

"It's an ancient mark depicting the Tuatha De Danaan. We carried this mark on our shields. Behind the stones, you will find a disguised cave entrance. This is, in fact, the entrance to a small vault secreting our Talismans. Here..." He handed them another parchment with neatly printed copperplate writing. "...is what I need. I want you to bring them to me." He sat back in his chair with a sigh as if this had been an ordeal for him.

Peter leaned over Annie to see the list she held:

Cauldron of Rebirth.

Nuada's Sword.

Sling Shot and pebbles.

Potions and powders, spices and herbs.

Peter looked at Lugh. "How large are these items? I mean, how many people will it take to carry them? We don't wish to involve more people than is absolutely necessary."

Lugh gave a rasping chuckle. "They are not as large as one might imagine. A sword is a sword and a sling is a sling. The Cauldron is symptomatic, irrespective of its usage; it is merely an ornate cooking pot in the eyes of the uninitiated. The only thing of weight or bulk is the Stone of Kings and I do not require you to bring that."

"We had better make a start then, if we are to get all the way over to Ireland and back." Said Peter.

"Yes, indeed." Agreed the sun god. "By all means leave and return in all due haste. I bid you farewell, and a safe and successful journey."

Back in the car, Peter teased, "He called you Aine again."

"Just a slip of the tongue." She said defensively.

"Hmmm well, you do look like her. I mean from the visions he gave us." He smiled.

ooo000ooo

An hour later, Annie and Peter were sitting in the car outside the Colliery.

"So," said Peter, breaking the silence, "what do you make of it? How are we going to explain any of this to the Inquisition in there, and how do we convince them we have to go to Ireland?"

"I was just thinking the same thing." She responded thoughtfully. "We can say we were following a lead from a friend of mine at university, which came to nothing directly, but indirectly points to certain clues related to very early scripts on buildings on Great Blasket Island. Photographs do not show up nuances sufficiently to decipher, so I need to see them first hand?"

"Hmmm, that might work, for you anyway…but how do I explain my having to go?" Peter asked.

"Do you need to go?"

"What? Are you suggesting you go on your own? No way! Besides, Lugh implied there might be danger. No. I'm going with you."

"Fine, I'll just tell them I need an assistant to carry my books!" She giggled. Peter playfully slapped her thigh.

"Seriously, though, I think it best if you leave this to me." Annie said." I think I can handle Harry better than you can."

"Well, if you need any help, I'll be in the Lab. Have to do some research on this map Lugh gave us." He kissed her softly on the check and she squeezed his hand, then they left the Capri and went into the building.

Shortly after, Annie rejoined the Geologist and told him all was well.

"Great! How did you manage it? What did you tell them?"

"I have my womanly wiles." Annie smiled and winked. "He balked a bit at the expense after I told him it may take a few days. I considered offering that we might save some cost on accommodation by sharing a room, but, on second thoughts, I decided against it."

She was smiling again. "I thought best be safe and estimate a few days, one day travel to get there, one, maybe two to excavate, then another day travelling back. We have no idea about how involved the dig may be, or whether we may have to recruit local labour."

"I think you're right." Peter conceded, holding up a sheet of paper he had been scribbling on. "I've made a few phone calls, and we can get to Dingle pretty easy, but I can't find the island he's marked An Blascaod Mor; apparently there are dozens there."

Annie took the parchment from him. "Blasket Island, I think it is?" she looked at the map of Ireland Peter had found.

"There!" She said in triumph. "Great Blasket. That's the one!"

"I wonder if it's inhabited." Peter thought aloud. "It looks pretty small. Anyway, when do we go?"

"No time like the present!" She said. "How do we get there?"

"By air seems to be the fastest way. We can fly from Turnhouse airport to Dublin, change for Shannon airport in Limerick. I need to call the airport and find times for flights."

"Do we need passports for Southern Ireland?" Annie asked.

"That's a thought. I think so, best to take them just in case anyway. You got yours. I threw mine in my bag before I left."

Annie thought for a minute. "I'm not sure, let me check." She began rummaging in her handbag. "Yep! Got it." She exclaimed triumphantly.

Peter smiled as he picked up the phone and asked Directory Enquiries for the number of Edinburgh Airport. After he dialled the number and had a short conversation with the information department, he announced to Annie.

"We're in luck! It's just after eleven now, so, if we're quick, we can get the two o'clock flight to Dublin, arriving around three thirty and there's a five o'clock shuttle to Limerick, arriving around six pm. How soon can you be ready?"

"If I don't change, I can throw some things in a bag in less than half an hour."

"Great. I'm the same." Said Peter, looking at his watch. "Grab what you need, and let's get out of here."

At 1:20 pm, they were buying flight tickets, arranging a hired car for pick up at Limerick Shannon airport, and at 1:45, they boarded the Aer Lingus flight to Dublin. The clear sky they had that morning had given way to scudding grey clouds as the plane taxied for take-off.

"Did I tell you I don't like flying?" Annie mentioned nervously as the Boeing picked up speed on the runway.

"Bit late now!" Peter remarked, but held her hand as the plane soared upwards.

Within minutes, it cleared the clouds into a sunny blue sky. Due to the clouds below, they could not see Central Scotland whiz by below them, nor, the Irish Sea as they left the estuary of the Clyde; through a break in the weather, they saw Dublin approach beneath them and the plane following the course of the river Liffey to Dublin Airport. They didn't have too much time to collect baggage and transfer to the domestic terminal for their onward flight, so it seemed little time at all before they were landing at Shannon Airport. They collected their bags and preceded through customs, an easy exercise since there was not a soul to check them through.

At the Airport enquiries desk, they picked up the documents for the car they had arranged to hire (a dark bottle green Hillman Hunter) while the Receptionist was assisting them in finding accommodation. Having ascertained where they meant to reside, she came up with a standard accommodation in the city centre of Dingle itself, Benner's Hotel. The brochure seemed to convey a three star respectable establishment and they booked two rooms for two nights. Peter bought a map of South West Ireland covering Limerick and Kerry counties and, having thrown both their travel bags in the back seat of the Hillman, they drove off on their adventure.

The weather was somewhat better here, the wind was a bit blustery, but there were lots of sunny spells between the fast moving clouds, making the journey more enjoyable since they could see their surroundings.

They drove through Limerick city and, having previously studied the local road maps, opted for the N69 minor route along the coast, rather than the N21, the busier internal road. This took them through the village of Foynes where they enjoyed views over the Shannon estuary and Foynes Island, then on to the picturesque hamlets of Loghill and Glin, the Hillman dragging itself up the steep slopes and Peter controlling the descents into green valleys on their left, their right being at times a sheer drop to the estuary below. They passed the 17th century Glin castle, and after half an hour or so, drove through Tarbet where the road headed south.

202

In a short while, they passed through a small town called Listowel, which Annie read off the road sign in Gaelic, "Lios Tuathail: the earthen fort."

"Tuathail?" repeated Peter. "Doesn't that sound familiar? Isn't that like the people of the Danaan?"

"Hmmm yes." She replied. "It does have a similar ring to it."

They drove on through Listowel, looking down on the river Feale, and up to Carraigafoyle Castle and eventually into Tralee.

"This reminds me of my father." Peter said absently.

"How so?"

"Oh, he was always singing that song, you know, Rose of Tralee?"

They stopped for a coffee at a sweet little cafe with a hostess just as sweet and friendly, then headed west along the N86 through Camp Anascaul and on to Dingle itself. The view was different here being so close to the sea, which was now on their left as they headed out along the peninsula. They found little traffic and managed to find the main street in Dingle easily enough where they came upon their hotel, a large old building in the centre of town. Peter parked directly outside the entrance, and they collected their bags and checked in.

ooo000ooo

Mrs. O'Connor was matronly and extremely friendly. She had a wonderful accent although she spoke at around a hundred miles an hour, but did stop to give a knowing smile with a glint in her eye when Peter and Annie checked in for two separate bedrooms. She and her

203

ently deceased husband had run the hotel with a few staff (all who seemed related) for the last twenty years or so. Nothing seemed to be too much trouble.

Annie wanted to go to her room to freshen up, but Peter took the offer of immediate refreshment. He walked through the small, wood-panelled foyer on an elaborately patterned carpet, through a mock archway into a tiny, dimly lit bar. From what he had heard or known of the Irish, Peter was surprised to see the bar was almost empty. He ordered a gin and tonic from the barman, a small balding man in his fifties, who Peter later found out was Mrs. O'Connor's cousin, and looked around the room. His eyes soon accustomed to the gloom and he saw a few barstools, a few chrome edged tables with matching chrome chairs, and a couple of bench seats with low coffee tables as adjuncts.

The decor was dark, carpet and wallpaper, but the walls had a multitude of photographs, the majority shared between fishermen and their catches and scenes of the surrounding area, beaches, hills and islands.

It was eight when Annie arrived in the bar; she had changed and was now wearing tight black slacks with an equally tight high necked but sleeveless Arran sweater. Peter ordered her a gin and tonic. While Sean, the barman and porter, was fixing her drink, Mrs. O'Connor asked if they wanted to go to the dining room. They collected their drinks and followed her down a dark passageway towards a large wooden door. Mrs. O'Connor apologized on the way for what they might find there, since the dining room apparently doubled as their function room. Peter realized why the apologies were necessary when she opened the large door to a cacophony of sound as they entered a large room full of people.

"Ah," he thought, "now this is more how I expected things to be!" It seemed the whole population of Dingle was assembled within. Annie seemed to recoil against an almost tangible atmosphere of noise, odour of beer and pall of cigarette and pipe smoke.

Their hostess ushered them to the back of the room where she cleared a table for them with thumb gestures to locals sitting there. They moved readily enough, and the couple were seated and presented with a menu consisting predominantly of fish.

Peter smiled at Annie and asked, or rather yelled, what would she like to eat. It was difficult to attract Annie's attention since she was totally engrossed in people watching and mesmerized by her surroundings. Finally, she looked at the menu and told Peter she would be happy with a simple grilled salmon steak. Peter agreed and ordered two.

They sat quietly for a while sipping on their drinks, taking in all that was around them; the older Irishman getting his point across, with frenetic hand gesticulations, the young couple arguing over something or other, the group of what looked like Students, rowdy and happy, some seated, some standing and waving to others across the room, or simply sitting drinking their pints of Guinness.

Their meal arrived, and they ate with relish. The salmon was delicious. They considered ordering wine with it, but 'when in Rome' they both ordered Guinness, Peter a pint, Annie a half-pint.

They tried conversation, but found it difficult, and when the meal was finished, Peter leaned across the table to ask Annie if she wanted anything else.

"Do want a sweet, or cof...?" he was interrupted by the local band starting up on the podium at the other end of the room.

The band consisted of a banjo, a fiddle, some Irish bagpipes a drum and an accordion. The room erupted in a cheer, which died off into singing along with the entertaining group. Peter laughed and, shrugging his shoulders, fell back into his wooden and plastic leather bucket seat. Annie laughed too, and threw her hands up in a submissive gesture. Peter left his seat and went round to the rear of Annie's chair.

He leaned over, yelled in her ear-

"If you can't beat 'em, join 'em!" And helped Annie to her feet.

They watched the band and the people between some singing and some dancing; it progressed that way throughout the evening, laughing and mingling, dancing and singing.

Mid-way through the night there was an intermission, or respite, when the musicians had a break. During that time, the couple chatted with some locals, but when the band struck up again, conversation was impossible. After a few more songs and dances, they gave in and retired for the night. Outside in the passageway, Peter grabbed Annie's waist and pulled her towards him; he kissed her hard on the mouth, then looking into her eyes he joked-

"Your place or mine, Baby!"

Annie pushed him off with a shove to the chest and said, "Well, considering that you're three sheets to the wind, and that you don't know where your place is, it had better be mine!"

With that, she led him upstairs.

Annie awoke next morning around 7 am, disorientated and confused. She was unsure of her surroundings, and there was a body in bed beside her. Slowly, the circumstances fell into place and she watched Peter sleep, a smile turning up the corners of her mouth at the recollection of his amorous attempts and waxing poetic about never ending love as he fell into a drunken sleep. She had had to complete his undressing for him and manhandle him into bed. In a way, Annie was thankful that the evening had ended that way, for she felt that, had they made love, it would not have been a five-minute affair, and they would have both been exhausted this morning. As it was, they both needed rest for the escapade they were embarking on. She left Peter to sleep a few more minutes as she headed for the shower. When she returned to the bedroom, he was already sitting up in bed, nursing his temples.

"Ah, it's alive." She said ungraciously.

"Only just." He muttered. "That was some night. I feel sore all over. Probably the dancing, haven't danced in a long time."

"Well, I'm sure a shower and shave will revive you. Get your arse out of bed, and let's get this show on the road!" She dragged the covers off the bed, leaving him naked and chilled.

"Hey!" He yelped, trying to drag them back. "You're feisty this morning!"

"Yep. We got a lot to do today, move it!"

"Yes, SIR!" He saluted, and disappeared into the bathroom.

Ten seconds later, he was back out again, looking confused.

"Wrong bathroom." Annie explained. "Yours is next door."

An hour later, having had a light breakfast of cereal and toast, they were down by the wooden pier awaiting their motorboat to take them to the island. They had previously decided to leave from Dingle rather than drive to Inisnabro and take the shorter three-mile boat trip from there. Both Peter and Annie had dressed in suitable clothes for the trip, wearing jeans, sweaters, hiking boots and carrying heavy jackets. Even though it was summer, they had been pre-warned about the chill winds and unpredictable weather. This seemed a good choice since the morning was dull and grey with a fresh breeze coming off the ocean. They each had backpacks with some food; flashlights and ropes together with rolled up heavy duty plastic bags to carry things in.

At 8:30 precisely, they heard the chug-chug of a small motor boat approaching round the point, and were soon on board what looked like an old rowboat, badly in need of paint, with an outboard motor and makeshift tarpaulin canopy.

Brendan, the owner of this craft, greeted them with a touch of his cap.

"Top o' the mornin' tae ye! Ye'll be the strangers that wants t'be goin' t' th' island."

He gestured to them to come aboard and sit in the stern under the canopy, while he busied himself with loading a few packages from the dock, presumably for delivery to the inhabited islands on his route. Within a few minutes, they were underway, and Brendan introduced himself to the couple above the constant chugging of the outboard.

Even although the distance to the island was only around ten miles, the trip took almost an hour in the small craft, battling against choppy seas. Visibility was only a few miles, which meant all they could see was the Dingle coast on their right. It was, however, an entertaining sixty minutes, as they watched the coast slip by; white sandy beaches, sloping up to hills, the village of Fahan, then becoming more rugged as they approached Slea Head and it's sea-bird festooned rocks and cliffs. Brendan was commentating on the view as they progressed, almost as if by script, having done it so often over the years for the various tourists who ventured this far west. He also was knowledgeable on the history of Great Blasket and told them of the old village and how the island was eventually evacuated, the last known residents leaving around 1953.

Soon, the island itself appeared before them extricating itself from the grey gloom like a mystical monolith, dark and overbearing. As they approached closer, the feeling of malevolence altered as the features of the island became prominent. The guests could see greenery and hills, the cliffs just south west of Gurraun Point giving way to white sands and remnants of dwellings on the hill behind.

They disembarked by a wooden pier jutting out from the lower, south end of the beach. "Tra Ban." Explained Brendan, pointing up the hill, "White Strand." They looked up from the mooring and saw the ghost town of the deserted village return their gaze. They bid goodbye to him and said they would meet him at this point around 4 pm, giving themselves more than six hours to explore. Peter smiled as he saw Annie subconsciously massage her prim rump, testament to the uncomfortable seats on the craft and the slightly bumpy ride. As the motorboat heaved and leapt over the incoming surf, they began the trek up the hill to the old village. They were conscious of the fact that they were the only persons on the island. One thousand, one hundred acres of hills and beaches, four miles long by half a mile wide and not a soul to be seen, their only escape being by boat; when Brendan decided to return.

At least the weather was improving. As they reached the summit, visibility had increased and there was a suspicion of blue in some parts of the sky trying to creep out from above the blanket of low clouds.

Peter brought out the map drawn by Lugh, and they both sat down on the front step of a deserted cottage, which appeared to have doubled at one time as the village store, evidenced by the posters in the window. They caught their breath, and found their bearings. They had been set down on the north-eastern part of the island and their route was to follow the coastline south almost to the southern end of Great Blasket. Peter estimated a hike of around two miles.

"Half an hour or so." He said encouragingly.

"Yeah, right!" Said Annie, unconvinced. "Uphill and on paths we hope don't peter out, if you pardon the pun."

The geologist smiled, pocketed the map, took her by the arm and led off down a slope on a well-rutted dirt road.

They continued along the track, which circled the island, following the ridge of the central hill. The views to the sea were quite spectacular and, looking inland, there were green hills, a few stunted trees and the occasional ruin of a crofter's homestead. The path undulated with the terrain and parts were quite steep and heavy going. Eventually, they came across a sort of grassy plateau, which led off to what seemed like a sheer drop to the sea. On the plateau, stood a few random stones about three feet high; Annie examined them as Peter cautiously looked over the edge of the precipice.

"Look here, Annie." He cried. "It's not a sheer drop, there's a kind of grassy terracing leading down to a lower level. Is this what Lugh was talking about?"

"According to these stones, it sounds like it. Didn't he mention these stones on his map?" she said distractedly, as she strained to read the Ogham script carved in the stone.

"What have you got there?" Peter was interested in Annie's find.

"Well, as you would expect, the Ogham writing is much more recent, and seems just to refer to people and dates, but the stones themselves are ancient, as is the earlier Celtic script here." She traced the faded carving with her finger, "But it is really weather worn and difficult to identify let alone decipher." She moved from one stone to the other, searching, and then shaking her head. "Best I can make out is some kind of religious reference and some sort of warning."

"Warning?" Shouted the geologist. "What sort of warning?"

"Oh, just some reference to tread carefully, stick to the path you know- that sort of warning".

Peter sighed with relief.

"There's also a part that's a little clearer, and seems to be much more recent, although it is still in ancient Celtic and pre-dates the Ogham. Hmmm…Trying to translate from ancient to modern and then to English is tricky, sometimes you lose the emphasis, but as far as I can tell, it goes something like Mar na beidh ae leith eidi aris ann."

211

She stood pondering the words, her back to Peter. After a while, he said sarcastically, "Oh…well. Thanks for clearing that up, now I'm much happier!"

She turned round, saw his smile and returned it. "Sorry, it's just that it's so poignant, my mind was wandering contemplating who would write such a thing so many years ago and what was the significance. It means, roughly translated, because our like will not be there again."

They both mused over this for a few moments then Annie asked, "So, what did you find?"

"Over here." Peter took her hand and led her to the edge of the plateau. They both looked onto what seemed like a natural hill terrace: they carefully worked their way down on to it. It led round a small bluff, completely out of sight from above and below due to the overhanging ledge and stony outcrop. They followed it for a few yards, and saw that it began to descend onto what appeared to be a further terrace. They both remarked that it was a perfect hiding place. Peter looked again at Lugh's map and saw that there was meant to be a cave nearby where they would find the items they had come so far to retrieve. They inched their way along the outcrop warily easing past a few bushes and outgrowing miniature trees embedded on the side of the terrace, and came to a dead end.

"Hmmm." Said Peter. "That's not good."

"Bit of an understatement!" Annie observed.

"Maybe we need to go in the other direction?" he suggested.

"OK." She agreed, and turned around, retracing her steps. As she passed one of the stunted trees, she slipped and grabbed at the branches to catch her fall. Peter lunged to grab her and, holding her under the arms, asked if she was all right.

Her reply was strange, since she yelled, "There! There!" trying to point, but Peter still held her arms.

"Let go!" She urged, shrugging him off. "Look, there!"

Behind the trees branches, visible now since Annie had disturbed it, was a craggy rock area with a gaping entrance.

"The cave!" She shouted with glee. "That must be the cave!"

"That is not a cave." Peter muttered sceptically. "That is a hole in the ground!"

"God, you've no sense of adventure have you? Help me clear this bush."

They both worked at the foliage until they had cleared enough to see that it did seem to be some form of entrance. There was just enough room for them to squirm through one after the other, Peter went first and assisted Annie to squeeze in.

On the inside, they found the small entrance belied the interior. It was indeed a cave, and seemed, so far as they could see in the gloom, to be almost seven feet high, four or five feet wide, and of an unknown depth. Peter searched in Annie's backpack for her flash-light, then used it to retrieve his own. In the beam of the lights, they could see the cave was about thirty-five feet deep, but, they could also see that it was completely empty; rock ceiling and walls, dirt floor, and absolutely nothing else.

Peter set about checking the walls for cracks or crevasses that might lead to some clue or hidden opening while Annie wandered back and forth kicking the accumulated dust and dirt on the floor of the cave. Her foot struck something solid and made her stumble. She shone the torch down at her feet expecting to see a tree root or hidden rock. What she saw made her heart pound.

"Peter! Here!" She said, in an urgent sharp whisper.

Peter came over to her and they stared at the outline of an old rusted metal ring. He bent down, uncovered it, and tried to pull on it. It wouldn't budge. They both tried; still nothing. Whether with the effort, or the closeness of the cave atmosphere, they were both sweating, beads of perspiration on Peter's forehead and neck, while Annie's face glistened in the torchlight.

They both froze when they heard the frightful moan behind them. They looked at each other, then towards the entrance. They could see nothing.

"Weird," suggested Peter.

"Bloody scary!" Offered Annie.

Then they heard it again, and Annie felt her hair lift in a chilling breeze. Peter laughed, more out of relief than anything else.

"It's just the wind. This cave was probably chosen for its scary acoustics, or else the entrance shaped to funnel the wind and produce noises to scare the potential robber away. Probably what Lugh meant by sentinels."

"Phew, I hope you're right!" Retorted Annie, feeling none too convinced.

"Let's clear some more dirt and find the edges of whatever this is."

They got down on their hands and knees and began scraping away dirt with their fingers, tracing the edge of the trapdoor by feel.

214

After a few minutes of panting, they had cleared the perimeter of a secret entrance some four feet square. They tried again to lift it, both heaving on the metal ring. It was stuck fast. Peter stood upright again and thought aloud-

"Hmmm, what have we got in the bags we could perhaps use as tools?"

After some rummaging, the best they could come up with was a nail file, a Swiss army knife and a couple of flat metal dinner knives the landlady had put in their lunch pack.

"Let's give it a go." Annie encouraged. They both got to work, Annie with the nail file, Peter with the Swiss army knife blade, scraping out more debris from the crack they had made with their fingers. Then they eased the blades of the dinner knives into the crevice and levered gently. Just as it seemed the knives would bend, something gave. There was movement. Peter told Annie to keep her weight on the two knives while he jumped up and grabbed the ring. He bent his legs for maximum effort and heaved with all his might. With a rending crack and groan, the seal gave and the trapdoor flew open, firing Peter across the cave floor ending in a heap against the stonewall.

Annie was caught between the shock of the noise of the opening, the urge to giggle at the sight of Peter, and her concern for his welfare; not knowing if he had injured himself. The result was an indecipherable mixture of noise that she uttered, then giggled, held her hand to her mouth and whispered.

"Are you OK?"

Peter was now standing, brushing himself off.

215

"I'm not sure, I think I hurt my pride; I have a severe bruise on my self esteem."

Annie was standing back from the void the trapdoor had opened, a puzzled look on her face.

"What is it?" asked Peter.

"I don't know; the smell - musty, but…spicy?"

Peter inhaled from the opening of the exposed cellar. "I see what you mean, a bit like a brewery, I would say, hops? You know?"

"Nope, I don't know; you have the advantage over me there; I've never been in a brewery." Annie answered sarcastically. Peter gave a wry smile. Peering into the gloom, he said, "Well worn steps apparently hewn out of the rock itself, looks pretty safe to me. Shall we go?"

"After you." Annie gestured flamboyantly with her arm.

Peter seemed to have second thoughts and scanned the interior with the beam of his flashlight. "I can see about eight steps down, then another floor. OK, Once more into the breach."

He tested the first step with his weight, and found it sound. He continued down and called back when he had reached the floor.

"It's OK. Seems like another chamber, room to stand, floor solid, some things stacked towards the far end."

Annie followed him down, gingerly at first, then with more confidence. The atmosphere in the hidden chamber was indeed heady and spicy. They moved slowly along the floor, the beams from their torches being the only light to penetrate the absolute blackness. Peter reached out to touch the collection of items at the rear of the cave - a neat stack covered in sack clothing. He pulled back with a yelp as a light blue flash exploded from his fingertips.

"Jesus! It's electrified!"

"Can't be." Annie argued. "This is so old, they wouldn't have had electricity, must just be a build up of static. You've probably earthed it now, try again."

"Ummm, why don't you try?" offered Peter, stepping back magnanimously.

"Owww!" Yelped Annie as the atmosphere was charged with a blue flash.

"Ha!" Scoffed Peter, "Earthed, huh?"

Annie was nursing her fingertips, looking petulantly at her lover. She stepped back and scoured the surrounds with her flashlight.

"Look!" She urged. "Up there, on the wall, writing!" Peter followed the torches beam, and saw a series of Hieroglyphics above the stored items. "What does it say?"

"Hmmm." Said Annie. "It's very old. Can't make it all out without reference books, but basically, it says, Don't touch."

"Terrific!" Peter gasped in exasperation, thinking of The Curse of the Mummy's Tomb.

"All this way, just to find the thing we want is protected. Thanks a bunch, Lugh!"

"Wait." Mused Annie. "There's more."

She traced the writing with her torch, muttering to herself, going over and over the ancient markings. Finally she said, "It's obviously a warning of sorts, maybe even a curse or spell, but it does imply no unauthorized touching. I wonder how we can convince it we are authorized."

217

"You have GOT to be kidding me! Spells? Magic? Curses? What else?"

Annie became very condescending. "Can you tell me that meeting a mythical character, the god of light and the sun is something normal? Like someone, you meet every other day. Come on, Peter! Nothing should surprise you now!"

"I suppose." He sighed. "So...what's plan B?"

"So it's down to me all of a sudden?"

"Well, you are the expert on all this legend and myth and mumbo jumbo stuff!"

"I am? Well thanks for admitting it, but this is not mumbo jumbo and, frankly, is way outta my league. Right now, any ideas are welcome!"

"OK." Said Peter sheepishly. "Point taken. So, what do we do? I guess we have to try to think in ancient terms. How does one overcome a spell? With another spell? I mean, should we say something? Or do something? Or throw some rats tails at it? I don't mean to be flippant, but I don't feel like going all the way back with nothing just to ask Lugh what's the Celtic equivalent of Open Sesame."

"Well," Annie suggested, "let's try the modern logic way first. Get the back packs down and see if there is anything we can throw over it to reach the floor and see if that can earth the...whatever it is."

"Worth a try." Conceded the geologist, and he climbed the steps and returned in less than a minute. "Rope?"

He threw the rope at the pile, one end landing on the sacks, the other trailing the floor. Nothing happened. "Gloves? These woollen ones are non conductive." He put one glove on his right hand and

218

gingerly approached the stockpile. About three inches from the first sack, there was a crackle.

"Ow! This is seriously pissing me off!" Whined the young man, furiously shaking his tingling fingers. Annie had to suppress a giggle.

"Let's try an incantation." She suggested.

"Like what?"

"Oh, I don't know, just tell it who we are and why we're here?"

"I suppose it will have to be in ancient Celtic, so, you go for it then." Urged Peter.

Annie thought for a while then, speaking in old Gaelic as best she could, she said in a loud voice, "Protector of this secret place, we come in peace on a mission for Lugh, god of light and sun."

"I caught the word Lugh in all that," Peter said, "but that was all...what do you think?"

"I don't know." Annie confessed. "Nothing physical changed and I'm certainly not going to stick my hand in again. Let's try the metal option. Do we have anything?"

"Only my small knife and the cutlery; nothing big enough to touch the stuff and earth it. Hey! Wait a minute, though, not in the bag, but the bag itself! The structure support of the backpack is metal! Now, if I can just get close enough, without getting zapped again." He held the bag in front of him, the metal frame facing towards the sackcloth, and inched closer to the target. He got to within six inches, then-

"Crack!"

"Yaiee!" He howled and in a reflex action flung the backpack

in the air; it came down with a thump on top of the cluster of sacks, spilling its contents.

Annie went to Peter to add comfort to his third shock and examined his fingers for burns. They were distracted however, by a faint blue light emanating from the store, gradually growing in intensity. Their eyes followed the light and both noticed at once that it came directly from Lugh's hand-scribbled map, which had fallen from the knapsack. The map seemed to glow, pulsed slightly, and then faded.

Annie and Peter looked at each other, and then back at the map, now reverted to its original parchment. They looked at each other again.

"You thinking what I'm thinking?" asked Peter.

"Authorization!" Nodded Annie.

Peter moved cautiously towards the sacking, and slowly extended his arm and hand closer, inch by inch. Finally, he touched the top sack, closing his eyes in anticipation of further punishment. Nothing happened.

"Yes!" He whispered, and extended his other hand until both were on the pile of artefacts. No reaction. He lifted the top sack to reveal a host of small folded parchment containers. He took one in each hand and gave one to Annie. They opened each to find dried herbs, spices, stems, seeds, powder and dried leaves.

They systematically went through the whole storage content, carefully opening each sack and parchment envelope, examining the contents and replacing them exactly as they had found them. Under the sacks, they found two small chests and a four-foot long item wrapped in embroidered cloth, old and rotten. One chest contained what looked like a small cooking pot, but was obviously not used for cooking, as it was ornately decorated with ancient embossed writing motifs and inset with precious gems.

"This must be the Cauldron of Rebirth." Annie suggested. "I had imagined something somewhat larger."

"Me too." Agreed Peter. "I suppose it's symbolic rather than practical then?"

"Oh!" He added excitedly. "And this must be Lugh's sling shot!"

He opened the other chest and took out a leather thong patch with long leather laces. The chest also contained a few small polished pebbles.

They set the chests aside, and pulled out the long item.

Carefully unwrapping it, trying not to destroy the rotting fabric, they both gasped at the beautiful sword within; a perfectly polished metal blade and an elaborately decorated handle.

"The Sword or Nuada!" Annie whispered.

"Wow!" Peter exclaimed.

"Well, we found it all." Annie said after a while. "Now we have to work out how we get it all back."

They realized that the way the items had been stock piled, there appeared to be much more than there actually was, and found that, with careful packing, they could get all of the herbs and powder envelopes in their knapsacks. Also, with each carrying one of the small chests and Peter strapping the sword to his back, they could comfortably carry everything out of the cave.

Well laden, they set off back along the old path having made sure the trap door had been replaced, re- covered with dirt and the cave entrance had been concealed once again.

THE CAULDRON

The sky had cleared of its earlier morning misty shroud and, although there was still a slight breeze, it was now a wonderful summer day. The couple had taken the best part of four hours to hike to the cave, extract the artefacts and climb back to the deserted village above the pier. From the wider part of the street, which probably served as the town square, they could see almost all round the island, the west and east shores, the mountain in the centre and across the sound to the mainland of the Dingle Peninsula. The sea was calm and mirrored the blue of the sky, the tranquil waters only disturbed by the wakes of small craft going about their business between onshore and offshore habitats. The view presented a perfect picture of beauty and solitude causing Annie to sigh as she sat on an old watering trough on the north side of the square.

Peter caught the sensation and walked slowly over to sit with her; neither said a word as he took her hand in his. She turned slowly to look at him only to find herself staring into his eyes. He leaned into her and kissed her softly on the lips. Goosebumps popped up on her arms and neck at his embrace and she shivered, with pleasure, not cold.

His hands caressed her shoulders and her hair, then her breasts; she closed her eyes as her body responded to the advances, her nipples growing taught to his touch. It was then they heard the familiar chugging sound of Brendan's boat.

They broke the embrace, looked at each other with a mutual hint of frustration, laughed aloud and began gathering their belongings.

They were still smiling as they reached the pier just as Brendan was pulling up alongside.

"Guid day tae ye' again!" He called out jovially. "Would ye' be gettin' whatever it was ye' were after gettin'?"

Annie and Peter exchanged glances, then Peter said, "Good day to you too. Yes, it was quite successful from an archaeological point of view; we have a few items of historic interest to take back, but nothing major."

They climbed aboard the craft and placed the items with their backpacks beside them on the seat. Brendan looked at them, and then at the objects they had brought aboard, shrugged his shoulders and restarted the small outboard motor.

It was not until they had been back at the Hotel and had eaten, that they both realized how tired they were. Whether it was the overdoing of it the night before, the fresh sea air or the exertions of the hike and the find, they were not entirely sure. They confirmed their travel plans for the next day, driving and flights, arranged an early call, and were about to retire to bed around 9 pm when Peter said chipped in.

"I'd better give Harry a call at the colliery, touch base with him."

Annie sighed and stretched.

"Hmmm, I suppose one of us had. But it's pretty late, and I don't think you'll get him at Easton - better try his home number."

The geologist called reception and put in the call. It took five minutes to make the connection and not a very good one at that, there was a lot of static on the line. When Harry finally picked up the receiver, Peter began-

"Hi Harry, how are you? It's Peter Graham, calling from Ireland."

The colliery manager did not seem particularly impressed, "Peter? Peter Graham? I knew someone by that name once, a long time ago, he used to work for me! What the hell are you guys up to? I hope you have something concrete in your research to substantiate this excursion!"

Peter looked at Annie and elaborately held the phone away from his ear, grimacing.

"Well, we have found some similar types of hieroglyphics, which helps to date the script we found..."

"Great!" Interrupted Harry, "And just how might that help us?"

"Uh, I'm not sure as yet, it's just another part to the jig-saw, I guess." Peter blurted out, thinking on his feet.

A pause.

"Bloody scientists! Just get back here and report P.D.Q! When do you think you might grace us with your presence?"

"We're leaving in the morning, should be with you day after next." Peter grimaced again.

"Fine! I look forward to seeing you both." The manager said sarcastically, and hung up.

Peter replaced the telephone, shrugged his shoulders at Annie and flopped on the bed.

"Expect a hostile reception, I'd say." He moaned.

"As much as I would have anticipated." Annie agreed. "We're

gonna need a good couple of night's sleep, don't you think? Come on, let's get to bed."

They showered and slipped into bed immediately. Their nakedness and proximity again aroused the sexual instinct, which had begun on Great Blasket. They held each other, caressed, then made slow, sensuous love before slipping exhausted into a deep sleep.

Twenty-four hours later, having risen early and vacated the Hotel, driven to the airport, flown to Dublin and on to Turnhouse, Edinburgh, they were driving into Bathgate once more. Peter dropped Annie off at her hotel, having already agreed with her that they should have another early night in preparation for the next day.

"That was an eventful trip, but nonetheless enjoyable." And she kissed Peter goodnight.

"Mmmm." Agreed Peter. "I thought we were going to have problems with Customs with all that gear. Lucky for us they didn't seem to give a damn!"

Annie laughed. "Yes. I guess they were on overtime and didn't really want to be there."

"Pick you up at eight?"

"Sounds good to me, I'll be ready." She blew him a final kiss and let herself into the hotel foyer.

Peter returned to the Fairway where he was met with confused looks. They could not understand the concept of someone booking a room, yet residing elsewhere.

ooo000ooo

Next morning, at 7:45, Peter arrived again at the hotel's car park. It was a typical Scottish morning; chilly and grey with low cloud covering and the constant threat of rain or drizzle. He was making his way to the Reception when he met Annie coming through the revolving door. She pecked his cheek and headed for the car, leaving him in her wake as she swept by. He looked on, smiling and shaking his head at her dedication and enthusiasm to get started, smiling at the pleasure her form gave him as she walked away from him, her sensual gait in white blouse and tight black pants, sweater and jacket thrown over one arm, her brief case and files in the other. She came to a stop at the car and smiled sweetly at him, a subtle hint for him to open the door.

"I like your hair up." He remarked, as he unlocked her side, referring to the neat, tight bun she had arranged.

"Thank you." She said modestly, but then gave a mock curtsey.

Minutes later, they arrived at the colliery administration building and noted that all seemed to be back to normal; the lift wheel was spinning, there were people roaming around, going about their normal business. They headed straight for the manager's office and found him there already with the police inspector.

They exchanged pleasantries (a grunt was as pleasant as Harry was prepared to offer) and sat down to discuss the update.

Bob Mathieson began, "It appears we have come to a dead end down on Level 17, I'll let Harry elaborate on that, and we seem to have become unstuck on all other avenues of investigation too. None of our *experts* have come up with any explanation, reasonable or otherwise. We have been chasing one red herring after another, clutching at straws, trying to find one piece of evidence or clue of any sort to lead us in a focused direction. It beats me, that's for sure.

"Have you people come up with anything?"

"Er, let's, get back to that." Peter hesitated. "I'd like to know more about the dead end underground?"

Harry looked tired again as he sighed, "It appears that the going was relatively easy, as you know, our machinery was coping with those sealed openings, or whatever they were, but now it seems they have all been strengthened or modified in some way, much thicker, harder, denser. It seems the further we tunnel in, the more reinforced they are. It's taking a full day to bore through one now, whereas we were doing six or seven a shift. I'd like you to look at the samples they have brought back from these more difficult seals when you get a minute, Peter."

"Sure." Said the geologist, scratching his chin. "Doesn't make sense, does it?"

"So," continued Harry, "apart from the mystery, the tunnels, the entrances, the suspicion of the miners, the hassle from the unions, the ever presence of the police, and the constant haranguing of the Press, not to mention the pressure from my seniors - everything's just fine!"

"Well," began Annie, "I'm afraid we aren't going to be able to resolve any of those headaches for you right away. We found other types of similar writing in Ireland, dating 'way back to pre history, but nothing that gives us anything tangible to focus on, all we have is a series of words, if that, mostly just letters and numbers, symbols and such. We have to sift through it all, decipher and try to interpret; other than the theory of map grids, we have little to go on."

"Damn!" Harry cursed. "I have a board meeting on Monday where they will want lots of answers, and what you are all telling me is we don't even know the questions?"

He sighed deeply and rubbed his temples. "I suppose you had better get down to it then, but remember, time is of the essence here."

"OK, but today, we need to get some assistance, some input; we have to go visit that lecturer at Edinburgh University, what was his name? D.D. or something?" Peter lied.

"Fine! Just do it!" Harry said, exasperation showing in his voice.

ooo000ooo

The couple lost no time in getting into Peter's Capri.

"Good thinking." Annie said. "About going to Edinburgh, but I'll have to remember just how readily and convincingly you lied."
Peter ignored her insinuation and said, "Looks like Lugh has been busy in our absence."

"How so?" She asked, curious.

"The tunnel accesses; how else could they have suddenly become impenetrable? He's been out re-sealing them all. It's the only logical explanation."

"Of course!" She said with realization. "I was wondering about that at the time. You're not just a pretty face, are you?" she dug his ribs with her elbow.

229

The hour or so spent with Harry and Bob hadn't improved the weather. As they drove north to the Knock Hill, the gloomy greyness was darkening under heavier thunderclouds and already large spots of rain were splattering on the car's windscreen. He drove the car alongside the closest access point to the Silver Mines valley so that their carry would be diminished. Between them, they managed to convey everything down to the cave entrance in one go, just as they had carried them to the boat on Great Blasket. Thunder rolled ominously in the distance as they approached the entrance.

The cave was open all the way to Lugh's interior domicile. As they entered, his voice was low and rasping.

"I sensed your return. I've been waiting for you. Did you find all I asked for?"

"I think so," said Peter. "we brought everything that was in the vault."

"Good. And I see you came to no harm? That is also good."

"Well, all except for a few energy shocks! Thanks for warning us!" Peter said indignantly.

Lugh chuckled. "Show me what you have."

They unpacked their bags and boxes, Lugh's eyes glinting at every little package. An audible gasp left his mouth at site of the cauldron and Nuada's sword.

"You have done well - very well. I too did well to trust you." He placed one scrawny hand on each of their shoulders. Peter winced at his touch; a feeling of immense energy seemed to pass through him. Annie shivered visibly as the hairs stood out on her neck.

"And so, to work!" Lugh was animated now, inspecting each package, discarding some, carefully placing others on the table beside him. He picked up the cauldron and, closing his eyes, muttered some prayer or incantation in the old language. Annie thought she caught some words, Cauldron of Re-birth, Tuatha De Danaan.

Lugh took the vessel over to the area where he cooked. He poured in about a cup of water, added a sprinkling of dirt from the

231

ground and then, taking a small knife, cut his finger and dropped his blood into the mix. He replaced the jewelled pot on the counter, and closing his eyes again, still muttering, placed his hands round it. The couple saw the container glow, then hearing the unmistakable gurgling of boiling liquid. He flourished over to the table and opening selected packages in turn, sprinkled minute quantities of each systematically into the boiling concoction, whispering incantations as he proceeded. The whole process took nearly an hour during which Annie and Peter stood mesmerized and speechless.

Finally, Lugh approached them.

"It is done, but for one more ingredient. This element of the conjuring is fraught with danger. It is better that you leave now."

"No way!" Protested Peter. "We've come this far, we want to see it through!"

Lugh looked towards Annie. She moved to Peter and hung on his arm, nodding vehemently.

"As you wish." He conceded resignedly. "But I must insist, that whatever you might see or hear you must remain still and silent!"

ooo000ooo

Annie and Peter watched with fascination every move Lugh made, every arm or hand gesture, raising goblets and phials to the ceiling, uttering ancient incantations. Then finally, with a deep rasping sigh, Lugh gently but methodically poured in a precise measurement of a dark odious liquid he had previously mixed with a pestle and mortar. Again, he clasped his hands round the cauldron and heated the mixture.

Smoke and vapour immediately ensued from the Rebirthing Pot; it filled the air in the cave, the acrid consistency making Peter cough and Annie gag. Then the thick cloud seemed to flow back to a spot near the cauldron as if sucked in by a vortex, whirring and spinning and thickening. Annie's eyes shifted from the mini tornado to Lugh. It seemed he was holding his breath, agitated and apprehensive. Back to the whirlwind, and she thought she saw a form within it. She looked more closely, and yes - there was a shape! Peter gasped at the same time. The form grew denser as the mist dissipated until, before their eyes, stood an old man with huge whiskers and beard dressed in some old grey robe.

"Calatin!" Hissed Lugh, making his audience start at the sound of his voice. The form seemed to turn toward the voice, then crumple in a heap on the floor.

Annie and Peter both jumped up but Lugh stopped them with his hand.

"Be still!" He commanded. "This is usual. He has been dead a long time."

The two lovers exchanged glances, their minds struggling to accept what they had just witnessed.

Lugh went to the body and effortlessly lifted it onto a bench, then pulled up a chair and sat watching and waiting. After a while, the body stirred and a hideous moan emanated from its mouth, although the sound seemed to come not from vocal chords, but from the soul itself. The eyes flickered and a hand moved stiffly to its forehead to shield them from the light. The body moved, seeming to slip off the bench, but steadied itself and sat up with difficulty, slowly looking around at its surrounds, taking in everything. The face turned towards Lugh, then to Annie and Peter. A chill ran through their bodies as they saw the coldness and emptiness of the stare. The head turned back to Lugh, grimaced with recognition, gasped in horror, looked around the cave once more - frantically this time - then, finally, it spoke.

"What place is this? By what means have you conjured me into Hell?" The voice was faint and distant, and rasped audibly. The language was unknown to the two observers although Annie picked up a few recognizable sounds.

"Do not dare to ask questions of us, Foul Servant of Evil!" Lugh chided in the same language. "You are here at my behest to do my bidding. You will speak only when commanded to!"

The Druid recoiled at Lugh's words then once more, his eyes explored the domain. They rested again on Annie. "Aine?" Calatin asked, but did not wait for reply as his eyes now saw the Cauldron of Rebirth and he gave a short, sharp gasp as if realizing the means by which he had been resurrected.

Lugh grabbed the druid by the scruff of his neck and lifted him off the ground.

"You evil dreg of humanity; you cursed me and banished me to this prison. Now you will undo your black witchcraft!" The Sorcerer quivered before the Sun God. Peter and Annie watched, mystified, but mindful of Lugh's warning not to interfere. Calatin was thrown to a corner of the cave where he sat cowering and shivering.

Lugh explained to his guests what had transpired and Peter questioned, "What happens now?"

"Now? Now I have to force this parasite to remove his curse!"

234

Rasped the sun god.

He walked over to the quaking magician and hauled him on to his feet.

"Get to work you mangey scum, or I will have you wandering the Land of Sorrows for all eternity! I am not without power here."

Calatin whimpered something about herbs and potions, and Lugh dragged him over to the collection of powders and artefacts Annie and Peter had retrieved. He spent some time looking over the ingredients, sniffing some, discarding others; he asked for a pot and a pestle, some water and blood from Lugh. Although the cursed God monitored his every move, by slight of hand Calatin extracted something from a pocket in his garb - a white object the shape and size of an egg - and crumbled it to dust in his hand, pouring the content into his mixture. He stirred and shook the concoction, all the time muttering in his archaic language. He asked Lugh to boil it for him with his special skill then intimated all was prepared. Lugh had to lie down and prepare to be bathed.

Whilst the sun god's attention was distracted in removing his cloak and top shirt, Calatin, with speed belying his age and demeanour, raced past his captor and poured his brew into the Cauldron of Rebirth uttering screeching incantations as he did so. Before anyone could react, the concoction hissed and bubbled and the room filled again with that misty gas. Before there eyes, a monstrosity formed within the fog and Lugh gasped, "Balor!"

ooo000ooo

235

Peter and Annie couldn't believe their eyes as they witnessed the rebirth of this vile creature. It was almost nine feet tall, horrendously ugly and disfigured with one eye in the centre of its scaly face. Its arms were huge and muscular as were its legs with its whole body covered in leathery protrusions like an alligator's hide. It's bellowing seemed to fill the cavern such that the couple had to cover their ears. Peter had never heard such a noise; a mixture of pain, rage and triumph.

Lugh was quickest to react; seeing that the creature was between them and the enchanted weapons, he grabbed Annie's arm with one scaly hand, Peter's with his other, and dragged them through the caves nearest exit into the labyrinth west of the entrance the couple had used from the Silver Mines. With a flourish of light and flame, he sealed the exit behind them, shutting out the bellowing rage of Balor.

The sun god stood in his self-generating light, gasping for breath, the speed and urgency of his defensive actions having sapped his energy. Annie and Peter gazed at each other, then at Lugh in fear and ignorance. They recognized Balor from Lugh's memory projection of the battle scenes, but neither appreciated the horror of the beast, but how was the tacit question in all of their minds.

Eventually Lugh recovered and whispered-

"Calatin, that deceitful trickster, that weasel! He must have had something of Balor secreted on his person, something small he could carry with him forever...Balor's eye!" He almost yelled. "That was never found after the battle! He and his hellish entourage must have run off with it!" He slumped to the floor of the tunnel and put his head in his hands.

"What have we done?" he reproached himself. "What have we done?"

ooo000ooo

Annie walked over to the distraught deity and laid her hand on his shoulder.

"Lugh?" she asked, her voice full of concern, "Just what have we done?"

Lugh raised his head and looked at each of his new friends in turn, then said,

"We have unleashed a demon from the darkest of hells. Not only that, but in my anxiety to see the artefacts you found I omitted to seal your entrance. The beast is free to roam your world!"

Peter and Annie exchanged glances; the young man saw nothing but fear and dread in his lover's eyes.

"What can we do?" asked Peter sincerely.

"I suggest you pray. Pray to your own god or gods; this one cannot help you!" Lugh whispered dejectedly.

With a sigh, he raised himself up and said, "Come." He led them through a couple of tunnels that seemed to backtrack according to Peter's sense of direction. They came to a dead end. Peter had been correct; they had come in a semi circle back on an alternative route to the sun god's cave. Lugh motioned silence with a bony finger to his lips and appeared to peer through the rock itself.

"They are gone." He said with relief sounding in his voice. He flourished his arms and the rock melted before him.

237

The two mortals looked around them in astonishment; Balor had trashed the cave; they could not conceive so much damage could have been achieved in such little time. The cave was a mess. Nothing, it seemed had been left whole. Lugh surveyed the demolition then raced over to the far corner of the room. He threw things from and about him in a frantic search then yelled in triumph and chuckled that hoarse rasping chortle.

"The fools! They were not aware that you also returned the Sword of Nuada and the other relics. We have weapons!" He stood brandishing the sword in one hand, the sling shot in the other.

"So, what do we do now?" asked Peter.

"Now!" Punching the air with the sword, Lugh proclaimed. "Now, we fight!"

"Oh my God!" Shouted Annie. "We have to warn someone!"

"I agree." Echoed Peter, "But how? And how do we fight something like that Lugh? It's daylight! You are trapped in here and it is out there!"

"I need time to think." Responded the deity. "But we can't stay here. They know where I am located now, they will be back."

"But won't your seals make it secure?" asked Annie.

"Ha!" Scoffed Lugh. "Nothing is secure to that monstrosity and its phenomenal strength. The only reason it didn't destroy the seal I made on our escape was because it was still hot. Cooled, and Balor could punch through it in a matter of minutes. I can't keep every seal perpetually heated. I can simply lose him within the labyrinth, over so many years I know every twist and turn, but that doesn't help us meeting…we need an alternative."

238

"Down the mine?" suggested Annie.

"No." Lugh rejected the idea. "That would involve too many people. I will think on this and visit you at your place of residence tonight." As an afterthought, he added, "Assuming anything survives this apocalypse."

"Lugh." Urged Peter. "We will think on it too, but for now, we have to get back; we have to try to make people believe us before too much harm is done. By the way, didn't you say something about his eye being a weapon? I looked in his eye before you rescued us and I didn't feel any affect."

"That is because Calatin's conjuring has long since lost its influence. I have no way of knowing if he can replicate that spell in this world without ingredients or his hellish cohorts. Let us pray he cannot. Now, go! Until tonight, stay safe my friends - Do not tackle this beast on your own, you will need my assistance. Believe me, there is no earthly weapon capable of stopping him! If you see him, run for your lives!"

oooOOOooo

The two scientists cautiously worked their way back to the cavern entrance, taking care lest their enemy lay in wait. They came out into the open air and were relieved to see no sign of the hellish pair.

"Which way do you think they went?" asked Annie, not really expecting an answer.

"Good question!" Conceded Peter. They hurried up the hill

and sat in Peter's Capri catching their breath.

"Just a thought -" Peter began, "neither of them knows this area, towns, roads, and buildings, whatever. That Wizard guy may know something of it from way back when, remember Lugh saying he chose it well? But that was eons ago...if I was to make a guess I would say they probably will head for Cairnpapple, make that their base and head out from there on the forage. I don't think they will venture too far since they need to eliminate the only threat to themselves...Lugh. If that's the case, they may well be camped out right above Lugh's head without even knowing it!"

"Good thinking!" Annie said. "Let's hope you are right, that gives us time to get back to Bathgate and warn people. What the heck do we tell them?"

"Damned if I know." Peter swore. "Let's cross that bridge when we come to it."

With that, he gunned the car into life and sped down the narrow back road into the north end of the town. An hour or so later, having had to trace all relevant personnel and get them convened at Easton Colliery, the two were trying to explain the circumstances to an incredulous audience.

"You what? A monster? One eye? You're having a laugh, aren't you?" The Police Inspector was adamant, and not amused. "Are you two on something? I have never heard anything so ridiculous! There has to be some other serious reasoning behind this. I am not going to call out reserves and brief headquarters and cause panic with defence tactics to fend off a...a...a...Loch Ness Monster? I'd be a laughing stock!" He huffed and hawed indignantly until he was red in the face.

Both Annie and Peter sat with their heads bowed like naughty school children caught playing truant. This was as much as they expected. They had told the whole story amidst a few gasps but also a few smirks and a full-bellied guffaw at one point. Peter's Uncle Tommy sat stunned by the revelation.

"Peter, you are saying that our mine was attacked by a monster who has been burrowing down there for centuries and..."

"No Unc, that was Lugh, the sun god...he's not a monster. Balor is the monster..."

"Are you going to continue with this ludicrous story?"

"It's true, Mr. Graham, every word is true." Said Annie in the faintest of whispers. "And, be warned, if this beast makes its way to town, there is no way to stop it - just get out of its way and limit the damage it is capable of wreaking."

"Poppycock!" Yelled Bob Mathieson. "This is some sort of practical joke and I don't think it's funny! I have a good mind to put you both behind bars for wasting all of our time here! Instead, I suggest you both get a good night's sleep; you are probably tired from your trip and hallucinating. Go on - get out of here before I change my mind. Maybe tomorrow your heads will be clear and we can get something sensible out of you!"

The two could do no more to convince the group. As Peter passed Alex Phillips, he leaned over and whispered. "Trust me, this thing is real!" The young policeman nodded, then blushed as he saw his boss giving him the eye.

Annie and Peter headed for the car, and having agreed there

was nothing further they could do there at risk of imprisonment, nor had they any brave inclination to go looking for the monster by themselves, they decided to go back to the Golden Circle to await Lugh after the hours of darkness.

The young geologist was right; Calatin had vague telepathic memories of this area, but he remembered only forests and beasts of the wild. They had sought the higher ground after leaving the cavern and the warlock led them north. They walked on it, following its winding progress into the scenery, leaving it at the entrance to Cairnpapple Hill. From the top, Calatin tried to configure some bearings, but it was hopeless as it had all been so long ago and so much had changed now. Balor looked into the old burial ground excavation at the top of the mound and with one swipe of his mighty fist, he shattered the glass top and ripped off the padlocked doors. He jumped inside as Calatin followed him using the stairs.

In their own dialect the Sorcerer remarked, "You brute, Balor. This would have been ideal shelter if you had not ruined the roof! Can't you just open doors? Do you have to smash everything?"

Balor eyed the Wizard with scorn.

"Take care, mortal, how you speak with your superiors. You have resurrected us; let not that achievement spell the end of your usefulness to us. What place is this? Why are we here? Who was that old man and the strange creatures with him?"

"That was Lugh, god of the sun, your grandson and your murderer. I have no idea who his minions were." Calatin explained.

"Lugh! An old man? How so? What trickery is this?" Demanded Balor.

Calatin spent the next half hour trying to explain the course of

243

events since his demise all those years ago; the going was tough since Balor was not too bright. When Calatin was done, Balor's only comment was, "Eat! Then slay Lugh!"

With that, he climbed out of the burial chamber and surveyed the countryside. To the east, he saw some sheep grazing, while to the west, he spied a few cattle lying on the meadow chewing the cud. His mind made up, he loped across the open fields and startled the cattle, one of which was too slow in getting up and instead dropped down dead as a result of one fatal blow to its head. Balor dragged it back to their new abode and, ripping bits off the animal with his huge claw like fingers, proceeded to eat it raw. Calatin witnessed this, but it came as no surprise to him as this was Balor's and most of the Fimorii way, although generally their taste was for raw fish.

Balor rested after his repast, his one huge eye closing as he burped and snorted into a sound sleep. The sun had set by the time he awoke, and while Lugh, sixty feet below him had set out through his caverns on his way to meet his friends, the beast decided it was time to explore. Calatin had said from the hilltop he could see smoke, evidence of life, hostels, a town maybe to the south of where they were.

They set out on foot over the fields to begin with until they realized that the route was easier for them if they followed the manmade footpaths. They had travelled almost two miles when they saw strange beams of lights following them, then the roar of some kind of beast racing down the road behind them. Calatin made for the tree lined roadside by way of retreat and concealment; Balor, fearing no man or beast stood in the middle of the road to challenge the oncoming adversary.

Jack Henderson was in a hurry. He was supposed to be at his parents' 25th silver wedding anniversary in Bathgate Co-operative Hall by 9 pm. He had been delayed in Linlithgow at his work. To try to make up time, instead of driving the main route, he had opted for the quicker 'crow flies' direct narrow roads over the hills. He figured there would be little or no traffic and he could travel safely at speed and gain at least ten minutes. He drove off the Knock Hill road, turning right into the reservoir road leading into Glenmavis. As he turned the corner at speed, he gunned the throttle to the floorboards knowing there was a stretch of straight road ahead.

He reacted automatically when his headlights picked up the beast; he slammed on his brakes and his Vauxhall slewed to a screeching halt directly in front of Balor. The creature interpreted these circumstances as an attack and retaliated with venom, pounding on the vehicles body with its huge fists. It pummelled the car; the front, the back, the roof until the engine died and all that could be heard were the screams of the occupant. He was unhurt, but terrified, cowering on the floor of his vehicle since Balor's inhuman strength had caved in the roof of the car until it was flush with the bodywork. As a parting gesture, the monster picked up one side of the car and rolled it over on to its roof where they left it lying in the ditch by the side of the road. He and Calatin continued their march on the town leaving Jack trapped inside the crushed shell.

As they passed through the outskirts of Bathgate, people ran from them. If the strange man in the ragged clothes wasn't enough to scare them, the huge roaring monstrosity in the Halloween costume certainly did. Cars and people who came too close, or didn't see the duo in time were swatted like flies as Balor swiped left and right, cars and vans dented, windows smashed, telegraph poles and street lighting all became victims of the beast's wanton destruction. The pair looked at the housing, but ignored it for the brighter lit town centre. They wandered down Hopetoun Street and the giant smashed a shop window displaying scantily clad females, grabbing one from inside the neon lit frontage. He threw away the mannequin in disgust when he realized it wasn't real. A bus drove past them and Balor launched another plastic lady in lacy underwear through the window, showering the passengers with glass and fabricated body parts.

They heard noise and music emanating from Flannigan's Bar and burst in through the door. Firstly, there was absolute silence, and then pandemonium as the clientele rushed for the nearest exit as far away as possible from this terrifying apparition. Within seconds, the room was clear all except for the Barman and a drunk. The drunk gave a stupid grin and held his drink up in a cheers fashion then fell off his chair. The Barman stood, frozen by fear. Balor clomped over to the bar, looked at the glasses of liquid left by the fleeing visitors, picked up a pint glass which looked like a wine glass in his huge paw, sniffed the beer, tasted it, finished it in one gulp then smashed the glass to the floor, thumping the bar demanding more. Calatin joined him at the bar as the trembling patron poured another pint, then another and another. The alcohol addled the brain of the monster such that he continued to wreck the place even as he was being served. Calatin tried to speak to the mortal, but neither understood the other.

A door opened and Sheena Watson wandered into the lounge from the ladies' toilets; her head was down as she fussed with a clasp

246

on her ornate cosmetic belt. She sensed the silence and looked up slowly. She screamed and turned to run when she saw the monster in front of her drooling in her face, but Balor's long arm sprung out and grabbed her by the hair. He pulled her towards him and turned her face around. She screamed and fainted. This did not deter the beast as he held her in one huge hand almost encircling her chest and ribs, ripping off her skirt with the other. Whether he was already aroused and frustrated from the uselessness of the mannequins is uncertain, but it was evident he wanted this female. He lowered her limp body onto his huge member and forced entry. Sheena came to with the shock and pain, and then passed out once more with the realization of what was happening to her.

The beast used the inert body as if it were a masturbation aid, finishing quickly with an almighty roar, and then tossing her ravished body aside like a rag doll. She landed in an unconscious heap on one of the bench seats in the corner of the pub lounge bar.

In the meantime, reports were making their way to the Police Station - one or two frantic calls to begin with - but within a few minutes, the switchboards were jammed. All the calls had two things in common, panic and a twelve-foot monster. The Police didn't know what to make of it, but the duty sergeant dispatched two men to the last known whereabouts of the alleged disturbance whilst he put a call into Bob Mathieson, his boss.

"Ten-foot monster? What they hell are they on about! Is every one on drugs?" yelled the police Inspector. "Get someone out there to give us a sensible report."

The desk sergeant advised his superior that two men had

247

already been sent to investigate.

"Good! Call me again when they return." The receiver was slammed down.

"You're welcome." Said the sergeant sarcastically and then turned to the WPC at the switchboard. "Where the hell are those two? I told them to phone in as soon as they had some explanations?"

"I don't know, Sarge. I'm trying to raise the pub on the blower but there's no reply." She told him.

"Bugger." He commented in frustration.

While the policewoman was trying to contact them, PCs Erskine and Murnin were lying unconscious on the floor of Flannigan's bar.

They had arrived to find a public house devoid of all the regular customers, the furniture in a state of broken shambles, but the room seemingly filled with a monstrous presence. Foolishly, they had approached the horror and had been sent sprawling by a backhand swipe from the beast.

Someone, seeing the havoc from a distance, ran into the Hopetoun Arms across the street and called the police. The sergeant called his superior immediately, and Bob Mathieson was at the station in fifteen minutes. He told his sergeant to call around for off-duty policemen and a couple of on-call Special constables who helped in emergency situations.

In less than an hour, the inspector with his sergeant and four PCs (two regular, two special) arrived at the bar in time to see Calatin and Balor leave.

"Jesus Kerrist! What is that?" yowled the inspector. All had vacated their vehicles and he advised them to approach with caution. Balor turned on them and roared a challenge; they stopped dead in their tracks. He crunched an old Morris Oxford with his clenched fists as a warning. The Police began to back peddle.

"We need guns." Said Inspector Mathieson. "Big guns!" A crazy story from a historian and a geologist flashed through his brain. "Bollocks!" he had thought at the time, but now the thing was approaching them.

"Back in the cars!" He yelled, that being the first order his men were happy to obey that night. The sergeant managed to reverse out of range, but Balor grabbed the rear end of the other squad car, which was now revving to no avail as its drive wheels were off the ground. The beast tossed the vehicle out of its way as if it were made of cardboard; it rolled twice and came to rest upside down twenty yards away. Bob's sergeant was a good driver and managed to turn his vehicle at speed. He raced away from the scene where they watched the progress of the reincarnated couple from a safe distance.

They checked on the other car, no one was seriously hurt. They left the officers there to see to the vehicle and direct other traffic around it while the other policeman was to check up on the two original investigators; meanwhile, he and Sarge were to follow the monster and its human familiar while trying to determine their next move.

Calatin and Balor turned left into George Street and headed down towards The Steel Yard. En route, the creature smashed the windows of a few shops and checked out their wares, looking for something edible. Blair's bakery held their attention for a few minutes.

The police inspector knew he was out of his depth in this situation and told his sergeant to head down North Bridge Street and back track to the police station; he had to have assistance with this.

His main priority was to warn the public and avoid any further bloodshed. Sarge remembered there was a bullhorn in the stores and went to fetch it. Bob got on the phone and having called adjacent precincts for assistance and back up, tried to get hold of Peter Graham at the Fairway, if for no other reason, than that motel was in the direction the entity appeared to be headed. He was unsuccessful since the geologist was with Annie at the Golden Circle. However, he did leave a message with the proprietor, for Peter to call him as soon as he returned. As an afterthought he told them about some out of towners, creating a disturbance, and for them to send customers home and lock their doors.

He got his assistant to drive him through the main streets of the burgh while he leaned out the window with the bullhorn.

"Attention! Attention! This is a police message. There is a disturbance in the town centre where a person or persons unknown are causing damage to property and injuring citizens. These people are dangerous and must not be confronted. For your own safety, please return to your homes and lock your doors until further notice."

He repeated the message over and over until, on passing the Steel Yard going onto King Street, they spied the cause of their situation exiting the Commercial Hotel having tasted the fare within and then trashed the furniture and bar.

The inspector ceased his broadcast mid sentence, but not before Balor had fixed his eye on the source of this annoying noise.

250

Before the sergeant could react, Balor rolled a Volkswagen Beetle at them, smashing the front of their vehicle and stalling the engine. This seemed to satisfy the creature as he walked on with the sorcerer in tow, out of sight of the two policemen.

"Damn!" Cursed Bob as they extricated themselves from the police car. "Now where are they going?" where the hell is our back up?"

It was to be twenty minutes before the first reinforcements arrived on the scene from Armadale, and another ten minutes before a squad car turned up from Whitburn. By that time, the reincarnates had continued east into King Street and for some reason ignoring the Fairway, were heading up towards Bathgate Academy on Marjoribanks Street. At the top of Academy Street, Balor saw the large edifice and said in his own language.

"I like. We sleep." He was about to smash down the main entrance when Calatin stopped him. "Do you want everyone to know where we are? Discretion!"

He got the beast to force open an adjoining window where Calatin climbed through and opened the door from the inside. It was dark, but that suited his plans, and Balor wouldn't need much light if all he wanted to do was sleep. Being late evening on a Saturday night, the school was deserted. They found the Gym Hall and both settled down for the night on the exercise mats. Before falling asleep, Balor said, "Lugh, near, I feel him."

ooo000ooo

Sheena Watson came out of her faint to loud shouts and yells from outside the bar. People were panicking, running all over the place. She tried to figure out where she was, what had happened, and why she hurt so much. Then she saw her own nakedness from the waist down and it all came back to her. She was embarrassed and ashamed of her nudity and looked around for her clothing. She found her skirt but had to hold it around her since the fasteners had been damaged when it had been ripped off her. She couldn't face anybody right now; she just wanted to be home and to bathe, to wash the filth out of her. She took advantage of the pandemonium outside, left the bar and scurried off home, favouring the alleyways and shadows.

oooOOOooo

Lugh was indeed near. Having surfaced at Easton Colliery and having discreetly evaded the night-shift there, he was making his way in the darkness to Blackburn Road not half a mile from, but oblivious to the havoc being wreaked in Bathgate. Annie and Peter had finished an early dinner at her hotel and had retired to her room when they heard a tapping on the window. They welcomed the sun god in, and dimmed the lights as he grimaced against the overhead luminescence.

"Are we glad to see you?" said Peter. "We are at a loss here as to what, where, why or how!"

"I am afraid I have little more to offer. I have brought Nuada's sword and my sling, but I have no plan as yet." Confessed Lugh. "All I know is that we have to find the beast and slay it!"

"Yes." Agreed Annie. "But we have one major problem with

252

that. You can't operate in the daylight. Either we do something at night, or we have to lure it somewhere dark. That has been our quandary."

Peter nodded. "I have been trying to think of somewhere we can lure it to where both worlds of light and dark meet. And we would have to accomplish this in daylight as any attempt after dark would scream...*Trap*...in any language. He would have to feel confident as to his safety. I have thought caves, mines, Cairnpapple, but nothing seems suited to an ambush. Failing that, we have no alternative but to try to flush it out at night and take our chances."

"That will not happen." Said Lugh sadly. "Balor is a demi-god; he has telepathy, he can sense me in the open, they will not be duped. He has to be brought to a place he least expects to meet me."

They all sat dejectedly hoping that between the three of them a plan might be formulated. After what seemed an eternity, Peter said excitedly.

"Wait! I have an idea! Where day and night meet - I recall that the Lindsay High School was built to teach trades...they had a dummy mine shaft laid in the basement of the school!"

"Yes?" encouraged Annie, "And...?"

"Well," continued the Geologist, "if we could break in there, it should be empty over the weekend, Lugh can hide in the shaft and we could lure Balor and Calatin to this side of the shaft, it's in the basement so there will be little or no natural light and Lugh will be in his element, so to speak!"

"Sounds good!" Said Annie, enthusiastically.

Lugh however reserved judgement. "I will need to see this place. Then if it is suitable, we still need to design a plan for luring them there and that is fraught with untold danger."

"Agreed." Conceded Peter. "But first things first, let's see if we can get into that school."

With that, he picked up his jacket, motioned to Annie to follow and invited Lugh to join them. Lugh said it was best that he remain undetected and so left they way he came, meeting them in the car park.

ooo000ooo

Back at the police station, Bob Mathieson was just about at the end of his tether. Firstly, what was happening just shouldn't be happening; next, the people who might be able to help weren't available, and, on top of that, it seemed the entire population of Bathgate was trying to call his Station and all he could do was offer empty reassurances. In addition, he had men injured and vehicles out of action, and all their reports and witness accounts were met with incredulity from the assisting forces.

"OK, OK - it's not a *monster* alright? It's a huge deformed man with incredible strength; does that make you feel better?" he was heard yelling down the phone to an officer in an adjoining precinct.

He had men out in the streets with walkie-talkies, but no sightings of the two aliens had been recorded now for over an hour. Bob assumed they had gone to ground, and that could be anywhere. His officers, the only other eyewitnesses from the police force, were either injured or beat, and the newcomers were sceptical. Bob felt like he was on his own.

"Where the hell are Graham and Wilde?" he asked the heavens.

BACK TO SCHOOL

Lindsay High School was built in the early thirties next door to Bathgate St. Mary's Roman Catholic school. Around 1964, a new school was built on the outskirts of Boghall, and Lindsay High became amalgamated into St. Mary's Senior Secondary, which was then renamed as St. Mary's Academy. They were formidable buildings but Peter always maintained they looked more like prisons than schools with the iron bar fencing, huge windows and the art deco fascia, grey and foreboding. It was around the corner from Blackburn Road and they arrived at the entrance within a few minutes of leaving the Golden Circle. The main gates proved no obstacle to Lugh, being secured by chain and padlock, which the sun god simply melted. Once in the gate, in pitch-blackness, it was just as easy to gain entry to the building, the old locks succumbing to Lugh's powers. The deity became their beacon inside the walls as he emanated sufficient glow to light their way. Peter directed the small group to the basement and the entrance to the mock pit shaft.

Annie was fascinated; she had no idea such a thing might exist in a school; she had been a pupil there for more than a year and had had no knowledge of its existence. Lugh had the locked entrance to the shaft open with a flourish of his hand and Annie screwed her nose up at the mustiness oozing from the long disused cavern. Lugh checked out the Foyer area before the entrance.

"This is perfect!" He announced. "I can conceal myself within and enter this hall when the trap is sprung. There are no windows, so no direct sunlight can enter. I can remain within this environment safely. Now, we have to devise means to encourage the monster here."

"I have been thinking about that." Annie stated. "I can see only one way; bait. Peter and I must find them, let them see us, keep a safe distance ahead of them in the car, and lead them here. It's the only way."

"Hmmm," said Peter, "I agree, but why both of us? Wouldn't it be better for you to stay here safe with Lugh?"

"Much as I would prefer that, I figured we still have to find them, and it would be much easier for one to look as the other drove else we might miss something." She answered logically.

"Well, if we are gonna do it, we'd best get some sleep tonight. Lugh, what about you?" asked Peter.

"I have eaten and I can rest here. I require few comforts." He replied.

"OK then." Concluded Peter. "That just leaves one thing outstanding. If this works, we are going to be headed for here with a huge monster hot on our tails. How are you going to know we are on our way?"

"Peter," said Lugh condescendingly, "I am a god. I will know. But beware, my friends, the beast is close; he sleeps, and he dreams of revenge!"

Peter drove Annie back to her hotel and, with a kiss on the cheek, told her to be ready around 8am. She nodded and blew him a kiss as she went in the door. Peter made his way back to The Fairway, unprepared for the reception he was about to receive.

The Motel was buzzing because of the golf tournament; there

257

were around thirty people in the establishment all drinking and jabbering about what was going on in this little burgh. There was silence as he walked in the door as all heads turn towards him in alarm, then settled back to their conversations. The hostess and her husband came running up to him. "Haven't ye heard?" She asked anxiously.

"Heard what?" he replied.

"There's some kind of beast about, wrecking places and killing folks." She said, in an exaggerated stage whisper. "And the police are looking for you! You've to call this Bob Mathieson as soon as you get back. He told me to tell you!"

Peter's face went ashen. Balor was on the rampage and he had been here, in town!

Instead of calling the police inspector, Peter about turned, got back in his Capri and drove the half-mile to the Police Headquarters. The senior policeman's mood hadn't changed. "Ah! There you are! Where have you been?" he yelled.

"Woah!" Yelled Peter, holding his hands up in front of him, "I'm not one of your constables!"

Bob seemed to mellow a bit. "Fair point, but I have been trying to reach you at The Fairway, you and Doctor Wilde."

"You didn't think to call the Golden Circle?" Peter retorted.

The inspector sighed meekly.

"Didn't know that's where she was staying. Anyway, impossible as it seems, it looks like you two were right; there is something unbelievable out there, I've seen it with my own eyes. What the hell is it?"

"It's what we told you, the reincarnation of a mythological

creature." Answered Peter. "Tell me what's happened. Where is it now?"

Bob Mathieson related all the information he had relative to the previous few hours concluding with the confession that they had 'lost' an eight to ten foot villain.

Peter reluctantly advised the inspector that there was not much anyone could do right now. It was either resting or had probably moved out of the immediate area or bedded down somewhere out of sight, maybe even Cairnpapple or the Silver Mines. He suggested that everyone get a good nights sleep and continue their vigilance in the morning, perhaps with more reinforcements, maybe even the military?

Bob scoffed. "Huh! The military? And just what do I tell them? I am having the greatest of difficulty convincing my own people that this is not just a bad hoax. But I do agree rest is called for."

Peter asked where the creature was last seen. Bob told him King Street, headed towards The Fairway, about two hours ago. Peter figured because of Calatin, unless Balor carried him, they would not have gone too far afield. The Warlock was very frail and fragile. Still, he returned to his lodgings and called Annie to put her in the picture. That night with the memory of their proximity to the horrendous Fimorii, they both slept very uneasily.

ooo000ooo

Calatin had a rude awakening as Balor prodded his ribs.

"Hungry; eat."

The wizard took a moment to gather his wits, then told Balor

259

to stay indoors while he scouted about. Due to either the late night previously or the alcohol that had been consumed, he saw that it was well into the day, the sun high in the heavens.

The sorcerer carefully let himself out the main door of the academy having checked through the windows that no one was about.

He walked to the back of the building where there was a raised mound of grass and a few outbuildings. He climbed to the top of the knoll and saw open fields beyond, but no livestock. He was about to return when he heard a cock crowing from somewhere over the brow of the field behind the school. He followed the sound and found a chicken farm. With still nobody visible, he quickly rounded up three chickens, wrung their necks and hustled back to the building.

A dog began to bark in the distance.

Balor in the meantime had found the school kitchen and was in the process of trashing it, ripping open drawers and cupboards. He found the fridge freezer and destroyed that too when he found only frozen meat inside and could not eat it. He pulled the sink away from the wall and the burst piping deluged him with water adding to his foul temper. His servant, hearing the commotion, rushed in to quell the disturbance, leading the now drenched beast back to the gymnasium.

Looking over his shoulder, Calatin observed that at least they had water and, thanks to the uncontrollable demi-god, they also had a supply of firewood - it would be easy now for the wizard to cook the chickens he had stolen, Balor probably opting for the raw variety. He showed the chickens to his master who scoffed and in Fimorii language ordered "More!"

Calatin cursed at the greed of the beast but went out once

more to increase his plunder. This time however, he had to wait some time since there was a mortal with a dog checking out the chicken run, the man probably alerted by the earlier commotion to which his guard dog had responded. The smallholding farmer was counting his birds and tutting to himself wondering what might have caused his loss as he could see no evidence of break-in or any carnage that might imply a fox or other predator. Eventually he returned home, out of sight of his coop, and called the police to report the theft.

Calatin waited until the coast was clear then helped himself to another two birds. The dog whimpered in the distance.

While the wizard attempted to satiate his master's hunger, Annie and Peter had been busy all morning following false leads and reports to the police. Bob Mathieson was beside himself in panic and frustration. It seemed the whole town was in a state of hysteria and people were seeing and hearing monsters everywhere. The couple had already been to Cairnpapple and had seen the evidence of the break-in, but no culprits; they had followed the police to other venues of disturbance either real or imagined, all to no avail. Everywhere they went they had drawn blanks. The prey had obviously gone underground, somewhere...but where. Even if they found them, how were they going to entice them to follow them to where Lugh was waiting? Annie pointed out, quite correctly, that if the two misfits were camped miles away from the town, then it would be difficult for Calatin in his aged form to follow for more than a few hundred paces. Could they deal with Balor and then the wizard thereafter?

The police inspector was sifting through the most recent complaints; a dog howling in Glenmavis; a domestic argument in

261

Marchwood; some farmer losing a few chickens.

Peter looked at Annie; reincarnations or not, the beasts had to feed. The geologist asked the police chief if they could check out the poultry complaint for him. Bob was only too glad to get it off his desk.

The young man with Annie in tow, set off driving up Hopetoun Street and into Marjoribanks Street, heading for the farmer's address which Peter knew he could access from Haig Crescent just off Council Road (now Crosshill Drive). As they drove, the historian was idly looking out the passenger window, when suddenly, she grabbed Peter's arm and urgently shouted. "Stop!" but as Peter applied the breaks she changed her mind.

"No! Don't stop! Turn off here!" Peter swung the car into Academy Street and came to a halt, looking inquisitively at Annie.

"Calatin!" She said.

"Where?" asked Peter.

"In the academy. Looked like he was plucking chickens!" She observed

"Balor?" enquired the geologist.

"No sign of that brute." Annie hissed.

"Well, he won't be too far away. Thoughts? Plan 'B', 'C'?" asked Peter.

"Plan 'X' I think. Solve two problems in one. How to get Calatin to the party and how to entice Balor to follow - kidnap!" She suggested.

"Yep, that will work...I don't think! How do you suggest we do that?" Peter was none too impressed with this strategy.

"Not we." She emphasized. "You!"

262

"Huh?" was all Peter could utter.

"We wait for an opportunity, you grab him and hold him then I drive up in the car and we take off making enough noise for Balor to hear. Once he sees his slave in the vehicle, he'll follow. Trust me." She said, emphatically.

"I see!" Said Peter sarcastically, "So glad I got the easy bit!"

"He's an old man, for goodness sake! You can handle him!" She scoffed.

"Sure, but how do we – sorry, I...get to him while he has a ten-foot, armour-plated Rottweiler looking out for him!" Peter added exasperatedly.

"We wait, and we watch." Annie explained.

Peter turned the car and parked it facing the Academy where they could observe their victim and wait for an opportunity to act.

They didn't have long to wait before they saw the wizard go inside with a denuded chicken and return a few minutes later to begin plucking a second one. Annie saw that there were two birds left, still in full plumage. "There!" She said. "When he finishes that one, he will go inside then come out for another.

That's your chance! You have just over a minute or so to sneak up there before he returns and grab him when he emerges!"

"Uh-huh! And what if it's not Calatin that comes out?" Peter said, with no degree of confidence.

"Then it's back to plan 'A'; I pick you up and we run for it!" Annie stated as if it were obvious.

"Shit!" Cursed Peter, as he grabbed the car keys, opened his door and went to open the boot.

263

"What are you doing?" she asked.

"I'm looking for something I can use to make this a bit easier." He replied, as he rummaged in the junk he had collated in the trunk. After a minute, he returned with a large, black, plastic, garbage bag and an old leather trouser belt. He handed the car keys to Annie and told her to scoot over into the driving seat. He stood outside the vehicle, out of sight of the sorcerer, and waited for his chance.

"If this works, he will probably squeal like a pig, so Balor won't be far behind us - just keep the engine running and as soon as you see me make my move, gun that throttle and get to us quick as you can. The gate is open isn't it?" He asked as an afterthought.

"Yep." Confirmed Annie, craning her neck. "I can see it from here. Mind you, I have no idea what you are going to do with a belt and a rubbish...wait! He's going inside! Go! Go!" She urged.

Peter needed no second invitation. He sprinted across the road and slipped in through the open gates, ran across the yard sticking close to the perimeter wall, then cut across adjacent to the stone steps to the entrance. He passed the area Calatin was using as his plucking station and took up a position behind a huge stone pillar. He waited as Annie held her breath, her foot on the car's accelerator.

Calatin came out half a minute later, muttering to himself in his own language, mostly derogatory references to Balor. He had picked up the penultimate chicken and began roughly ripping off its feathers. Peter saw his chance as the warlock turned his back to the pillar Peter was squatting behind. He jumped out, the garbage bag held open in front of him and pulled it over the old man's head. Calatin dropped the chicken and howled in fright at the sudden movement and darkness. Peter was quick to strap his belt around the victim's arms and fasten the buckle just as Calatin realized he was being attacked and screamed for his master.

Annie had seen Peter's action and gunned the Capri into motion, hurling it up to the stone steps and turning in a screech of brakes. Peter tossed the old man into the back seat of the car just as he heard banging and crashing from inside the building as Balor made his way to the main door.

"Go!" He yelled at Annie. She released the clutch, but in her anxiety, too quickly. The engine stalled; she made two attempts to start it but all she got was the starting motor whining.

"C'mon!" She squealed in panic.

"Hell!" Yelled Peter, "This only happens in horror movies!" He jumped out, told her to put the car in second gear, and keep her foot on the pedal and to pop the clutch on his say so. He rushed to the back of the car and began pushing; fortunately, the vehicle was stalled facing downhill and was beginning to pick up speed when the geologist heard the crash behind him as the monster smashed its way out of the building making matchwood of the main door.

"Shit! Nooow!" He yelled at Annie, slapping the roof of the Capri. She lifted her foot off the clutch and the car jolted and kicked into life. She had to brake to allow Peter to run round the car body and fling himself into the passenger seat. "Go! Go! Gun it!" He yelled. This time there was no mistake and the vehicle thrust forward.

Balor shook an angry fist at it as it pulled away from him.

"Damn!" Swore Peter looking out the rear window. "He's just standing there".

"Does he know you have Calatin?" asked Annie, slowing down.

"Well, he will now." Answered the young man, as he ripped the garbage bag open around the wizard's head forcing his face onto the rear windscreen. Balor bellowed his rage and thumped the ground with his mighty fists cracking the concrete under him. He waved both fists in the air then took off in a lope after them.

"Here he comes!" Peter yelled to Annie." Go, but keep this distance between us, I'll tell you to speed up or slow down." They headed away from the school and down Academy Street where it comes out onto King Street just before it changes to Edinburgh Road and headed east towards the old Lindsay High School. The road there is practically straight, so they could put a few hundred yards between themselves and their pursuer and, remain within sight of him. He loped after them at a fair pace. Before they knew it, they were turning into the yard at the school, Annie braking hard and Peter tumbling out, grabbing their prisoner and dragging him up the steps and in the entrance with Annie close behind.

"OK." Panted the geologist. "He can't fail to surmise that we went in here, so we will have a few minutes before he finds us as he won't know which floor to search…time enough, I hope, to get to Lugh and set the trap."

Peter dragged Calatin into the Foyer before the mine entrance and closed the door behind them when Annie was safely through. It was dark; being interior to the corridors and little light penetrated that far into the building. Before the wizard's eyes had accustomed to the lack of light, a voice addressed him in his own language.

266

"Filth! Now you will witness my wrath!" The old man howled in despair and cowered to the ground.

"Balor is right behind us." Began Peter, but Lugh cut him off.

"I know; I feel him!" Rasped the sun god. "Let him come, we are ready!"

He gave the young man his slingshot and a couple of black pebbles rescued from Blasket Island. "Using this is easy. Look at your target, swing, release and the sling will do the rest; it cannot miss. Hopefully you will have no need of it; I intend to finish this with the Sword of Nuada!" He concluded, brandishing the talisman in the air. Lugh then generated a glow around them so that they might see more clearly. They heard the bellowing of the beast somewhere above them and the crashing and smashing of doors and furniture as the monster swatted them aside in his search for Calatin and his abductors. They waited, following his progress by the din he created. He seemed to be coming closer but the noise suddenly stopped. Then they heard an almighty bellow of rage, which dropped in pitch to a low roar, a growl-

"Luuuuuggghhhhh!" Then there was silence.

"He has sensed me." The sun god explained. "Now we must be aware, he will be more cautious now."

The silence was more frightening to Annie than the crashing was, at least then they knew where the beast was and in what direction it was coming. They waited and waited, Lugh standing at the furthest point of the area facing the door; Annie to the right guarding Calatin, and Peter on the left breathing heavily and balancing a pebble in the wide part of the sling, ready to begin it spinning at a moment's notice.

That notice came with a thunderous crash as Balor two fisted the door with all his strength; the door catapulted across the room, its supports and masonry flying everywhere. A huge piece of plaster struck Peter on the head knocking him unconscious. Annie screamed and was about to go to his assistance when Calatin seized his unguarded opportunity and rushed at Annie with his head down colliding with her, his skull meeting her full in the mid riff, winding her and knocking her to the floor where she struck her head and lay there dazed. Lugh began a charge at Balor holding the Sword of Nuada aloft ready to strike, but Calatin continued his momentum and careened into the sun god taking him by surprise. Lugh stumbled as the sword went flying out of his hands to land at the far end of the room.

Balor smirked as he looked down at the once proud deity, then with a vicious backhand sent him sprawling across the room and landing against the wall in a crumpled heap. He scrambled to his knees and began to glow as he summoned his firepower, but before he could release a projectile, Balor had him by the throat and lifted him clean off his feet. They were eye to eye and Balor could not resist the opportunity; in Fimorii, he said, "Proud Lugh! Favoured one! See what you have become!"

Lugh was not to be outdone and responded. "However I may be, I can never become as low as thou, Balor, god of evil!"

The monster tossed Lugh to a corner of the foyer like a rag doll; the sun god rolled over on to his knees again as Balor sauntered up to him, Calatin cackling in the background.

"You defeated me once, god of the sun, if you could only imagine what I taste. Revenge is so sweet! Prepare to die, god of

268

nothing!"

The monstrosity raised both of its huge arms above its head to deliver the killer blow.

Balor never struck that blow; instead, his body jerked in muscular spasms; he stopped dead in confusion as he felt the searing pain enter his lumber region and slice through his belly; he moved his head slowly downwards so that his one eye could see the cause of this distraction and gave a bellow of disbelief as he saw the Sword of Nuada protrude beyond his abdomen, dripping with blood; his blood. His head swivelled slowly to his rear where he saw Annie, a stream of blood running down her face, braced against the wall driving the mystical sword through his body with all her might. His tormented face took on an air of utter confusion as he looked again at the dripping sword, then he staggered first one way, then another before toppling like a felled tree face first onto the concrete floor.

Peter had come to just in time to witness the demise of the creature and staggered over to hold Annie who was now faint with exertion. Calatin dived over the rubble screeching in panic as he tried to revive the monster, then stood back in horror as the giant body began decomposing in front of him; first into a putrid slush, then into a gelatinous creature and ultimately into nothing more than fetid sea water which flowed into a drainage trough and disappeared into the mine shaft.

Lugh had regained his footing and stood shakily absorbing the scene. He walked slowly over to his friends cuffing Calatin into a corner as he went.

"Thank you Annie." The God said. "You have succeeded

where we had failed. I am in your debt, forever."

They sat together on the floor, all three, in silent acknowledgement, the wizard whimpering in the background.

Peter brought a handkerchief out of his pocket and mopped the blood from Annie's face. She allowed it for a moment, and then insisted she was fine. Peter held her tight, stroking her arm.

"What now?" he asked of the sun god.

"Now?" sighed Lugh. "Now, I have to take this excuse for a human being back to Cairnpapple. He has some tidying to do and a curse to undo. Then? I will have to think on it."

Peter looked at his watch.

"It's a few hours till dark yet and it's a long way to Cairnpapple with an old man in tow, what if we come back for you after nightfall and take you there?"

"That would be appreciated; in the meantime, I will consider our next course of action." Lugh said. "But for now, Annie? Let me look at your wound."

She walked over to him and he gently pulled her hair back to reveal the cut and bump on her head. He closed his eyes and stroked the wound with a feather like touch of his fingers. She felt a tingling sensation followed by a warm glow where her head hurt most, then a cooling and a relief from the throbbing.

"You should be fine; it is not a deep cut." He stated, then releasing her. Annie was surprised at just how good she felt, as if a current of energy had passed through her revitalizing all her tired muscles. She smiled and mouthed, Thank you.

He returned the smile. "And you, Peter?"

"I'm fine," he said, "really, just a bump and a bit of a headache."

With that, they left their friend with his captive and drove to the Golden Circle hotel where Annie insisted on a shower and a change of clothes. After, she became aware of how hungry she was and so they ate at the restaurant in the hotel. It was relatively early for dinner, and the place was almost empty due to the Police broadcasts as they enjoyed a quick and easy steak and salad, with a glass of house wine each.

Dusk was settling in when they finished and went out to the car park.

"Your wheels or mine?" asked Peter.

"Yours." Replied Annie, without a moment's hesitation. "If we have to take that cretin Calatin on board, I'd rather he stank out your car than mine!"

They arrived at the school just as the streetlights came on and found Lugh deep in thought. The wizened creature beside him looked as if he hadn't moved a muscle since their leaving three hours previously.

Peter drove them to the Silver Mines and the two ancients set off down the valley, Calatin propelled most of the way with occasional prods from the sun god. Lugh had said he would contact them the next day with a view to further discussion.

The couple returned to the Golden Circle where Peter felt they ought to make contact with the police inspector. He called the station and found out from the receptionist that they were still on full alert, but when he told her who he was, she said that the chief had been

271

expecting his call, so she patched him through.

"Where the hell have you two been?" was the hostile reception Peter got from Bob Mathieson. "We are at our wits end here, no sightings, no updates, heaps of hoax callers and paranoid spinsters…what is going on?"

"Bob," chided the geologist, "calm down. All I can tell you is the good news. It's over; done; taken care of. You can send your men home, there is no danger now, trust me."

"What do you mean? Look, you can't…explain yourself!" Bob yelled into the telephone.

"Bob." Peter waited until he had the Policeman's attention.

"We are exhausted. We have had one hell of a day. It is too complex to try to explain over the phone and we are too tired to sit round a table and try to convince sceptics right now. Just believe me, OK? It's ended. There will be no more mayhem; the…how do you say it? The perpetrator has been dealt with. We will stop by tomorrow and give you chapter and verse. In the meantime, cancel the curfew, release your reserves, get back to normal working, and you, go home and get some rest - that's what we are going to do right now." With that, Peter replaced the receiver without waiting for a response.

Annie raised her eyebrows as Peter lay back on the sofa. She had expected that sort of reaction, but had agreed with Peter that was the best approach. She leaned over, took her lover's hand and led him to the bathroom. She assisted him in undressing, turned on the shower and pushed him in. She undressed herself and joined him in the flow of hot water. They languished in the warmth, washing, caressing and drying each other then fell into bed where they held each other before succumbing to the pleasure of uninterrupted sleep.

ooo000ooo

About a mile away from them in Belvedere, Sheena Watson was not enjoying the luxury of rest. She had told no one of her rape, who would believe her? She had come home, run a bath and soaked in it for ages. Now, although she felt clean, she was still in pain - her vagina felt like it had been ripped apart and she had bruises and scratch marks, more like claw marks, across her abdomen and breasts. Her sleep was troubled with the recurring nightmare to such an extent that she thought she might never sleep again. Eventually exhaustion took over when she could cry no more.

Annie jumped up from a complicated dream where she was being pursued by something or someone in slow motion when she heard the telephone. At first, she wasn't sure what had so rudely interrupted her dreaming.

She snatched at the receiver gasping at the same time when she saw on her small travel alarm clock that it was almost nine.

"Yes?" she finally managed.

"Dr. Wilde?" the Hotel Receptionist asked.

"Yes. What is it?" Annie said almost impolitely.

"I have a gentleman at reception asking to see you." Came the terse reply.

"Who? Just a minute." By this time, Peter was awake and was questioning Annie with raised eyebrows. She put her hand over the mouthpiece and whispered. "There's someone downstairs asking for me." She removed her hand and asked the girl, "Who is it? What's his name?"

"Hold on…" There was a moment of almost inaudible conversation as the Receptionist spoke with someone else. "Uh, it's a…Lou Dan…Anne?"

Annie looked at Peter, "Lou Dan Anne?" she repeated to him, her face screwed in confusion, and then almost immediately, it dawned on her. "My god, Lugh! Lugh Danaan!"

"Send him up!" She yelled at the receptionist as she jumped off the bed, slamming down the receiver at the same time.

"Lugh!" She yelled at Peter.

"Here! Now! But how? It's daylight?" she threw on some clothes and chucked Peter's at him.

"Quickly! He'll be here in a minute!"

Annie answered the knock on the door and stood back totally confused. Before her stood a tall, golden-haired, extremely well built and attractive man with a wonderful smile on his face. It took her a few moments to realize that this was indeed Lugh; he had been transformed into the God he had been before his imprisonment. She gasped at the recognition; Lugh could help but laugh at her bewilderment. He walked in and laughed again as he experienced the same reaction from Peter.

"Well, well, well." Said the younger man. "You do look good! And the clothes, all modern and...Ummm, familiar? Hey! Wait a minute! These are my clothes!"

"Ah, yes, indeed." Explained the deity with a sheepish grin. "I wasn't sure where you might be, so I went to the other residence first and finding you gone, I sort of, well, took the liberty? I entered and left unobserved. Hope you don't mind!"

"No, not at all, in fact they look better on you than me." Confessed the geologist.

Annie agreed as she looked at Lugh's (or Peter's) cream turtleneck sweater, grey slacks and tan shoes.

"They fit pretty well, don't you think?" said Lugh, turning around; it was fortunate that both men were of similar height and build.

"Wow!" Peter agreed. "Yes indeed. I'll take a while getting used to seeing you like this though, it's like we just met!"

275

"I need a coffee, right now!" Said Annie. "Throw your shirt on Peter and let's head for the coffee shop. I'm hungry too."

Peter put his shirt on, and a few minutes later, they were seated in the small breakfast restaurant.

When they were settled, Peter asked, "Er, where is Calatin?"

"Where he deserves to be, wandering the Land of Sorrows for all eternity!" Lugh spat.

"You killed him?" Annie said, almost shocked.

"I prefer to think of it as releasing his spirit from the grotesque mortal shell it was trapped in, as a reward for removing his curse." Lugh suggested with a sly grin.

They ate some eggs and bacon with toast and while they were enjoying the percolated coffee, (It was Lugh's first taste of the beverage and he seemed to enjoy it) Peter brought them all back to earth asking, "What now? We have to show up with the police inspector and have a hell of a lot of explaining to do. Just what to tell him, I don't know for sure as to the credibility, and what about the clean up and explaining to the Press? I'm at a loss, I can tell you."

Annie nodded; she too had no idea where this was taking them.

The sun god raised his hands for quiet. "I have been giving this much thought. After thousands of years in darkness, I saw my first dawn rise; feeling the sun on my face after so many years was wonderful, so much so, that I decided to walk to your abode. It was while walking that I considered this solution. Here is my plan. I need you two to arrange a gathering of all those involved in the events of the past few days. Can you do that?"

276

Annie looked at Peter, then back to Lugh. "I suppose a public meeting could be called by the local authority or the police, but there would be two problems. First, it will be very difficult to convince either of them that they should, and secondly, there could be no guarantee that everyone involved would attend."

Lugh continued-

"Leave the first problem to me; I have the power to convince." He smiled. "As for attendance, if we make the reason for the meeting interesting enough, then there would be few absentees; a promise of a full, concise explanation might be sufficient. I will address this meeting and shall use my skills to imply that it did not happen as they 'imagined', and auto- suggest an alternative scenario."

"And what might that be?" asked Peter.

"Ah!" The God sat back and folded his arms. "That's where I need your input!"

"Oh, great! Fine! Hey Annie, all we have to do is think up an alternative reason for miles and miles of underground caverns, disappearing miners, monsters firing thunderbolts, Godzilla trashing the burgh and its schools, cars and vans crashing of their own accord and everything returning to normal! OK, you first!" Peter sounded exceptionally cynical.

"Come on Peter." She chided. "We needn't be alone in this. If we, Lugh, are going to advise the police to hold a meeting then we can seek their ideas on how to handle it. I'm sure they are used to cover up spin yarns; we've heard more than a few over the past week!"

Peter was not convinced. "Anyway, we had best be going before old Bob has a heart seizure. We need to stop by the Fairway; I need a change of clothes."

"And I need to shower and pretty myself up a bit." Conceded Annie. "Why don't you go do your thing and come back here when you're done? I will be finished too by then and we can all go to the police station fresh."

"Excellent plan, Annie." Said Lugh "I will await you down here. There are things I wish to peruse in the rack of books and maps and things in the foyer.

ooo000ooo

Peter was back at the Golden Circle within an hour, freshly kitted out in a light blue shirt and jeans. Annie and Lugh were having coffee in the lounge, the sun god having acquired quite a taste for Brazilian beans. The Geologist joined them.

"I was just thinking, Lugh, on the way over. I know your gifts are wonderful, but to convince so many people all at once - we are talking hundreds - it's a bit much, don't you think?" Peter asked, still doubting the logistics of such an exercise.

"Do you doubt my powers?" It was a matter of fact question from Lugh with no malice intended.

"It's not a question of doubt, really, its more ignorance I have to admit." Peter replied.

Lugh sighed.

"Peter, it is not so difficult to extract from ones mind that which one does not wish to believe or remember and superimpose something that appears more logical and believable. Given a choice and the opportunity, people will always accept the easier path, physically as well as mentally. They will see what they expect to see. Take these documents, for instance," He handed some papers to his young friend. "I intend to go to Ireland after all this and pursue my destiny. I understand I will require documents to enable me to pass from country to country. I have prepared these; do they appear to be in order?"

Peter looked at the items quizzically. "Yes, your passport looks fine, the dates seem true as to birth and place of issue; even your photograph looks as you do now. How did you manage to do this in a few hours?" he was about to continue when he saw the blond man smile and heard Annie chuckle.

"What?" he asked, puzzled.

Annie sniggered. "Peter, you are looking at a blank piece of paper!"

He looked again at the documents and confirmed what Annie had told him.

"Oh...Oh, I get it." He laughed. "Fair enough! Point taken! You made me see what I expected to see, right?"

They all piled into Peter's car and Lugh, winking at Annie, suggested that the geologist ought to think more seriously about personal hygiene.

"Very funny!" Peter replied sarcastically, knowing that Lugh referred to the remaining essence of Calatin on the upholstery.

Half an hour later, they were being shown into Bob Mathieson's office.

"It's about time! Do you know it's almost noon? And who is

279

this? Some other crazy scientist?" Bob yelled his frustration.

Peter did the introductions. "Inspector Mathieson, meet Lugh, sun god of Celtic mythology! Lugh, meet our chief of police, Bob Mathieson."

"This is no time for your off the wall humour, Peter! We have a serious situation here." Bob scoffed.

"He does not jest, Sir." Lugh took over the conversation. "You see, what you might have expected to see from my previous description..."

He continued to talk in a quiet monotone to the inspector, most of which was inaudible to the other two in the room. However, they did see Bob's expression relax and his eyes glaze slightly. He held this dreamy countenance until Lugh finished speaking, and then suddenly, he broke out of it saying, "Right! Right! OK. I know how we do this. Annie, Peter, thanks for all your help and your great report, but I haven't time to go over it all right now, I have to speak with the town clerk and the colliery manager and arrange an urgent Public Meeting! We need to put a stop to all these silly rumours. I expect you two will be on hand at the meeting to field questions in your relative domains?"

The two lovers could hardly hide their smiles at this change in reaction and attitude. Lugh had done his job well. They left and went back to Annie's hotel. As they sat in her room enjoying room service coffee and sandwiches, Annie asked-

"What did you say...what did you implant in his mind, Lugh?"

"So far as the mine is concerned, Level 17 has uncovered unusual pockets of dangerous gasses both flammable and

280

hallucinogenic, hence the strange reports. With regard to Balor, an extremely large mentally ill person escaped from custody and ran amuck. He has subsequently been captured and re-interred. The damage to the schools was the result of errant children who had no great respect for the buildings and who showed no willingness to attend there again." Lugh summarized.

"Cool!" Agreed Peter. "I can justify the mine readings in my report, but what about the tunnels?"

The Sun God added-

"I intend to be here for a few more days, I have much to learn from you both about present day travel, your flying machines, airplanes - for instance, I need to know procedure; I will also need some form of financial support, so I will require assistance in perhaps disposing of some of the items and artefacts I have, shall we say, collected, over the years? During that time, I will secure many of the tunnels that are in proximity to the mining shafts such that they will not be exposed in the foreseeable future. I must also secure the cavern under Cairnpapple."

Three days later, over a thousand people convened in the Co-operative Hall. Lugh addressed the meeting as an 'expert psychologist' and worked his magic. Bob Mathieson assured everyone that all was well, and the town clerk, to rapturous applause, intimated that they had set aside a special fund from a huge donation by the errant (unnamed) mental hospital so that anyone suffering loss from the experience would receive adequate reparation. The whole audience, including the miners, the shopkeepers, the publicans, even Martin Preston and his gang, the press, the police, all had come to the meeting expecting answers. All left the meeting feeling informed, secure and uplifted.

Sheena Watson also felt satisfied. Although her situation was now much better, the scratches beginning to heal, she was not really well enough to attend the meeting, but felt obliged to be there. She needed to know what had happened to her and why. She did not have those particular questions answered specifically, yet she felt better; the pain had dissipated and she was coming to terms with the belief that her discomfort was natural; a direct result of her own promiscuity when she allowed Martin to have his way with her in Cairnpapple car park; monsters being merely things of nightmares.

Annie and Peter had set Lugh up in the Golden Circle Hotel where they coached him on all things modern that were missing from his self-learning. He had cleared whatever he required from Cairnpapple, and they had taken him on a shopping outing for modern clothes and to explain the basis of cash transactions, using Peter's cash and chequebook initially. In the meantime, the geologist, through friends and acquaintances, had managed to offload various items from Cairnpapple to a myriad of buyers and auction houses whereby Lugh was to become a reasonably rich man. Peter whistled at some of the artefacts, roman coins, knives, shields, swords down through all the ages, old flintlock rifles and pistols, jewellery in gold and silver encrusted in gems. A treasure trove, for sure!

When all of this had been accomplished over a few weeks, it became time for Lugh to depart. Peter asked out of curiosity, "You say you are following your destiny in trying to trace Aine; yet I thought at times you believed Annie to be her reincarnation?"

Lugh smiled at the historian and took her hands in his. "Yes, indeed, you do strike a remarkable resemblance, but you are not She. You are mortal and may therefore be a successor of Aine's descendants inter- married with mortals, but you can not be Aine herself; no goddess can be reincarnated as a mortal; that is forbidden within our laws."

"Will we see you again, Lugh?" Annie asked, wiping a tear away from her cheek.

Lugh thought for a minute then replied. "Only if you really need me." He hugged the young woman and held her for a long time.

"But, how will we reach you? How will you know?" she sobbed and Lugh smiled.

"Take heart, young one, I will know; trust me; I'm a god!"

He embraced Peter and said his farewells, charging the young man to care for Annie, then made his way to his flight to Dublin and his destiny.

The two lovers made their way back to Blackburn Road in silence and sadness. They had a meal neither really had appetite for, before retiring to Annie's room. They were resigned to the situation and had consolation not only in that Lugh had trusted them enough not to wipe their memories, but also in the knowledge that the need may arise where they might once more be together. With that thought, they both cheered a little and snuggled up on Annie's sofa. Tacitly, she took Peter's hand and led him to her bed; she needed him tonight.

As they undressed, Peter said, "In all of this I still have one disappointment."

"What's that?" she asked.

"I'm disappointed that you are not a goddess." He said without

283

smiling.

Annie thought for a moment, and then realized he was teasing. "Why, you...!" And she set about hitting him with a pillow.

Peter protected himself with his arms and yelled through his outstretched hands, "OK, OK... you can be my goddess, alright? My own personal goddess." She laughed and threw herself into his arms as they both toppled onto the bed.

FIN

EPILOGUE

Sheena Watson was not a happy lady. Despite what she tried, she was still gaining weight. She also had been suffering from occasional stomach pains and was never far from nausea. She had missed a period and was convinced that she was pregnant. She arranged to meet Martin Preston and discuss the situation with him. The problem was that neither of them could recall actually doing it. They could recall the evening almost two months ago, the drive to Knock Hill, Sheena dragging Martin into the back seat, but thereafter was a blank for both of them.

Sheena put it down to her state of inebriation, but Martin was not too convinced; he had the car and he rarely got really drunk when he was driving. Still, he couldn't account for his lapse in memory, so if Sheena said they did, then he guessed they did. He talked Sheena into going to a doctor to confirm or deny the pregnancy; she did two days later.

"And when did you say conception occurred?" the Doctor asked.

"About two months ago, almost eight weeks, I told you." She repeated.

"And there's no possibility of it being before then?" he persisted.

"No, no way, it was just the once!" She insisted. "Why are you asking?"

"Ah well, it's just that, had you not told me it was only two months ago, I would have sworn that you were well on your way to six months' gestation, going by the size of the foetus!" He beamed at her. "But don't worry! You are going to be the proud mother of an exceptionally well developed baby!"

Lightning Source UK Ltd.
Milton Keynes UK
29 December 2009
147978UK00001B/27/P